WHATEVER CAME OUT OF HER MOUTH AND WHATEVER SHE THOUGHT OF HIM, HE WOULD HELP HER

Unless they killed each other first.

"A little gratitude wouldn't be a bad idea," he said.

She blinked several times, as if the comment actually shocked her. "For what?"

"Rescuing you. Feeding you. Not turning you in to Ted. Not throwing you in jail. Pick any of those."

He stopped making a list. Once he started he'd never stop. The goal was to make her comfortable, convince her to trust him and get some answers. Not antagonize her.

"Are you ever going to put me down?" she asked in a chilly voice.

Comfortable. Not antagonizing.

Yeah, great in theory. Impossible in practice.

BOOK YOUR PLACE ON OUR WEBSITE AND MAKE THE READING CONNECTION!

We've created a customized website just for our very special readers, where you can get the inside scoop on everything that's going on with Zebra, Pinnacle and Kensington books.

When you come online, you'll have the exciting opportunity to:

- View covers of upcoming books

- Read sample chapters

- Learn about our future publishing schedule (listed by publication month *and author*)

- Find out when your favorite authors will be visiting a city near you

- Search for and order backlist books from our online catalog

- Check out author bios and background information

- Send e-mail to your favorite authors

- Meet the Kensington staff online

- Join us in weekly chats with authors, readers and other guests

- Get writing guidelines

- AND MUCH MORE!

Visit our website at
http://www.kensingtonbooks.com

YOUR MOUTH DRIVES ME CRAZY

HelenKay Dimon

BRAVA

KENSINGTON PUBLISHING CORP.
http://www.kensingtonbooks.com

BRAVA BOOKS are published by

Kensington Publishing Corp.
850 Third Avenue
New York, NY 10022

All Kensington titles, imprints, and distributed lines are available at special quantity discounts for bulk purchases for sales promotion, premiums, fund-raising, educational, or institutional use.

Special book excerpts or customized printings can also be created to fit specific needs. For details, write or phone the office of the Kensington Special Sales Manager: Attn. Special Sales Department. Kensington Publishing Corp., 850 Third Avenue, New York, NY 10022. Phone: 1-800-221-2647.

Brava and the B logo Reg. U.S. Pat. & TM Off.

ISBN-13: 978-0-7582-1586-4
ISBN-10: 0-7582-1586-X

First Brava Trade Paperback Printing: July 2007
First Brava Mass-Market Printing: March 2009
10 9 8 7 6 5 4 3 2 1

Printed in the United States of America

*To Kate Duffy for everything
but especially for loving this book*

Acknowledgments

Some special words of gratitude are in order for this book. In addition to Kate Duffy, thanks also goes to everyone at Kensington who constantly take roughly four-hundred-page manuscripts and, through some miraculous process, turn them into marketable books. Also, thank you to Ethan Ellenberg for selling ideas when they only consist of a few lines.

As always, I am indebted to Wendy Duren for her willingness to take time from her own writing schedule to read the incomprehensible mess that was this first draft. Your friendship and assistance mean a great deal.

My deepest appreciation goes to Kunio and Miyuki Miyazawa for introducing me to Hawaii and, most importantly, for producing the amazing man I married.

And for James, your support, patience and inside information on Hawaii made this one—all of them, actually—possible.

Chapter 1

Three days into his involuntary vacation, Kane Travers realized one thing: he wasn't a vacation type of guy. He had enough home projects to fill exactly two days. He cleaned up the yard, painted the porch railing and ripped out the built-in bookcase in the family room.

He tried surfing. Running on the beach. Washing his sporty red pickup truck under the intense Hawaii sun. That blew another day.

And still six days to go. Six long, boring days until he knew his fate at work. Until he heard the results of the trumped-up investigation. Rather than dwell on the mess his life had become, he inhaled, breathing the scent of warm salt water deep into his lungs.

Just then, something moved off to his left. Squinting, he tried to identify the strange pile sitting about a hundred feet down the abandoned beach. Probably debris washed on shore or abandoned by the resort tourists earlier that day when the Pacific Ocean had unleashed a powerful storm on the rocky coast of Kauai.

He stood there, his feet sinking deep into the wet sand as pink and orange bands from the retired sunset streaked across the sky and dipped low on the horizon. How any person could hear the rhythmic beating of the waves against the shore and decide this was the perfect place to throw a used potato chip bag, he'd never know.

He'd bought the one-level cottage here as a place for escape. The edge-of-the-world feel appealed to him on a fundamental level. Having someone ruin the scenery with litter ticked him off. Also gave him something to do. Cleaning up the beach could knock ten or twelve minutes off his unwanted vacation time.

Wearing nothing more than a low-slung pair of faded jeans, he walked the waterline back to his house to fetch a bag. Along the way, chilly February ocean water splashed across his bare feet, and small pebbles pelted his chest.

He'd taken only a few steps when a strange sensation pricked at the back of his neck. His gaze slid back to the lump on the beach.

The thundering crash of water against the beach blocked out most sounds. But, no doubt about it, this time the damn thing moved. One step toward the mass, then he saw it. A slim, bare arm.

"Damn!" He broke into a blinding run, kicking up wet sand behind him.

He reached the pitiful bulge and dropped to his knees. Sweat broke out on his forehead as a wave of desperation hit him. The same frustrating mix of rage and helplessness he'd experienced before. The worry that he was one second too late. Again.

Sweeping the seaweed aside, he encountered a tattered blanket and tangled long hair. This time the bump groaned.

"Can you hear me?" He lifted the rest of the waste away from the crumpled form.

Not just any form. A woman. A naked woman with a slight blue tint to her pale skin. With two fingers pressed against the cool flesh of her neck, he felt for a beat. Despite the strong thumping, concern coursed through his veins, shutting out any of the normal interest that might have flickered to life at the sight of a nude female body.

Three months had passed since he'd scratched that particular itch. Not that long for some men, maybe, but about two months longer than he could tolerate without getting twitchy. On the small island, one rich in tradition, everyone seemed to know or be related to everyone else.

This sense of community, combined with a few too many pushy matchmaking mothers hell-bent on securing appropriate husbands for their baby girls, made dating rough on a single man. Especially on a single man who intended to stay that way. The resulting involuntary celibacy sometimes came with the job and the life whether or not he liked it.

And he didn't. Not one damn bit.

But now wasn't the time for those thoughts. He wasn't that guy. He'd never taken advantage of a woman in his life. Hell, this one wasn't even awake.

"Ma'am? Are you hurt?" It was an obvious question, but he didn't know what else to say.

He brushed her wet hair off her cold cheek. Soaked from head to toe, he couldn't even tell her hair color.

Marks and scratches marred her pale skin. Getting tossed around in the rough water had battered her a bit, but she looked relatively untouched. Even with the surface injuries and her bedraggled condition, he saw a hint of cheekbones, a slim refined nose and a full mouth.

If he didn't do something soon, she could be a fine-looking corpse.

"Talk to me," he said, as if ordering her awake might work. People told him his yell could raise the dead. He could now state with some authority that theory appeared to be wrong.

With hands planted on the damp sand on either side of her head, he leaned down. His ear hovered above her mouth so he could hear over the crashing surf. Steady small puffs of air brushed against his skin, calming his anxiety.

The coolness of her skin still scared him. He knew from training and experience that too long in the water and hypothermia kicked in. Tropical climate or not, a body could take only so much abuse from the elements.

"Ma'am?"

Her eyes stayed closed. Her body still. She needed a shower and dry clothes. Even then . . .

He tunneled one arm under her legs and the other around her shoulder. In one fluid move, he pushed to his feet with the injured stranger clutched to his chest. He looked up and down the beach. No one lingered except him.

Quick strides turned to a jog. He had to get to the front door of his bungalow. Two hundred feet, then he could warm her up, dry her off and get whatever help she needed. There was no time to waste.

He now had something to fill those long hours. He just hoped he wouldn't be spending the time checking her into the morgue.

Annie Parks refused to open her eyes. Open eyes meant facing reality. She wasn't ready for that yet.

She'd been in the ice cold waves only a few minutes. At least she thought that was the case. Time blended and distorted. Sluggish muscles and misfiring brain cells made thinking and moving almost impossible.

Nothing about the last few hours made any sense. She remembered standing in the small bathroom of her stateroom, looking over her crude drawing of the yacht's floor plan. She fiddled with her camera, unconsciously adjusting the settings to account for fading light. The steady beat of jazz music sounded from the main living area and adjoining dining room. With everyone enjoying a pre-dinner drink, she had the privacy she needed to study the layout of the rooms and decide where the owner would keep valuable paperwork.

She had slipped out of her stained dress. The spill of red wine had given her a reasonable excuse to leave the party. The fact she had to ruin the one fancy dress she owned ticked her off, but what was one more sacrifice to the cause. She'd sacrificed so much already.

One minute she was reaching for the black outfit she'd set aside for her snooping. The next, someone held a bag over her head, hands went around her waist and . . . splash. Then a mouthful of water followed by a hard skid to a beach landing and pain. She couldn't forget the pain.

Now someone held her. Sure, the guy didn't throw her back in the water, but that didn't necessarily mean things were looking up. Her back teeth slammed together with each one of his firm steps. The brisk walk cuddled against his chest had warmed her, but at this pace she'd be broken into little pieces before they got to their destination. Wherever that was.

The naked early evening jog with a perfect stranger was new, not to mention embarrassing. Plenty of fear ran through her, too. She thought about jumping out of this guy's arms and running as fast as she could in any direction but the water.

Thought about it. Even plotted out the escape. But, she knew the smarter move was to bide her time and figure out her next step. She'd spent her entire life biding time. Waiting for the right moment to get her revenge.

Panic and weakness were the enemies. Two of them, anyway. During the past few hours she'd discovered a new one of the human variety. She'd been knocked around, dropped into the ocean and nearly drowned due to her mediocre swimming skills. All that made washing up on the beach the highlight of her evening.

Not the normal day for a nature photographer. Of course, this wasn't a paid assignment. This one was a personal project. An investigation gone seriously wrong. Somehow she'd managed to stumble onto the right track. Got close enough to get tossed into the ocean. She'd lost her camera and nearly her life.

And now . . . well, she did not know what was happening. She lifted one eyelid in the barest move possible. She spied miles of muscular forearm. Tan and, she hoped, connected to the safe and friendly variety of male on the other end.

Before she could squawk, her rescuer balanced her body on his hip, reached for a doorknob and opened the door. She silently added *strong* to the list of her rescuer's attributes.

Looking through the slit under her eyelashes, she tried to scan her new surroundings. They stood in the center of a small room with a red sectional sofa as the centerpiece. Not what she imagined the home of a typical serial killer would look like. That was her first good news of the last forty-eight hours. The only good news.

He started to move. With each step, she saw a flash of his bare feet against the oak hardwood floor below her. She poised for fight or flight. Tried to concentrate on getting the hell out of there—even though she still didn't know where "there" was.

He threw her in the shower before she could make her big escape.

Chapter 2

The world spun beneath Annie until her feet landed on the cold tile floor of the shower stall. Strong arms banded around her waist, holding her in place.

Every cell in her body snapped to life. The lethargy weighing her down disappeared with the screech of the shower curtain rings against the rod. A rush of water echoed in her ears as steam filled the room.

"Here we go," the stranger said to the room as if the nut chatted with unconscious people all the time.

He balanced her body against his. Rough denim scratched against her sensitive skin from the front. Luke-warm water splashed over her bare body from the back, making her skin tingle and burn.

A gasp caught in her throat as her shoulders stiffened under the spray. A scream rumbled right behind the gasp, but she managed to swallow that, too.

"This should help." He continued his one-sided conversation in a deep, hypnotizing voice.

He seemed mighty pleased with himself. And since he had stepped right under the water with her, a bit ballsy for her taste.

"This will feel better in a second," he said to the quiet room.

He wasn't wrong.

Firm hands caressed her skull, replacing the frigid ocean with bathwater. He rinsed and massaged and rinsed again. The sweep of his hands wiped away the last of her confusion. With that task done, his palms turned to her arms, brushing up and down, igniting every nerve ending in their path.

His chest rubbed against her bare breasts until heat replaced her chill. With thighs smashed against his legs, the full-body rubdown sparked life into body parts that had been on a deep-freeze hold for more than a year.

"Better?"

She didn't answer him. Wasn't even sure she could speak if she wanted to.

"Open your eyes and say something."

The husky command broke her out of her mental wanderings and sent a shot of anxiety skating down her spine. This was the part of the program where she ran and hid . . . and then ran some more.

Naked. Alone. Strange man. Yeah, a very bad combination.

"I know you're awake." He sounded pretty damn amused by the idea.

The jig was up. Okay, fine, she got his point.

Not knowing if her rescuer counted as a friend or foe, she played the scene with the utmost care. Only a complete madman would attack a vulnerable woman who didn't know her own name. If her stranger fell into that category, she'd scream and make a mad dash into the kitchen for the nearest sharp knife. The nearest sharp anything.

She groaned in pain that was only half false.

"Your eyes are still closed," he said.

Yeah, pal, no kidding.

"You aren't fooling me."

Well, she could certainly try.

His hands continued to massage her sore flesh with

just the right amount of pressure to bring her blood sizzling back to life. If he kept this up, her eyes wouldn't open. She'd be asleep.

She couldn't remember the last time she slept through the night. Actually, she could. It had been fifteen months. Fifteen months of searching. The path led to Kauai. To the yacht. To flying over the side and into the water. To being in this shower.

"We can stand here all night for all I care," he said.

Nothing that extreme. Maybe ten more minutes.

He chuckled. "Doesn't bother me."

Lucky for her she found an accommodating potential serial killer.

"Because I'm the one with clothes on," he pointed out.

Her eyelids flew open.

The deep rumble of his laugh intensified. "Thought that one might get your attention."

Oh, he had her attention. All six-feet-something of him, with haunting dark eyes, straight coal black hair cut short and blunt, and chiseled high cheekbones that spoke to Hawaiian bloodlines.

Her gaze dipped lower and . . . damn.

That gasp she'd been holding finally escaped her lips. The part below his neck looked as impressive as his face. A broad muscular chest, every inch tan and perfect. Blue jeans balanced on lean hips.

Double damn. Obviously strong and in command, this guy could crush her if he wanted to.

That realization got her talking. "Who are you?"

One dark eyebrow kicked up in question. "That was my question. You are . . . ?"

A woman in deep trouble. A woman at home with a camera and in a darkroom. A woman with a mission.

The idea of confiding in someone tempted her, but she resisted. She didn't know this guy or his agenda.

Hell, she didn't even know who her enemies were and why. Until she did, she was not saying a word.

"I . . . I don't know," she stammered out.

She was playing a dangerous game. No other choice. Someone had pushed her off a party boat. Either Sterling Howard had figured out her real identity and ushered her off his yacht the hard way or . . . actually, she couldn't think of an "or" option.

"Don't know what?" he asked.

"My name."

Those deep brown eyes, almost black, narrowed. "For most people it's an easy question. You've likely had one since birth."

"I, uh, can't remember it," she said, making sure her voice held the appropriate mixture of concern and shock. Funny how those two emotions came to her without any trouble at the moment.

"Wait a second. You mean—"

"Yes."

His hands tightened briefly on her elbows, then relaxed. "Interesting."

The longer she stood there, the more pronounced their size difference became. "Not to be rude or sound ungrateful, but could we have this little chat later? Like, when I'm dry and fully dressed."

"You really can't remember your name?"

She lifted her hands and covered her breasts. A stupid move, yes. He'd already seen all the goods. Not that he cared one wit. He didn't appear to be staring anywhere but dead into her eyes.

"Trying the dry thing now would be good," she said.

He reached behind her and turned off the water. "You're saying you have amnesia?"

For a second she wondered if a person with a real case of amnesia would recognize the word *amnesia*.

Deciding that type of thinking would drive her nuts, she answered, "Yes."

"Seems a bit convenient."

The least the guy could do was have the decency to look a little worried about her made-up amnesia story. "There's nothing convenient about not knowing who you are."

He stepped out of the tub and grabbed up a towel for her. "Here. Dry off. We need to pump some heat into you and then . . ."

"Yes?" she asked, a bit concerned about what the rest of his sentence could be.

"Find some clean clothes for both of us. I'm guessing you'd like to be dressed when we talk."

She'd rather skip the talking part. "Talk about what?"

"Whatever it is you're running from."

Wariness washed over her. This time not about being naked, although she wasn't real fond of that either. The heart-to-heart he had planned was the bigger problem. She'd made a promise to her mother, although in her mother's catatonic state, she likely didn't understand the vow. But that wasn't the point. Annie had enough guilt for a lifetime without failing her mother a second time.

He turned away and lifted an oversized terry cloth robe off the back of the door. "Once you've settled in, we'll get to the bottom of who you are."

"I told you—" Whatever she was going to say stuck in her throat when he cuddled her in the warm material and gently tucked in the loose ends between her breasts.

"You can explain why you're in Hawaii, what you were doing on the beach and how you got there," he continued.

Now that the uncertainty about her safety with him had eased, she could focus on his habit of interrupting. Very annoying.

Other aspects about him were annoying, but for a different reason. Being soaking wet, his jeans clung to his body. Water dripped down his bare chest and lean frame, forming a puddle on the bath mat. When he wiped a hand through his damp hair, stray ends stood up straight. For some reason, the goofy look worked on him.

Shame she couldn't say the same thing about the intelligence lingering behind those dark eyes. He was going to be a problem. Hard to fool.

Time to leave. She had to track down the yacht and find her camera. Out of habit, she carried around her photography equipment wherever she went. Being separated from it made her nervous.

"I think it would be better if I got back and left you to your life," she said.

A sly grin tugged on the corner of his mouth. "You don't know who you are or how you got here. Hard to imagine you know where you're going."

She clenched at the cotton gathered between her breasts and adjusted the rest of the robe to make sure everything important stayed under wraps. "I meant that I should check in with the police. Look for a bag or some other type of identification, that kind of thing."

His smile beamed now. "You're in luck."

Lucky, right. That was how she felt. "How exactly?"

"I'm the police."

Her stomach dipped to the floor and took up residence there. "Excuse me?"

"I'm Police Chief of Kauai County."

"County?"

"That's a fancy way of saying Kauai."

"The entire island? That's not possible." *Please have that not be possible.*

"I promise it's true. I attended the swearing-in ceremony."

The last thing she wanted was to talk with a police

officer. She was operating under the radar on this. She didn't want justice. She wanted revenge and didn't plan to walk within the lines of the law to get it.

"Show me your badge." She wouldn't know a fake badge from a real one, but the request seemed like one a smart woman would make.

He grabbed a black leather billfold from the vanity and flipped it open. Shiny badge. He flicked it closed again before she could read the name.

"You wanted me. Here I am and with all the time in the world to listen to what you have to say." He paused, drawing out his comment. "Let's get to those questions."

"But . . ." That was all she had. The rest of the sentence just kind of died in the air.

He snatched up a towel and draped it over his shoulders. "Including your name."

"I don't—"

"Remember? Yeah, heard you the first seven times." He grabbed both ends of the towel and pulled it taut against his neck. "I just don't believe you."

The man was as smart as he looked, which was a damn shame.

Chapter 3

Copper. Out on the beach Kane had wondered. Looking at the mystery woman standing on his bath mat, now he knew. Her hair fell in loose copper-colored curls around her shoulders, drying as he watched. Those green eyes were the color of the grass in spring. The brightness a perfect opposite to her creamy pink-hued skin.

Lovely and delicate. A beautiful woman.

Except for the lying. She had not uttered a single truthful sentence since he dumped her in the shower and forced her out of her fake slumber.

His robe dwarfed her petite frame, making her look sweet and vulnerable. After talking with her for five minutes, he knew that was a sham, too. This woman could hold her own.

Now he had to see if she could tell the truth.

"I'm ready when you are," he said.

She clenched the robe even tighter against her breasts. "You can look somewhere else. I'm not interested."

It took a few seconds for her comment to settle in. When the words hit him, so did a twinge of guilt. The woman likely suffered from something, even if that something was her own stupidity. No wonder she expected the worst from him.

"I'm not offering," he said, hoping to ease her concern.

"Keep it that way, or I strangle you with this belt." She twirled the material a bit.

He wondered if she realized the move looked more like a striptease than a threat. The direction of his thoughts confirmed what he already knew—three months was too long to go without a woman. He'd started seeing sexual overtones everywhere, even from a nearly drowned woman.

He exhaled for emphasis. "Look, Trixie, we have a problem."

"Trixie?"

"Do you prefer Fern?"

"To what?" She stopped twirling the belt.

"I don't know. Mabel?"

"Who?"

"Or is it Bertha?"

A flush settled over her cheeks. "I don't even know what we're talking about."

Somehow he didn't believe that either. He'd been in law enforcement in some form or another since turning twenty-one. That amounted to fifteen years of intuition and experience. During his time with the Drug Enforcement Agency he'd seen everything. Tracked down money and drugs. Dodged bullets and knives. Hell, he'd broken unbreakable perps. Same with his current position with the police department.

This lady put on a good front, but she was playing some sort of game just like the rest of them. He just had to figure out which one.

"We're still working on your name," he said as he towel dried his hair. "I see you as a Gertrude."

She clenched her teeth together so hard his gums ached in sympathy. A lot of anger brewed under the surface with this one. He filed that information away for later.

"I told you I don't remember my name. Why don't you believe me?"

He threw the balled-up towel on the counter. "Maybe because you're lying."

She gasped.

Her acting needed some work, but he appreciated the effort. "Don't get me wrong. You're doing a convincing job, but the I-don't-remember thing is getting old."

She waved her hand in the air in a dismissive gesture, one that came very close to giving him the finger. When she did it a second time, he figured she *was* giving him the finger.

"Think whatever you want," she said as she curled her bare toes into his bath mat.

He couldn't figure out if she was cold or trying to hide her shocking pink nail polish. "Right. The amnesia. Any other disease or afflictions you're pretending to have? Just so I'm prepared."

The stain on her cheeks deepened. "For a supposed police officer you don't seem all that concerned about the fact I nearly drowned."

That thought sobered him. Despite everything else, trouble barked at her heels. "If you tell me how you got in the water, I can help. I can't do anything until you level with me."

"I have."

"Look, Fern—"

She lost some of her cool and started shouting. Even stomped one of those bare feet against the small carpet square. "Stop calling me that."

"It could be your name."

"It's not."

Tweaking her temper came easy. "You're saying you know what your name isn't?"

"That's right."

He'd received medical training. Knew how to identify injuries. "Did you read that in a book?"

"When?"

"Whenever you dreamed up this story."

"I was too busy drinking in buckets of saltwater and swimming for my life to read or dream anything."

"Touché." He grabbed his shield off the counter. "Let's go."

"I'm done showering, thanks."

"To my bedroom." He reached for her elbow.

She backed away and evaded his grasp. "Look, I'm not—"

"Not for that." The thought of a mutual and hot "that" had been hovering at the back of his mind ever since he stepped into the shower and felt her soft skin pressing against him.

Not about her. About any woman. Now that she'd brought the idea out into the open, he wouldn't be able to block it again until he found a woman to scratch that itch. Preferably one who could tell the truth for more than three minutes at a time.

"We're going to change," he said.

"If by that you mean change into someone less annoying, I'm all for it." She motioned for him to go first.

He figured the biting remarks were a defense mechanism. Either that or her entire personality consisted of sarcasm. "You need to stay in my line of sight."

"I'm still not interested," she grumbled.

"Me either."

"Right." She shot a bug-eyed glance at his zipper.

As far as he was concerned, she needed to keep his pants out of this. And stop looking. That type of encouragement he did not need.

He exhaled again to let her know his frustration, hoping this time she would get the hint. "I'm in wet jeans. Not comfortable. I need to get out of them and into something else so we can figure out what to do with you."

"You're not doing anything with me."

"I'm going to gag you in a minute." This time he caught her elbow before she could move away. "Since you strike me as a runner, you're coming with me."

He started to guide her down the short hallway. After two steps, her sharp intake of breath stopped him. "What's wrong now?"

She leaned down to rub her leg through the robe. "You make it sound as if I complain all the time."

"That's been my experience so far."

"Yeah, well, my knee hurts. Pain makes me grumpy."

Damn, she *was* hurt. "What happened?"

"I don't know."

He watched her massage her leg. "How can you not know?"

This time she was the one who sighed. "I was in that water for heaven knows how long. Maybe an animal bit me."

"Animal?"

"Fish? Mammal? Big-toothed water predator? Whatever crawls around in the water."

"Since you still have a leg, we can rule out shark. Not sure what crawling creatures you're referring to, but let me see." He dropped to his knees to inspect the injury. His fingertips barely touched the robe before she snapped the terry cloth back and away from his hands.

"I don't think so." She said a few other words, all profane and none in sentence form.

"What has gotten into you?"

"You."

This would teach him to rescue a woman in need. "What did I do?"

"Stand up. Now." She grabbed the edges of the robe and pulled the material tight against her legs in a big bunch. One hand clamped against the material at her breasts; the other held the wad around her knees. The contortion shielded every inch of bare skin except her neck, calves and feet.

The lack of trust irked him. "I'm a professional."

"Uh-huh. Get up."

"I'm trying to help you."

"Nice try." She waved a finger—this time not her middle one—in his face.

"You could have a serious injury. Something that re-quires immediate attention." He doubted that. More likely a sprain, but he should check it out to be sure. Maybe get her to a clinic or the emergency room.

"You've seen and felt enough. No more freebies. Thanks anyway." A dull red stained her cheekbones.

"What if—"

"No."

He blew out a breath. "I've seen you naked."

"That's my point. Show-and-tell hour is over."

She stayed calm when he saw her without clothes on and went wacky when he touched her knee. Women were bizarre creatures. Not exactly news to him, but still.

"Fine. You win." He held up his hands in surrender because conceding proved to be the easiest choice.

"Good."

"For now." He jumped to his feet and guided her down the rest of the short hallway to his bedroom. To keep the damage to a minimum, he balanced most of her weight on his arm.

Not that there was much to her. She probably clocked in at five-six or -seven and a hundred twenty pounds. Slim and small boned despite having some height on her. But at six-two he towered over her. The vantage point gave him a front-row view of the smooth skin at the tops of her breasts. The lawman in him looked away, but the man part snuck a peek or two.

As they walked through the doorway he tried to see the room through her eyes. Probably best described as practical and sparse. Nothing special or fancy about the mattress and frame on the floor or the oak dresser and nightstand.

He was a simple man with simple tastes. The room reflected his no-nonsense view of life. Getting tied to material objects went against his personal philosophy. The land, family and hard work mattered. It had taken losing almost all of his family for him to realize that fundamental truth.

Trade winds blew through the open window, cooling the two-bedroom house and filling the room with the scent of white ginger. Like everywhere else on Kauai, flowers bloomed in colorful disarray right under his window despite his tendency to ignore them. His front lawn consisted mostly of sand. Low maintenance for a man who rarely spent time at home.

Make that a man who *used* to rarely spend time at home. Right now he spent all of his time at home or on the beach or over on Oahu visiting his nephew at college.

Six days of vacation left. Today he'd found a woman. He could hardly wait to see what washed up on shore tomorrow.

"You could have left me in the bathroom," she said as she came to a halt in the middle of the room. "It's not as if I have anywhere to go."

He set her down on the edge of the bed and turned to search through his dresser drawer. "A very rational argument."

"Then?" She massaged her knee.

He made a mental note to double check the injury and wrap up her leg later. "No."

"Why not?"

He almost chuckled at the disbelief in her voice. "For starters, I don't trust you."

"You're not exactly Mr. Sunshine yourself. Working on that bedside manner of yours wouldn't be a waste of your time."

"I'm not a doctor."

"So you treat all crime victims this way?"

He caught the slip. "What crime?"

The color seeped from her cheeks. "Huh?"

Now he was getting somewhere. "You. Victim. Crime. Those were all your words."

"Well, I . . . ummm, since I washed up—"

This time he did smile. Couldn't help it. She flipped from sassy to flustered in a second. If she balled her fists together any tighter on her lap, she might break a finger or two.

"Still waiting on a full sentence, Fern."

Her toes curled again. This time, she buried the tops in the carpet just under the bed. "My name's not Fern."

"Right."

"I'd know if that were my name."

He kept his hands low behind his back to hide his surprise from her. If he lifted his palm, she'd be able to see him in the mirror set above the chest of drawers. "Try again on the victim issue."

He could actually see her mind working and waited for the next lie. Instead, calm washed over her. She sat up straight, clear-eyed and ready for verbal battle, as if she'd made some internal decision.

For some reason the change in her demeanor made him nervous as hell.

She shrugged. "I just figured if I was in the water, I must have been there by nefarious means," she said.

"Nefarious?"

"It means—"

He held up a palm. "You don't need to whip out the dictionary. I know what the word means. My point was that you could have been in the water for any number of innocent reasons, like swimming or boating."

"Naked?"

"Maybe you were skinny dipping?"

"I doubt it."

"You immediately assume something bad happened." So had he. An occupational hazard. Consistent with his life experience, too.

"I'm a pessimist." She looked him right in the eye when she said that.

"Not my Fern."

Those clenched hands now held fistsful of his comforter on either side of her legs. "If you call me that one more time, I'll . . ."

"What?"

"Something."

"Good comeback." He pulled out the handcuffs from behind his back. The metal clanked against the wood.

"What are those for?"

He dangled the cuffs in front of her face. "Insurance."

"No way. I'm outta here." She bolted from the bed.

He was ready for her. He looped one arm around her waist and pulled her back tight against his chest. He could smell his shampoo in her soft hair. His soap on her skin.

"Let me go!"

He held her still with one arm. "Can't."

"Of course you can." She squirmed and pushed against his hand.

He got his confirmation when her body fit snug against him. He needed a woman. Not this woman. One less temperamental and not water-logged. One night. Sex. Cleared head. Move on.

"Stop before you hurt yourself," he said as he blocked a shot to his temple.

"You mean, before you hurt me."

"Never going to happen." He grabbed both of her forearms, careful not to hurt her, and set her back down on the bed.

Before she could protest, he slipped one end of the handcuffs over her wrist. The other end snapped against the mattress frame with a click. The move forced her to lean on her left forearm low to the bed. Not the most comfortable position ever, but it would last only a few minutes.

"What are you doing?" She sounded more angry than scared.

"Holding you steady so I can change my clothes."

"You've got to be kidding."

"Almost never."

"This is ridiculous. Let me out of these." She rattled the cuffs, causing metal to screech against metal.

"Would you prefer I strip down in front of you?" he asked.

"I'd prefer you show a little common sense." The heat stayed in her voice, but the clanking stopped.

"That would require me to drive you to the hospital and have you checked out. After all that poking and prodding, if you still insisted you couldn't remember anything, I'd take photos and send them out over the wire to see if anyone had reported you missing. Contact the FBI for assistance. Put your face on the television and in the computer. Those things."

"Sounds like typical male overkill."

"Standard procedure." As if he had a plan for this sort of thing. Since beautiful naked women tended to walk through the front door rather than wash in with the waves, he didn't. "Just like putting you in jail would be if I found you were in that kind of trouble."

"Jail?" Her voice actually squeaked.

"But if I knew your name . . ."

She rolled her eyes. "Fine. It's Fern. Can I go now?"

"And miss your sparkling conversation? I don't think so."

"I am going to have your ass on a plate for this."

"We can talk about my ass when I get back." He winked, then disappeared into the bathroom.

Chapter 4

Annie sat on the corner of Kane's bed and drummed her fingers against the comforter. Being nearly naked and chained to a stranger's mattress should have been the scariest thing that had ever happened to her. This wasn't even the worst thing she'd had to deal with this week.

She'd forgotten to get her rescuer's name. Probably had something to do with the near drowning and public display of nudity. All that excitement made her mind a bit fuzzy. Of course, if she asked him about his name, then he'd insist on knowing hers. She'd say no. He'd call her some made-up name. With this guy's stubbornness, the cycle could go on forever.

The rescue and blood warming had helped. The robe and the hair wash weren't bad either. But the time had come—and probably gone—for her to leave. There was a difference between biding time and wasting it.

The yacht and Sterling Howard. She had to find her notes. Retrieve her camera. Hide from whatever goon had tried to drown her . . . once she figured out exactly which goon that was.

Yeah, not the most comprehensive plan ever contemplated. And, yeah, the handcuffs and six-foot watchdog caused a tiny problem.

But being confined made her crazed. She preferred the outdoors. Those slices of nature that defined serenity and peace: at the right angle, with the right light, framed by her lens and captured in a perfect moment that would never pass by again. Sunshine or dusk, hot or cold, didn't matter to her so long as the beauty of that wide-open space translated on film.

Make that *dry* wide-open spaces. It would be some time before she could look at an ocean view again without getting the shivers.

She pulled and shoved, trying to loosen the hold or snap the metal around her wrist. No chance he'd used joke cuffs. Nope. They were real which meant he was real. Not just a cop, this one claimed to be the cop in charge of cops. Better the police than a serial killer but, really, what were the chances she'd land on a police officer's doorstep?

Seeing his badge had eased the panic that kept bubbling up in her throat at the thought of being at the mercy of a strange man. Everything about him soothed her frazzled nerves. His straightforward attitude. His calm demeanor. His warm voice and hands.

Deep down, she knew she'd be safe in his home. The controlling-behavior thing would get old, but he wouldn't hurt her. The question was whether he would follow when she left.

She tugged again and let out a yelp when the cuffs dug into her soft skin. "Damn him."

"Kane? You here?"

She heard male voices first, then a door slam. At least two more people were in the house somewhere. The very small house.

That made three men she needed to avoid.

She jerked around, looking for something big and heavy to whip at whatever moron walked through the door. Furniture. A pair of old sneakers. That was all she saw. Not so much as a magazine in sight. The guy had the most boring bedroom on earth.

But, he did own a lamp. Now all she had to do was reach it. She scrambled to her knees, ignoring the shot of pain that moved up her thigh from her injury, and spun around until she faced the doorway with her back to the bathroom. One arm hooked to the bottom of the bed, and the other stretched toward the nightstand. If only she were fifteen feet tall.

The men kept calling out, walking around and otherwise making her nervous as hell.

"This is all his fault," she grumbled as she wiggled her fingers, trying to make her torso longer through sheer will.

"Hey, warrior boy, where are you? We're heading out for a beer and saw your car." The muffled male voice kept coming closer.

Warrior boy?

The bedroom door stood wide open. Two guys, polar opposites in looks, joked and laughed as they walked in. One, blond and light, with the scruffy start of a beard along his jawline and bright blue eyes close in color to his aqua tie. Despite the tailored suit, this one had a rough-hewn look about him.

The other, trim and dark and Hawaiian, dressed casually in a college tee and shorts. Throwing his keys in the air and concentrating on that task to the point where he bumped into the wall.

If she guessed right, the second was blood related to her captor. They possessed the same tall, dark and handsome gene.

"Hey, we're—" Blondie stopped and stared.

"Josh, what the hell." The young stud dropped the keys. "Whoa."

"I am going to kill him. Throw him right out the window." She mumbled the vow under her breath as she grabbed for the edges of her robe.

Blondie rubbed the back of his fingers over his beard. "Maybe we should give Kane a rain check on the beer."

The young one finally gave her eye contact. "What did Kane do now, or shouldn't I even ask?"

"Whatever it was, looks as if he hasn't finished," Blondie muttered.

"Yeah. Right. We should leave."

The young one talked sense. Annie decided she liked him.

"And miss the opportunity to give Kane shit? No way. Where is he?" Blondie looked past her. "Hey, Kane!"

Her mind went blank for a second. "Kane?"

Blondie's eyebrows raised in question. "Kane Travers. The man you're sleeping with."

Now, there was a wrong conclusion.

"I just need to talk to Kane for a second; then we'll get out of your way," the younger one said. "I promise."

Time to get the who, what, where and when basics. "He's your . . . ?"

"Uncle."

She would have guessed brother. Dark hair. Dark eyes. Unbelievable looks with an air of something exotic and forbidden. A younger version, probably somewhere in his early twenties. All torso with broad shoulders and long legs. Maybe a bit friendlier around the mouth and eyes.

Not that she was taking any chances. Not with one arm useless and a knee on the injured list. If needed, she could kick out the other leg. That one worked just fine, but she had limits.

"Why are you here?" She didn't know all of her enemies yet. Until she did, everyone was suspect.

"I actually live here, or did before college." The young one held up one of the keys as evidence.

"You still do." Blondie leaned back against the door frame and eyed her with a mixture of appreciation and skepticism. "Where's Kane?"

"Hiding like a rat in the bathroom."

Those narrowed blue eyes popped open wide. "Never known Kane to hide from anything."

"Never known him to chain a woman to his bed before either," the young one said.

She relaxed her stance a bit, still on her knees and ready for flight, but no longer stretched across the room. "That's fascinating and all, but could one of you get me out of these?"

"No, they can't." Kane walked back into the room, wearing another pair of faded jeans this time with a slim gray T-shirt.

"Damn," she whispered under her breath, both because of Kane's untimely entrance and because of how fit and athletic he looked in that tee. This guy cleaned up nice.

"What are you doing here?" he asked the younger one.

"I've been calling for three days. You didn't answer."

Kane shrugged. "I've been busy."

"Apparently." Blondie wiggled his eyebrows. "Sorry. If I'd known I would have taken him straight to my place."

Kane focused on his nephew. "You called Josh? You shouldn't be here. You have classes tomorrow."

"Because you never skipped a class in college," Blondie said.

"It's important that he—"

Annie cleared her throat. "Excuse me? Hate to break up the education lecture, but you have a woman in handcuffs over here."

Kane dumped his wet clothes in the laundry basket. "How could I forget? Josh Windsor, Derek Travers, meet Fern. Derek is the young one. Josh is the ugly one."

"My name is not Fern."

"Blanche?" Kane asked. Even managed to look serious.

"Stop doing that."

Kane motioned in her general direction. "Call her whatever you want. Doesn't matter since she'll answer even if you haven't asked a question."

Her head pounded. Her sore knee ached no matter how she sat. And three guys loomed over her as if she were a speck under a microscope. All in all, not the most fun she'd ever had while mostly naked.

"Guess you didn't get around to introductions before you—" The young one blushed under his deep tan.

"It's not what you think." Kane reached into his front pocket and pulled out the handcuff key.

"Yes, it is. He's holding me here against my will." She raised her handcuffed arm as evidence. The chain didn't reach very far, so her arm snapped back and jolted her shoulder joint. Add one more injury to the list.

The younger one frowned in what looked like confusion, not anger. "I guess women usually run too fast for him to use the handcuffs."

"Don't encourage her." Kane held the key right in front of her face. When she took a swipe at it, he yanked it back. "This is the only way out of the cuffs."

Nothing like stating the obvious. "The ocean water didn't affect my eyesight."

"I'm going to free you. In exchange, you're going to behave." Kane bent down to fiddle with the lock.

"Like hell," she muttered.

He stopped right before slipping the key in. "Excuse me?"

This time she shouted in his ear. "Like. Hell."

"That's quite a woman you have there. Feisty. I like

that." The broad smile on Josh's face suggested more than like.

Derek chuckled, but didn't take one step to help her.

Annie decided right then that these men could use a lesson or two in how to treat a woman. Handcuffs might have a place in the bedroom, but this wasn't it. She honed in on the one she suspected would be the weakest. Weaker in the sense of vulnerable to a helpless woman, and now she knew a name. Derek.

Playing the victim required a bit of acting. Pleading voice. Sad eyes. A scared shake or two. She'd learned this skill from the best. Her mother could put on a show that would have everyone around throwing pity and assistance in her direction.

Annie had spent most of her younger life with a frontrow seat to her mother's performances. Then most of her adult life on a series of freelance assignments far away from home to avoid the act. By the time her mother actually needed her, Annie knew only how to be away.

"You have to help me." Annie focused all of her energy on convincing Derek. When his smile faded, she knew the show had gotten his attention.

"Uh, Kane?"

Kane stood. "Ignore her."

"That's kind of tough. I mean, damn, look at her. She's—"

She liked this kid more every second. "Derek, please help me."

"She's playing you." Kane twirled the key ring on his finger.

"She can play with me." Josh's comment earned him a shove from Kane.

Derek looked around the room. "This is the weirdest one-night stand I've ever heard of."

Josh shrugged. "I've had worse."

"Shut up." Kane delivered the order, then turned on her. "Fern, you're embarrassing yourself."

The mention of the damn Fern name made her double her efforts to convince Derek. "Kane will lose his job over this if you don't put a stop to it now."

"When exactly did you learn my name?" Kane asked.

"You forgot to ask her name before you climbed into bed with her?" Josh shook his head. "Damn, Kane, what kind of example does that set for the kid here?"

"Doesn't bother me," the kid said with a big smile. "Nice to see Kane getting . . . out."

"Can we get back to business?" When the men didn't speak up, Kane folded his arms across his chest and continued. "I found Mabel, here, on the beach."

He was talking about her as if she did not exist. The toad. "I'm right here and—"

"—and then I brought her here to make sure she was okay. That's why she's in my bedroom."

Kane's speech got the other men's attention. They crowded in until she had to slide down farther on the bed to get some air. With them hovering, she wanted her feet on the floor, not tucked underneath her.

They stood like a matched set. Three handsome men. Three fierce frowns. Three men in control and in her way.

"Damn, is she okay?" Derek asked.

Just what she needed, a wall of testosterone on a problem-solving kick. "No, I'm not—"

"She's fine except that she's pretending to have a case of amnesia."

"That doesn't make much sense unless she has something to hide," Josh said as he leaned in even closer.

Derek's frown mirrored Kane's. "Why is she faking?"

"*She* is sitting right here, and *she* can hear and speak just fine. *She* doesn't need Kane answering for her." Great, now they had her talking about herself in the third person.

Josh flashed a megawatt smile. "She's bossy."

"Tell me something I don't know. You should try showering with her."

With Kane's comment, the men stopped looking at her and faced Kane.

Josh coughed. "What did you say?"

"Uh, hello?" She waved her hand but realized it was too low on the bed for the guys to notice the motion. "I'm chained to a bed. Let's get back to that little piece of the puzzle."

They treated her to another joint stare. She almost melted under the scrutiny of three pairs of eyes.

"Any injuries?" Josh ignored her tirade and continued as if she hadn't spoken.

"Cuts and bruises. Sore knee. Nothing too serious. She was lucky," Kane explained.

"Because I didn't actually drown? Yeah, lucky me."

"Drown?" The lazy look in Josh's blue eyes disappeared in a flash.

"She should go to the police," Derek said.

Good boy. The kid really was her favorite. "That's exactly what I said to Kane. That I wanted to check in with . . . Wait a second. I thought Kane was the police."

"Go back to the drowning part," Josh said.

Derek shook his head. "We should call the police first."

"Stop, stop, stop," she yelled. Surprisingly, they did. "Kane told me he was the police chief. The guy in charge of crime in this part of the state."

"I know I didn't say it that way," Kane said in a dry tone.

She pointed an accusing finger at Kane. "You lied to me."

Derek jumped to his uncle's defense. "He's police. It's just that he's not working right now."

"Derek." Kane said the kid's name like a warning.

"He's on a leave of absence," Josh added.

"Vacation, and that's enough," Kane said. This time the warning in his tone was pretty clear.

"You've never taken a vacation in your life," Josh muttered. "Do you even know how to have fun?"

She held her wrist up as high as it would go. She aimed for under Kane's nose but could stretch only to his crotch. "Take these off, or I'll call the *real* chief and burn your sorry no-good ass. When I'm done, you'll be damn lucky just to pull meter-reading duty."

"I'd like to see that," Josh said.

"Wow." Derek's voice filled with something that sounded like admiration.

Kane looked bored by the entire scene. "Impressive language, Fern."

A little profanity never scared her. The saltier, the better. Her career required her to travel with men and fit in. Men swore. She swore. No big deal.

"Wait until I get started. That little shower scene deserves a profane word or two. The damn handcuffs should be good for an all-out screaming fit."

"Notice how they keep mentioning the shower but won't give any details," Josh said to Derek.

"Shut up!" Annie and Kane answered at the same time.

Kane stared at her with those penetrating eyes. "No wonder you ended up in the water. You're lucky they didn't gag you first."

Derek threw his hands up. "I'm lost again. Who's they?"

"Yeah, let's get back to the drowning." Josh reached into his pocket and took out a small flip pad. "That's the subject on the table."

Her frustration boiled over. "I didn't drown, so you can stop talking about it."

Josh puckered his lips together. "But you were in the water."

"Yeah? So?"

Josh turned to Kane, all traces of amusement vanished. "We may have a problem."

Muscles tensed across Kane's shoulders, pulling his T-shirt even tighter over his chest. "Yours or mine?"

"Ours. Maybe hers. All I have is a report of a missing yacht, missing crew and missing owner. The boat was last seen near here."

Her stomach flipped at the word *yacht*. The chances of that yacht being her yacht had to be slim.

"Which one?" Kane asked the question on her mind.

Josh rubbed his palm over his stubble. "You're not going to like the answer. It's the *Samantha Ray*."

Yeah, not good. Annie did the calculation in her head. She goes overboard, then the yacht and people on board go missing. The chances of those events not being related were about zero. Maybe less.

Kane's eyes grew even darker as he glared at her. "Anything you want to tell me?"

Only that she suddenly didn't want to go anywhere since by Kane's side seemed to be the safest place to be. Getting him to agree to let her stay moved up as the new number one strategy. She needed to regroup and think. Kane's house would provide the perfect setting for that.

"Uh, yeah."

"What?"

"My name is Annie."

Chapter 5

Ten minutes later Annie, or the woman who claimed to be Annie, sat at his kitchen table wearing a pair of his sweats and one of his slim exercise T-shirts. On her, slim and form-fitting turned into baggy. The clingy material reached past her butt but did highlight her high, firm breasts.

Braless, shoeless and pissed as hell, she sat there with her elbows resting on the table while Derek sat on the tile floor at her feet. She muttered something about luck and a phrase or two, most of it profane, about fake police officers.

Kane assumed she meant him. "Are you done calling me an idiot?"

"Are you done being a damn idiot?"

"I dunno, Kane," Josh said. "The answer to your question looks like no."

Derek chuckled but didn't add a comment.

Disgruntled and bitchy. Well, Kane thought, she should join the fucking club—yeah, he could swear, too.

The second she'd given Derek the okay to wrap her knee, Kane felt a rush of heat sweep through his body. Not in a good way. The uncomfortable twinge hit him out of nowhere. He pushed it to the back of his mind and focused in on figuring out why Annie had washed up on his beach. "How 'bout a last name?"

He'd need first and last to do a proper search for her in the police computer. Or, ask someone else to do it. Police property, even his own office, was off-limits to him thanks to the Internal Affairs investigation. His desk temporarily belonged to that IAD idiot William Dietz. Kane refused to put his officers in the position of sneaking him in the building.

Josh sprawled in the kitchen chair across from her. One arm hung over the back. With his other hand, he tapped a pen against his front teeth.

"Annie is fine." She wrapped her fingers around a coffee cup, then turned her attention to Josh. "Can you stop that noise?"

Click, click. "It calms me."

"Drives me nuts," she said.

"You're not alone," Kane mumbled.

"It's not any better down here," Derek said.

Josh kept right on tapping. "Do you have something to hide, Annie?"

She looked down into her cup. "No."

Kane tried. "Is your name really Annie?"

"Yes."

Click, click. "You're acting like a lady with a secret. If the name is real, something else is wrong." Josh tapped a few more times.

"We all have secrets," she said before gulping down her coffee.

"Most of us have secrets that don't matter to anyone but the people involved. This is different. You say you have amnesia; then you remember your name. Annie, those aren't the actions of an honest woman," Josh said.

Kane had seen Josh's act a thousand times over the years. No one would know from his loose tie, wild hair and lazy smile that his ability to track down and destroy a drug ring was legendary. That steely determination and forget-the-rules attitude put Josh at odds with his superiors at the Drug Enforcement Agency all the time.

The bureaucracy. Yeah, Kane didn't miss that part of being with the DEA. Of course, if he'd known that the police job would come with an investigation into his personal life and monthly bills from lawyers, he might have sucked up the government bullshit and stayed where he was.

"Done." Derek got to his feet, then slid into the chair next to Annie. "Feel better?"

"Fine. Thanks." She flashed the younger man a sweet smile.

Kane tried to ignore the byplay. "Why are you in Kauai?"

"Sightseeing. Kauai is as beautiful as everyone says."

"Sightseeing underwater, were you?"

She shoved the mug aside. "Look, I know what's happening here."

Kane glanced around the kitchen. "We're sitting."

"The interrogation."

"I thought you didn't believe I was a police officer."

"Chief or not, you plan to blame the missing yacht on me. You're fishing, trying to gather information and then pin this whole thing on me."

Kane had to admit that she wasn't exactly wrong. He'd found her naked and soaking wet. She'd lied to him. She wouldn't tell him anything. A yacht just happened to go missing right about the time she'd floated onto the beach. A guy didn't need years of training at the Police Academy to know something strange was happening.

"I want a lawyer." She delivered her ultimatum, then clamped her mouth shut.

Kane felt a nerve in his cheek twitch. "What?"

"Oh, boy," Derek said as he moved his chair a few inches away from Annie.

"Have you ever noticed how the guilty ones always ask for an attorney just when the questions get interesting?" Josh stopped tapping and started scribbling in his notebook. "Happens every damn time."

"What are you writing?" she demanded to know.

This woman could make even the sanest man lose his mind. Between the hot looks, pouty mouth and sharp tongue, Kane couldn't decide whether to admire her or strangle her. In the last few minutes, the strangling idea had edged ahead.

Somehow, he kept his hands at his sides. "Annie, let's be adult about this?"

She shook her head.

"You can't ask for a lawyer." Kane tried to reason with her. The task would have been easier without Derek's laughing and Josh's loud scratching of his pen against the paper.

Kane took a deep breath and fought for patience. "You're not under arrest."

She shrugged.

"This is a bit juvenile, don't you think?" Kane asked, hoping to tweak her ego and get her talking.

She stuck out her tongue.

So much for tweaking "Another fine comeback by Ms. Annie No Last Name."

She did it again.

"Does this mean you're done talking?"

She tried to take a sip of coffee but stopped when she figured out the cup was empty. Kind of ruined the effect of ignoring him.

Josh leaned forward in his seat. "I say we skip the chitchat and arrest her."

Her eyes bugged a bit, but her mouth stayed closed.

Kane thought the idea had some merit. "Tempting, but probably wouldn't be fair to the other inmates to stick them with her."

That one earned him a glower. Her green eyes flashed with fire. He doubted the red specks on her cheeks meant she was warm. Ticked off was more like it.

Since she'd opened her eyes in his shower, she hadn't closed her mouth. Kane figured it must be killing her to keep quiet now.

"Okay, new strategy." Kane stood up and dumped their empty mugs in the sink. "Derek, you're going to do some shopping."

"And miss this? Screw that."

"She needs clothes."

Derek's jaw dropped. "Damn, Kane, you can't mean—"

"Watch your language. Just because Annie swears doesn't mean you should." Kane noticed how her hands balled into fists at that comment.

Kane glanced at the phone. He could continue to play this game, or he could call his officers and let them figure out what was going on. With six days left until he found out whether or not charges would be filed against him relating to the officer-involved shooting, he needed something to fill the hours. Annie qualified as being far more interesting than his planned house-rewiring project. Probably more dangerous, too.

"Come on, Kane. Why me?" Derek's voice stayed just this side of a whine.

"This will teach you not to cut classes," Josh said.

Kane grabbed the pen and Josh's notepad and dropped them in front of Annie. "Make a list of what you need. Personal stuff, clothes, whatever."

She frowned up at him.

"You can make the list or I can guess your size." He

looked her over, pretending she could be anything other than a small. "Do you need an extra large or something bigger?"

She snatched up the pen and scribbled hard enough to carve lines into his wooden table. Two words. Not a clothing size on there anywhere, but a comment that was more of a temptation than she knew.

Josh read upside down. "I see the 'you' but can't see the first . . . Oh, now I get it."

"Fuck you," she said before she closed her mouth again.

"Nice language," Josh said with mock shock.

"That was your last chance." Kane reached over her shoulder and picked up the pad. He listed a few items, then handed the paper to Derek.

Annie jumped up and tried to peek over at what he'd written. Kane just raised his arm higher to block her view.

Derek scanned the list. His head shot up. "Panties?"

"What?" Annie squealed.

"Now you're talking? Interesting." If Kane had known a comment or two on her underwear would get her talking, he would have shouted "panties" long before now.

"I am not having a kid buy my underwear."

"Hey, I'm twenty-one," Derek said, obviously insulted.

"And I'm twenty-nine. You're still not buying my underwear." She tried to grab the list back, but Derek slid his chair farther out of her range. The squeak against the tile echoed in the room.

Giving her a gentle shove, Kane pushed her back into her chair. "Would you prefer to go without?"

"I am right now," she shot back.

The reminder telegraphed a wake-up call straight to Kane's lower body. He had been trying to block out the memory of her body. The feel of her slim waist and soft skin. Talking about her panties or lack of them, sure as hell wasn't helping.

"Should Derek be listening to this conversation?" Josh covered Derek's ears. "'Cause I can send him outside. Just don't say anything while I'm gone."

Derek and Josh traded shoves.

"You're leaving, too." Kane wanted them both out. Alone he might be able to get Annie to talk. "Your job is to go figure out what's happening with the yacht. Is the DEA on this?"

"Not yet. There's not much to know. Someone at the marina gave a call with some concerns about foul play. That's it so far."

"Any news and information you can find would help," Kane said.

Josh gave him a quick nod.

"Why can't you find out what's happening, Mr. Police Chief?" she asked.

"The leave of absence thing," Derek rushed to explain.

Kane knew Derek would defend him to the end, but he felt his temperature rise anyway. "I'm not on—"

She talked right over him. "Let's talk about that topic for a second. Why aren't you working? What's with the leave of absence?"

"It's a vacation."

"It's not a vacation if you're forced," Josh mumbled.

"Sounds to me as if Kane is the one with secrets." She gave Josh a conspiratorial wink.

Enough of that, Kane thought. First Derek. Now Josh. Yeah, if she was going to flirt and smile, she needed to do it with him. Not that he was interested, because he wasn't. He just didn't need a turf war over Annie on top of everything else that was going on.

"You won't find any stores open now," Kane told Derek.

"We'll give it a shot. If we don't find anything, his stuff's in my car so he can bunk at my condo tonight," Josh offered.

Kane nodded in agreement. "Fine. Just bring the items back in the morning."

"She's staying?" The question came from Josh, but the confused look in Derek's eyes asked the same thing.

"Of course."

She stared up at him. "I am?"

"You have somewhere else to go?" Kane didn't bother to hold his breath waiting for her answer because he knew she didn't. If she did, she'd be there.

"Uh, no."

"Then you're stuck with me." Because he sure as hell wasn't letting her out of his sight. "Derek, go."

Derek saluted, then ripped out the page with the list. "Yes, sir."

One down, one to go. "Josh, do some digging. See what you can find out. My research resources are limited at the moment, so I'm depending on you."

"Gotcha." Josh stood up and tucked his notepad back in his jacket. "Children, no fighting while I'm gone."

"You're asking the impossible," Kane said.

"True, but the fight wouldn't be fair," Josh said.

Kane snorted. "I won't hurt her."

"I was talking about her fighting skills, not yours. I'd put money on her to take you out," Josh said in a deadpan voice.

Annie did some snorting of her own. "Damn right."

Before Annie and Josh could join forces. Kane escorted the men to the front door. When Josh threw Derek the keys to his precious vintage Mustang and told him he could drive this time, Kane knew he was in for a man-to-man chat.

"The kid's worried about you. He thinks you're turning into a freak out here by yourself. When he called me, I put him on one of the hourly flights in from Honolulu and ran him over here."

"You should have told him I'm fine and to get back to studying," Kane said.

"I'm not convinced you're fine." Josh tore a leaf off the tree next to the front porch and crumpled it in his fist. "What's up with you and Red?"

Kane appreciated the concern, but his friend had it all wrong. "Nothing."

"I've got eyes, warrior boy."

Kane ignored the nickname. He'd heard it for all seven of the years he'd known Josh. And regretted providing the Hawaiian meaning for his name for every single one of those years. "She's a guest. Nothing more."

Josh frowned. "Tell me another one."

"Found her on the beach. Was I supposed to leave her there?"

"You could have turned her over to your officers or taken her to the hospital. You kept her."

Kane felt that familiar knot in his chest. "I'm still the police chief around here no matter what Derek or anyone else might think. I have responsibilities."

"Do those responsibilities include showering with strange women and chaining them to the bed?"

"She's hiding something. I want to know what."

Josh rubbed his beard. "Look, you've had a hard run. You're under a lot of pressure."

"That's nothing new."

Kane thrived on pressure. He made a career out of chasing the drug trade. That type of work demanded long hours and a piece of his soul. Since he lost everything else, work became his focus. Work and Derek. With Derek grown and making his own way, work filled the void. The same work Internal Affairs threatened to take away.

"You deciding to add a woman to the mix is new. Ever since Leilani died—"

Kane refused to have this conversation. "This is different. She isn't Leilani. She isn't my wife. She's a woman in trouble, and I'm trying to help. It's my job."

"This one's dangerous."

Kane thought so, too, but wanted to hear Josh's theory. "How?"

"I don't trust Red."

"She's under control. I can handle her."

Josh nodded. "Right. None of my business. I get it. Just be careful."

Kane watched his friend climb into the passenger side of the car and drive off. When he returned to the kitchen, Annie sat in the exact same position. She hadn't moved an inch except to retrieve her mug and fill it again.

He sat down across from her. "Well, Annie, looks like it's just you and me."

"This day just gets better and better."

"Not yet, but there's plenty of time left."

Chapter 6

Annie finally found something scarier than being alone in the dark ocean. Being alone with Kane. The man had walked back into the kitchen a few minutes after the crowd left, and everything stopped, including her breathing.

His tall, looming presence should have scared the hell out of her. Instead, he made her stomach tumble. He was the only man who had made her look twice in over a year. There was something about him that pulled at her and made her want to know more.

She hoped it was one of those freaky things where a victim mistook gratitude for her rescuer for interest. A good night's sleep, some food and an hour or two of planning her next move, and she'd be fine. Everything would go back to normal. She'd get back on Sterling Howard's trail. Kane would get back to whatever it was he did all day on this secret vacation of his.

The time between now and getting back to normal made her nervous. Sure, she'd eventually forget all about Kane, but right now he was on her mind. That made Kane Travers, alleged Police Chief of Kauai, the number one threat to her plans.

Unfortunately, he was also her best chance for protection and information. Without him and his resources, she'd never track down the missing yacht. If the police and DEA couldn't find it, neither could she.

That wasn't an option. No, she needed to stop Howard before he hurt another woman.

"It's time for a chat." Kane grabbed another mug and the coffee pot and sat down in the chair across from her.

"Isn't that what we've been doing?"

"You've been evading and posturing." He set a bowl of sugar packets in front of her.

"I didn't—"

"Flirting and ignoring. Not talking about anything that matters or that I want to hear."

"Flirting?" That one stunned her enough to make her ignore the nastiness behind his other comments.

"I'm serious, Annie. I want answers." He poured a fresh cup of coffee and topped hers off. "It's just us. No more audience to play to. No more time for games."

She ripped open a pink packet and dumped the contents into her drink. Maybe some sugar would help jumpstart her brain cells. For some reason, they seemed to be frozen from all that ocean water.

"You sound like a cop," she said.

"I am a cop."

She sat back and folded her arms across her stomach. "Not according to Derek."

"Tell you what." He drained the cup and poured another. Black and strong. "I'll answer one of your questions if you answer one of mine."

"Okay."

He smiled. "That was too easy."

"You're not the best winner I've ever met." Of course, he really hadn't won since she didn't plan to answer anything.

"Truthfully this time, Annie. No more lies."

"I said okay."

"Ever been on the *Samantha Ray*?"

Did being thrown overboard count? "Who is she again?"

He made a face. "Do I need to define what truthful means?"

"A woman should be able to ask for some clarification without being called a liar." She twisted the empty pink wrapper between her fingers.

"Fine. The missing yacht. She docks at Port Allen. Owned by Sterling Howard, wealthy businessman and all-around scumbag. Any of this ring a bell?"

All of it. Especially the scumbag part. "That's more than one question."

"It's a description." Kane leaned forward with his elbows on the table. "Right now, I'd settle for you telling me how you know Howard."

Kane hadn't said how much of the truth he expected, which was good, because he wasn't going to get much. This was her battle. Not his. "I'm in town to photograph him."

"What the hell for?"

She made a tsk-tsk sound. "I answered your question. Now it's my turn. How did you get kicked off the force?"

He hesitated for a second before answering. "I didn't."

"What does that mean?"

He tsk-tsked right back at her. "One question only, remember? Your rules."

"You're a—"

"Don't say it." He stood up.

She decided to push him. "You're telling me that if I called police headquarters right now, someone would pick up the phone and confirm your job. Your title."

He grabbed the phone off the wall and pushed the receiver under her nose. "Ask for Ted Greene."

Okay, fine. He was the police chief. That still didn't

explain the vacation-versus-leave debate. She'd get to the bottom of that mystery once she solved her own.

She slapped the phone away from her face. "I'm sure you could get this Ted person to cover for you."

"Not very trusting, are you?"

"The handcuffs and interrogation ruined my mood."

"I asked one question, Annie. Not exactly a white-light-in-the-eyes shakedown." Kane hung up the receiver.

"You say potato . . ."

"As fun as this is, it's late. We should get to bed."

The word *bed* shot through her. "I'm not tired."

More like exhausted. The adrenaline rush had died down, leaving a trail of sleepiness in its wake.

"You should rest. You'll need it."

"A threat? I'm terrified," she said in a bored, flat tone.

He ignored the sarcasm. "Tomorrow you're going to give me the answers to all of my questions."

"More tit for tat?"

"Then we're going to go on a little field trip to your hotel."

"What makes you think I have one?"

"Unless you're sleeping in a car. Where is it parked again?" He poured another cup of coffee.

By her count, that made five. The guy must have a rock-hard stomach. At two cups, she tested her body's tolerance. The hanging out and drinking part of her job never got easier. Alcohol or coffee, it didn't matter. She preferred her own company. Just her and her camera and the room to explore.

"A hotel," she admitted.

"Which one?"

There was no use in hedging. He'd figure it out, so she gave him the name of the beach resort where she'd stayed before boarding the yacht. She should have checked out by now. She'd get right on that as soon as she figured out what to do about not having any identification or a key or her stuff.

With the yacht missing, she needed everything in her room. She'd also need protection to escort her inside in case the same someone who pushed her off the yacht was waiting in there to finish the job. And Kane would fill the role of escort just fine. Once there, she'd figure out how to get him out of the way.

"Hotel first, then we're going to the marina," he said.

She couldn't figure out if that was a good idea or a bad one. "Not to state the obvious, but the yacht isn't there."

"I've heard."

She toyed with the sugar packets, piling them in a neat stack, knocking it down, then building again. "Then what's the point? We can see the water from your front yard. Lovely view, by the way. Oceanfront on a policeman's salary? Hard to imagine."

"There was a time when people could afford to live here. I bought then. Before the overbuilding and before everyone from . . . Where are you from?"

"Seattle."

"Everyone from Seattle barged in, acted like they were the first to discover the beach and ocean, and started building street after street of overpriced houses."

She photographed the outdoors for a living. She understood the swell of anger and frustration when people took nature for granted or acted as if they owned it rather than borrowed it as a caretaker. "Bitter much?"

"Just honest."

"We don't need to drive around the island looking for beauty. It's right at your doorstep." She had had enough trouble lately. Tracking down more was not on her agenda.

He watched her fingers, his stare following the placement of every pink packet. "Yeah, but this way if you continue to lie, I can always open the truck door and throw you back in the water."

He acted as if he meant it. "You don't have to sound so damn happy at the thought. Where are we now anyway? I mean, I know we're on Kauai, but where exactly?"

He leaned back against the sink with his ankles crossed in front of him. "Your new temporary home is in Kapaa."

"Home? You keep thinking I plan to stay the night and hang out with you tomorrow." She did, but that wasn't really the point.

"That's not up for debate. The only question is where. You can sleep on the front porch. The trade winds are cool this time of year, and the waves tend to be loud, but you should be fine if you curl up under the deck chair."

She refused to dignify that comment by responding. "How many bedrooms do you have?"

"Two. One for me. One for Derek."

She should have been happier to hear that news. "Problem solved, then."

"You can't have Derek's room."

She didn't want to displace the kid. "A gentleman would let me have his bedroom while he slept elsewhere."

Kane frowned. "Then you should have washed up on that guy's beach."

A scream rumbled up the back of her throat but she shoved it back down. "You're infuriating."

"Strange talk from a woman who claims to want to sleep inside tonight." He rinsed out the coffee pot and dropped it in the sink.

"Were you fired for how you treat tourists?"

"One last time, I wasn't fired." He stepped back to the table and knocked over the pink packet wall she'd been building. "I'm the police chief and, from what I can tell, the only person you know on Kauai. So, left side or right?"

She forgot all about the sugar. "You're serious? You expect us to sleep together?"

"*Sleep* being the operative word." His face stayed blank and his voice neutral.

The thought of lying next to Kane, of having his scent and arms curl around her, sent her nerve endings tingling.

She hoped that rescuer gratitude wore off soon. With everything else she'd been through, all those months of putting her needs behind her mother's, her resistance lingered at an all-time low. The idea of a meaningless one-night stand with a hot Hawaiian guy tempted her more than she cared to admit.

If his white-knuckled grip on the back of the chair was any indication, she guessed Kane fought his own battle on that front. Unaffected, her ass. The guy felt the tug and pull between them just like she did.

"I'll take the couch," she choked out.

"Not an option."

Okay, maybe not a good option, but the only option. "Of course it is."

"Only if you want the handcuffs back on."

"If you even—"

"Yes?"

"I'll kick you square in the—"

"Understood, but the answer is the same," he said with a wink. "I don't trust you not to run."

The wink should have been swarmy. On him, it came off as sexy. "I have nowhere to go."

"You're a resourceful woman, Annie. So, you either

sleep next to me, where I can feel you and hear you, or you sleep on the couch with the handcuffs to keep you warm and toasty. You choose."

Did he have to say "feel"? "That's not a choice."

"It's the only one you're going to get." Kane walked to the doorway and shut off the light, leaving her sitting in the dark kitchen. "Ready?"

"Would it matter if I said no?"

"Not one bit."

Chapter 7

A few hours later Kane decided that being in bed with Annie could be described only one way: pure torture. Lying on top of the covers in sweat shorts and a tee with her tucked underneath the bedding provided a small barrier. A thin cotton shield between his body and hers. Too thin.

He could feel the heat radiating off her through the sheet. Could smell her scent, a mixture of his shampoo and her skin, on the pillow. When she turned on her side and snuggled her firm bottom against his thigh, he broke out in a cold sweat.

"I'm hot," she grumbled.

That made two of them. "You're wearing four layers of clothing. You could trek through the Arctic and not worry about frostbite."

She sat up and punched her pillow. Probably pretending the defenseless thing was his face.

"I'm wearing what I had on before bed," she said between shots.

"Plus my robe."

"The air was cool." She slapped the pillow a few more times.

"It's eighty degrees." He didn't own an air conditioner, preferring to throw open the windows and let the trade winds drag in the breeze off the ocean.

"A cool eighty," she said.

She'd said she lived in Seattle, but now she found Hawaii cold. Interesting. Made him wonder if the Seattle story suffered from the same problem as the amnesia one—being false. "So you needed the robe and my sweatshirt?"

She stilled in mid pillow fluff. "How did you know about the sweatshirt?"

"I saw you digging through my drawers." Leaving her alone still wasn't an option. Not until he knew her story. Having her last name would be a start. Until then, he'd piss with one eye on her and one on the toilet.

This time she punched his shoulder. "You were in the bathroom."

"Hey!"

"Were you watching me?"

The woman packed a punch. "Don't hit me. Ever."

"What are you going to do about it?"

Absolutely nothing. "Throw your pretty little ass in jail. That's assault."

Even in the dark room, he could see her mouth fall open. The woman had to know how enticing her butt could be. Her shock must have been a result of the threat.

"Just answer me." She balanced her head on her elbow and hovered over his left shoulder.

Her soft hair brushed against his cheek and tickled his nose. He could see her sexy auburn curls in the pale light from the window. A deep, dark sultry red.

"It's my damn house." Unexpected desire whipped through him, making his voice gruff.

Maybe he should try a real vacation. Fly to Arizona. Take in a football game. Find that nice woman who could tell the truth for more than three seconds at a time and sleep with her. Meaning not sleep at all.

"You invaded my privacy," she insisted.

Was she kidding? "You mean like you did when you went into my drawer without asking?"

She flopped back on the bed. "Anyone ever tell you how annoying you are?"

"Never."

Plenty of folks used stronger language than that. Being in law enforcement guaranteed a wide variety of enemies. He counted a few of Kauai's finest families on that list. Busting up their baby boys' drug-selling operation had been his most recent task. A task that had earned him the families' wrath and an internal investigation.

"They should try sleeping with you. You're a bed hog."

"Never had any complaints before." Not on that score.

Of course, since Leilani, he hadn't kept any woman around long enough to move to the disgruntled stage. The women in his life tended to die young, so he didn't see the point in getting attached. Breast cancer, car accidents, the reason for the death didn't matter. Death was death.

His mother. His sister. His wife. He took the hint and backed off. He was done burying the women in his life.

She flipped her pillow over once, twice, and smacked it with her fist a few more times.

He waited until she settled back into the pillows. "You done squirming?"

Lying on her back with her hands folded across her chest, she did a great impression of a corpse. "Unless it bugs you, then I'll keep moving around."

"While you're flopping all over the place, you may want to take one or two of those layers off." If he got a vote, he'd choose removal of all the layers.

"Keep your nose out of my clothes . . ." She choked a little. "Well, you know what I mean."

"Where did you say I should put my nose?"

"Shut up."

"I've seen you naked. The mystery's gone." He tried to sound uninterested, as if her body were nothing special.

"Don't remind me." She tugged the covers up to her chin.

"We're grownups."

"One of us is. The jury's still out on the other."

He could not drop the conversation for some reason. "We should be able to talk about this like adults."

"We're not talking about it at all."

He was. "Why not?"

"I'm not going to answer that."

He turned on his side and watched her chest rise and fall in a steady rhythm. His gaze traveled up to her face. The small upturned nose. The deep-set eyes. Flawless complexion.

"There's no reason to get shy all of a sudden," he said. In my line of work, I've seen—"

"Forget what you've seen."

Like that was ever going to happen. "Fine."

"About my body, I mean."

"Already forgotten. Couldn't even tell you were a woman. Seen hundreds better than you. Happy?"

The mattress dipped in front of him as she rolled over and fell right into him with an "ompf." Her breasts crushed against his chest for a second before she reached across him and clicked on the light next to his head.

To keep from being blinded, he threw an arm over his eyes. "What the hell are you doing?"

The woman had some trouble taking a hint. Instead of going to sleep, she poked and shoved against his shoulder. "Wake up."

"What the hell makes you think I can sleep through your acrobatic routine?"

He dropped his arm next to his ear to get a better look at her. All wrapped up in his robe and glaring, she kneeled next to his hip.

"What's wrong with you?" he asked.

"You are."

"I thought we weren't talking anymore tonight."

"We're not talking about the nudity. On every other topic, we talk when I say we talk."

"When did you start paying the mortgage?" He closed his eyes. Not looking at her fine-boned beautiful face might ease the tension building in his groin.

"The guest is always right."

He opened one eye. "You're a guest now?"

"You invited me to stay over."

He had. The move had surprised him more than her. He'd had sex since Leilani. Sleepovers, no. "Who could argue with that logic?"

She poked him again. Put all her strength behind it that time.

"Stop that." He lifted up his arm and looked at the scratch. "You broke skin."

"You deserved it."

"For what? I'm trying to sleep." He got a good look at her face. There on her cheeks and forehead. "You're sweating."

"I'm trying to get our relationship on an equal footing. We started off wrong, what with me being naked and you . . . not."

"That part was fine with me." More than fine. Amazing. Call him an insensitive bastard, but healthy men looked at that kind of thing.

"I don't like the imbalance of power between us," she said.

"And to adjust this alleged footing issue, you've decided to wear all of my clothes at one time. Yeah, that makes sense, Annie."

"It does."

"The tropical heat has rotted your brain. Maybe you're allergic to the smell of plumeria."

Her eyes grew dreamy for a second. "I love that smell. As soon as I got off the plane, the scent hit me. That unique mix of greenery, rain, ocean water and flowers. Then on the way to the hotel I saw this amazing bougainvillea with mountains in the distance and white puffy clouds filling the sky. The shot would have been perfect for this calendar . . ." The faraway look vanished. "Never mind."

"What calendar?"

She ignored the question, just as she had most of his questions. "My logic makes perfect sense. You know it."

He didn't. Women spoke a language all their own as far as he was concerned. "Let's try this."

He sat up and reached for the belt to the robe. She pulled back just as he grabbed the end. The move untied the knot without any effort from him. "I didn't save you on the beach to have you die of asphyxiation in my bed."

"Guess that wouldn't look good in the paper. I can almost see the headline: Police Chief Smothers Female Companion With Clothing. Very catchy."

She was too busy chuckling at her lame joke to complain about him sliding the robe off her shoulders.

Or the sweatshirt over her head. In about a minute he had her striped down to his washed-out Arizona State University T-shirt, which on her looked oversized but sexy. The same one with a picture of Sparky the Sun Devil, the school's mascot, right in the center of her chest. Devil. How appropriate.

His skin itched with the need to touch her. Not the robe. Not the clothes. Her. All that creamy skin. Those full red lips. Her hard little nipples.

"Kane?" Her tongue swept across her lips, wetting them.

All he wanted to do was pass his own along that seam, dip inside and taste her. He shook his head to wipe out all of those erotic thoughts.

"Go to sleep." He didn't recognize his own voice.

"I think we should—"

"Go to sleep." Maybe if he said it over and over, he'd actually believe it.

But she wasn't moving. She sat straight up, as if frozen in place right there in the middle of his mattress.

The situation called for fast thinking, quick action and absolutely no touching. Letting his fingers wander over her skin, slide under that tee, comb through that silky hair. All tempting, but his pants would catch on fire. Worse, he'd lose it like a teenage boy touching his first breast.

"Here. Let me help." Against his better judgment, he balanced his hands on her slim shoulders and eased her back into the pillows.

Then whatever remained of that better judgment expired.

He followed her down until his palms rested against the mattress on either side of her head. With his chest pressed diagonal against hers and his knees still on the bed beside her, he leaned in until his lips hovered just above hers.

"You comfortable?" he asked.

"No."

At last an honest answer. He could see from the heat banked behind her eyes and sharp kick in her breathing that his closeness affected her. The fact she didn't hide her reaction or pretend disinterest filled him with pure male satisfaction. Made him wonder how fast he could bring her to orgasm.

Her mouth fell open the slightest bit, luring him in. He pressed a palm against her chest, right on the upper crest of her breasts, and rubbed her skin with a gentle massage. "You still feel warm."

"Probably because I'm covered by a hundred and eighty pounds of warm male."

He brushed his lips across her cheek. "Very warm male."

Her fingers caressed his shoulder. "One could even say hot."

"What now, Annie?"

Her sweet smile turned mischievous. Like, he-should-cover-his-balls-and-duck-for-cover mischievous.

"We go to sleep," she said in a sing-songy voice.

The sensual spell evaporated. The mood changed that fast. If he were the pessimistic type, he'd think she planned this seduction scene to teach him a lesson.

"Now, Kane. Sleep." The caress against his chest turned into a full-fledged shove.

The push caught him off guard. He fell back and only by kicking out his legs did he manage to stop the tumble before he landed on the floor and on his ass.

"What are you—"

"Sleeping." She turned over, facing away from him, and curled deeper under the covers with a deceptively sweet sigh.

"But—"

"Good night, Kane." Her voice sounded downright chipper.

That made one of them.

Chapter 8

Kane nearly gave Annie whiplash when he pulled his small red pickup truck into the marina parking lot the next morning. Good thing Derek had dropped off two khaki shorts and white polo shirt outfits because she was about to ruin this one with a rehash of her breakfast toast from a few hours ago.

"That was a lovely ride. Any longer and I would have thrown up all over your shiny dashboard."

Kane shifted the truck into park and stared at her. At least she thought he was looking at her. Hard to tell with his dark sunglasses. She couldn't see his eyes, but she could see his severe frown. Added to the unshaven chin and deep lines on his forehead, the look was a bit too menacing for her taste.

"Are you always so grumpy in the morning?" she asked.

"Frustrated."

"From what?"

"Last night." His lips flattened into a thin line. "Not funny, by the way."

She didn't pretend to misunderstand. Not with the mood he was in. "Oh, come on. It was a little funny."

"Hysterical."

"You're just mad because I didn't fall for your bedroom stud act. You expected me to throw off my clothes and beg you to make love to me."

"Would that have killed you?"

"You'll get over it." She hoped she would.

Kane acted as if he was the only disappointed one in the car. Wrong. Putting a fast stop to his heavy move was the only option last night. One more inch and he would have kissed her. Lips. Hands. Clothes on the floor. Him inside her. She could see it, feel it. Her body clenched inside at the thought.

That was exactly why she'd stopped him before they went too far. She'd come to Hawaii to gather information and settle a score. Not get laid. A side dish of Kane Travers, well, the idea tempted her more than she wanted to admit.

Making him angry, getting his masculine pride riled up, seemed to be the only answer to stop the seduction. If he had kept up the touching, she would have caved. She couldn't afford that right now.

"There are words for women like you."

"Adorable? Irresistible?"

He cracked a smile. "Try pain in the ass."

"I like my descriptions better."

She stuck her arm out the open window, palm up, and felt the healing heat of the bright sunshine. Across the hilly landscape off to her right, flowers bloomed in wild disarray. Scents from different plants and buds mixed together in a pungent aroma that assailed her senses. The same intoxicating smell she always associated with Hawaii.

And chickens. Everywhere she went on the island, the little feathered critters followed. "What's with all the chickens?"

"Hurricane."

Somehow she missed a natural disaster? She must have been in the water longer than she thought. "When?"

"Nineteen ninety-two."

"What?" He had to be kidding. "That was fifteen years ago. How could that have anything to do with these chickens?"

"One caused the other. Trust me, I was here."

"Let me get this straight. You're saying a storm fifteen years ago accounts for the dozens—"

"Thousands."

"Okay, thousands of chickens roaming around the island?" She snorted. "Is this a tale locals tell to tourists to make us look stupid?"

"We have other stories for that. The chicken one is true." He watched six chickens attack a piece of bread on the grass in front of the truck. "As late as the day before the hurricane hit, the weather service underestimated its force, called it a storm, and predicted it would miss us. Instead, it turned into Hurricane Iniki and slammed into Oahu and Kauai."

"But, to still feel the effects fifteen years later?"

"Hawaii experienced an economic downturn. Foreign investors pulled out. Took years to rebuild Kauai. Oahu fared a little better. Basically, the economy and the chickens have never been the same."

She watched another chicken walk over and join the group. She swore at the birds before. Now she wished she had a loaf of bread.

"Why doesn't someone round them up?" she asked.

"You ever try to catch a wild chicken?"

"In Seattle? Hardly."

Kane stopped watching the chickens and started watching her. "Want to volunteer for the duty?"

"Yeah, where do I sign up?"

Uncomfortable under the force of his stare, she gazed out over the clear water, docks and boats . . . and no hotel. She realized for the first time where they really were. Chickens weren't the only problem.

"What happened to the hotel stop?"

"Not necessary. I sent Josh over this morning."

Her heart galloped. "To my room? How?"

Kane turned off the truck and took the keys out of the ignition. "You told me where you were staying."

"You don't even know my last name." The words rushed out of her, each one louder than the one before.

"I do now, Ms. Annie Parks of Seattle Washington." His sexy grin came back in full force.

"But—"

"One of the perks of being in law enforcement is having access to information. Tracking down your room and getting in wasn't hard. Not for Josh."

"He went through my personal stuff?" The idea scared the hell out of her. Her private papers and journals. All the newspaper clippings. The report from the investigator she'd hired.

"Nothing to go through."

"Huh?"

"Your room was empty."

She couldn't process whatever he was trying to say. "What?"

"Cleaned out."

"I don't understand."

He balanced an arm over the top of the steering wheel. "You have a hearing problem all of a sudden?"

"I'm hoping." She tried to put the best spin on the situation. Maybe the hotel put her stuff in storage. That would be a perfectly reasonable explanation. And good news. No one would think to track down her personal property there.

"Yeah, well, Josh said the room looked as if no one had stayed there. Completely empty." The keys jingled in Kane's hand.

"That's not possible. Where's my stuff?"

"No idea. Josh couldn't even find a fingerprint."

Now she had something new to tick her off. "Wait just a damn minute. He ran my prints?"

"Tried to. At my request." Kane said that so calmly. The same way other people asked for a glass of water and tuna salad on rye.

She couldn't afford to be that calm. All of those months of hard work. All of that information. "How dare you!"

"It's my job."

"Not right now it isn't."

"Get angry, then get over it, Annie. You knew I would find out who you are sooner or later."

She'd hoped for later. Much later. "So, what else do you know?"

His smile faded a bit. "Is there more to know?"

Relief rushed through her. He didn't know much, and that was exactly how she wanted it to stay. "Just the name, huh? Aren't you just the super detective?"

"Chief. You're still having a hard time with my job title."

A police car pulled up beside them. She could see the officer through the window behind Kane.

"Ah, Kane?"

He turned around and glanced in the direction where she looked. "It's okay. Roy's meeting us."

Sounded like the exact opposite of okay to her. Hanging out with the police chief and a DEA agent was enough for her. She didn't need to meet a whole gang of officers following her every step.

"Believe it or not, I don't see the arrival as good news."

Kane pinned her with a narrow gaze. "That's because you're hiding something."

"Wrong." Okay, right.

"Uh-huh, let's go."

"I'm still furious with you over the privacy invasion at the hotel."

"Thanks for the warning." He opened the truck door.

"I want to know where my stuff is." Probably with the jerks who threw her into the ocean.

"We'll figure that out later."

Kane dropped out of the truck, leaving her no choice but to follow. If only he'd forgotten to take the keys with him. She could probably get a few blocks before the police trapped her in some kind of roadblock.

"Good morn'n, Chief." The other man rushed up to greet them.

The men shook hands before Kane turned to introduce her. "Annie, this is Roy Wallace of the KPD."

The twenty-something officer held out his hand. Eagerness bubbled out of him. Either he'd never seen a woman before, or he had a bad case of the nerves being this close to his boss. The younger man, all six feet, hundred fifty pounds of him shifted from foot-to-foot as if he had to pee.

"Ma'am. Pleasure to meet ya."

"Wallace." Kane's gruff voice demanded attention. "What's going on?"

"We found it, sir."

She almost hated to ask. "It?"

"The *Samantha Ray*." Wallace shot them both a hearty grin. "How 'bout that?"

The news should have filled her with relief. She was too busy fighting off a wave of anxiety to feel anything positive. The yacht could be lost forever for all she cared, as long as the crew and passengers were fine, except Sterling Howard. She wanted to know where he was at this moment.

Kane shook his head. "And?"

"And, sir?"

Kane stood, unbending and still, with his hands on his hips. "The people, Wallace. Sterling Howard? The crew? Is everyone okay?"

"Well, see, that's the thing."

"Spit it out, Wallace."

If the gray cast to Wallace's skin was any indication, Kane's strategy scared the hell out of the guy.

"Kane, is that necessary?"

"What?" Now he snapped at her.

Why Kane thought *that* was appropriate, she'd never know. "Your tone."

"Tone?" Kane's dark eyes grew huge. One more inch and they'd pop right out of his head.

She tried a strategy of her own. The strategy that worked for her most of the time. Ignoring Kane and going after the weaker link. "Roy, is Mr. Howard here somewhere?"

"No, ma'am."

She tried again. "Do you know where he is?"

"We can't find him, ma'am."

This time she screamed at poor Wallace. "What?"

The kid jumped twelve inches off the ground. "Well, I—"

"What was that about tone?" Kane shot her a shut-up-now look before turning his attention back to his sergeant. "Start from the beginning."

The kid opened up. "The marina owner called this morning. You know, Sid. The same guy who reported the ship—"

"Yacht," she corrected without thinking.

Roy misunderstood. "Huh?"

"Continue." Kane's scowl deepened.

Wallace shook his head, then kept on going. "Anyway, Sid said the ship was back in its slip, but no one was around. The radio was blaring and there's—" His gaze darted to her.

"What?" Kane asked.

"Why did you stop?" She wanted to give Wallace a shake but asked the question instead.

"Maybe the men should talk alone, sir."

She lost all semblance of calm. There was no way she'd go stand in the corner while the big boys talked. Nope. "Oh, I don't think so. Spit it out, Wallace."

Kane gestured for the younger man to continue. "She's not like most women. Go ahead."

What the hell did that mean?

"Blood. There's blood on the deck, sir. We have the entire area roped off. The bedroom is a wreck. There are some clothes and bags in there, but all the stuff inside looks as if it belongs to a woman."

Uh-oh.

Kane's eyes narrowed. "A woman's small, maybe?"

"A lot of women wear a small," she pointed out.

"Sir?"

"Forget it. Tell me where we are in the investigation. Anyone reported Howard missing?"

"Manning only. Since we can't find Howard and the crew, we're assuming they're together and gone."

The news just kept getting worse. She'd bet every dime she had that the bags on that yacht were hers, and that all of her paperwork would be gone.

"Manning as in Chester Manning the magazine publisher?" Kane asked.

"Yeah. He was a guest on this cruise. So was a woman. Something about a magazine article. The information on that isn't very clear." Wallace visibly gulped. "And, sir?"

"There's more?"

"Dietz is on the way."

Kane's good mood dissolved. "Damn it! Who told him?"

She noticed this news upset Kane more than the idea of missing people and blood. "Who's Dietz?"

"Internal Affairs," Kane said, almost as an after-thought.

She knew enough to know that was bad news. It wasn't a huge leap to figure out that this guy and Kane's vacation shared a link.

"I guess this Dietz guy shouldn't find you here," she said.

Wallace glanced behind them. "Too late. He's here."

She turned around, expecting Lucifer to get out of a big black limo and shoot fireballs at them. The real version was a bit of a disappointment. Just a guy. A normal guy. Tall, brown hair graying at the temples, maybe late-forties. No fire, but plenty of sparks.

Dietz saw Kane.

Kane saw Dietz.

Both men tensed.

"Dietz." Kane's jaw tightened.

Yeah, there was a history here. A bad one, she thought.

"Travers, I hope you're not dumb enough to be visiting a crime scene right now. You're in enough trouble." Dietz even sounded like a normal guy instead of the leader of the underworld. "Wallace, you wouldn't be feeding information to your former chief, would you?"

"I'm still the chief."

"For now." Dietz rested his hands on his hips in what Annie now recognized as the universal law enforcement stance. "Well, Wallace?"

"No, sir."

Kane shook Roy's hand. "Good to see you. I'll let you get back to work."

Roy took the hint and jogged in the direction of the marina office. Annie thought about running after him. Seemed safer than standing between Kane and this Dietz guy.

Dietz nodded in her general direction. "Who's the civilian?"

With that attitude Dietz moved right onto her assholes-to-watch list. "I'm Annie."

"Annie who?" Dietz issued the question like a command.

"Do I have to answer that?" she asked Kane.

"No."

"Yes," Dietz answered at the same time.

The wind ruffled her hair. She tucked it behind her ear so she could look Dietz straight in the eye. "A friend of Kane's."

Dietz's eyebrow raised. "Didn't know Kane had any of those."

"Which proves you don't know everything," Kane said.

"Speaking of knowing," Dietz wore a look of smug satisfaction, "does this young lady know about you?"

"Technically, I'm not sure I qualify as a young lady anymore."

Dietz ignored her and focused his anger on Kane. "All I need is ten minutes alone with you."

"Anytime, anywhere, Dietz."

"Whoa." She grabbed Kane's arm and held him back. She hoped the gesture looked loving. She also hoped he didn't drag her along with him.

"You should tell your lady to move aside," Dietz said.

"I'm staying, and nothing is happening here." She moved in front of Kane and glanced around for Roy. Reinforcements carrying guns would be good about now. "Kane's showing me the marina."

"Annie, don't help."

She rambled right over Kane's warning. "We ran into Roy. No big deal."

Dietz barked out a laugh. "Are you going to let your woman cover for you?"

The guy needed a punch in the jaw. Annie considered letting Kane land one. Just one.

"At least I have a woman." Kane looked bored, but anger threaded through his words.

The testosterone level kept rising. Any higher and she'd choke. "Gentlemen. Let's pretend we're adults, okay?"

· The red splotches on Dietz's face faded a bit as he stepped back and away from Kane's truck. "The lady's right."

"Her name is Annie." The roughness in Kane's voice decreased, but with his shoulders stiff and his hips squared, he still looked ready to pounce.

As long as she didn't get caught in the middle of the pouncing, she'd let this display of masculine puffery go on a little longer. Like, two more seconds. Whatever history these two had was not good, and she wanted to know why.

Suddenly everything about Kane interested her. And any guy who could make Kane's temper simmer like this was someone she needed to watch.

Dietz took out one of his business cards and held it in front of her. "Annie, may I call you that?"

"You won't be talking to her much longer," Kane said.

Dietz ignored the dig. "Do you have a last name ma'am?"

Apparently the obsession with her name extended to all of the males on the island. "No."

Kane squeezed her arm in what she assumed was a grateful gesture.

"Annie"—Dietz wiggled the card under her nose—"we should talk."

Kane snapped the square piece of paper out of the air. "Leave her out of this."

"Anyone who's messed up with you is in this." Dietz's smile turned feral. "Or doesn't she know?"

Kane pulled her toward the truck. "Let's go."

She didn't fight him, since she was in favor of getting away from Dietz. Her knee had other ideas. When he jerked her forward, a sharp pain shot up her leg, and she stumbled.

"Damn," she hissed out under her breath.

Kane immediately shouldered her weight. "You okay?"

"Let's just get out of here."

"Seems to me the lady has a right to know the type of guy she's sleeping with," Dietz called from behind them.

"I'm fine, but thanks." She plastered a fake smile on her face, trying not to let Kane know how much pain throbbed through her.

Leaving was the priority at the moment. Dietz creeped her out. His hatred of Kane rolled off him, filling the space around them like a living thing.

"Then you don't mind that Travers here is a killer?"

Her knee buckled as she skidded to a stop. Kane swore and reached for her as she turned back to Dietz. The guy looked pleased. Oh, yeah, he'd scored whatever points he wanted to score and he knew it.

Kane stepped between them so that all she saw was the back of his T-shirt. "You got a problem with me, Dietz, take it out on me."

"You should be in jail," Dietz spit back.

"Never going to happen." Kane grabbed her arm again, this time a bit harder so that her feet barely touched the ground. Even through his haze of anger he must have sensed her pain.

"Running, Travers?"

"Stay away from Annie or you'll deal with me." Kane shouted the threat over his shoulder.

"Wouldn't want that," Dietz said from behind them.

With shaky legs and a jittery belly, Annie slid into her seat and buckled up. When Dietz appeared at her window, she thought about grabbing his tie and telling Kane to drive off while they pulled Dietz behind them. Somehow, she refrained.

"Yes?"

"Annie, be careful of framers."

Kane leaned across her lap and threatened in a deadly soft voice. "Get away from my truck."

She tried to put the window back up, but Dietz stuck his arm inside the car. "You're not safe with him."

"Goodbye." She really meant get lost.

"I'm backing up." Kane shifted into reverse and started to roll up her window from his side.

"Go faster." She wanted Kane to gun it.

"Kind of obvious if I run him over, don't you think?" Kane mumbled his question.

"I'll testify for you."

Dietz touched her shoulder to get her attention. "Just think about something, Annie."

"I've had enough thinking today. Thanks."

"Sure, but seems to me if a guy would kill a kid, he wouldn't think twice about killing his girlfriend." Dietz finally removed his arm. "You might want to keep that in mind."

Shock clouded her vision. "Did you say—"

Dietz winked at her. "Call me. And don't forget what I said."

Chapter 9

Less than an hour later Kane stared at Annie over the top of his menu. She sat on her side of the red fake-leather diner booth, humming and studying the burger listings while activity buzzed all around them.

Apparently eating lunch with a killer didn't affect her appetite.

Or improve her singing voice.

He dropped the menu on the table with a thunk. "Okay, spit it out."

The soft singing sputtered out. "My gum?"

Her response threw him off stride. "Where'd you get the gum?"

"From your kitchen drawer." She blew a bubble.

"When?"

"This morning while you were on the phone." She stopped chewing. "What, were you saving the pack for a special occasion or something?"

He had the sudden urge to check for his wallet.

"Did you search every room of my house?"

"I think search is a strong word, don't you?"

"So is theft."

She popped a second bubble. "I guess that will teach you to hold a woman hostage."

"It will teach me not to use the handcuffs."

He added talk on the phone to the long list of tasks he could perform with Annie in his line of vision. So far, the only time he could trust her was in bed. Not that he'd exactly found peace then either. Tossing, turning, fantasizing and sweating—yeah, those he could manage with her curled up by his side. Not peace.

Every time something about her got stuck in his head, her eyes or her sexy legs or anything, he tried to remember how annoying she could be when she opened her mouth. How argumentative. How dishonest. Even that last one was losing its effect.

"If you try that stupid handcuff trick again, you'll pull back a stump." She dunked her teabag in a mug of steaming water.

Good. Eating and conversation, he could handle those. Could even take her smart mouth.

He exhaled, relaxing for the first time since they left the marina parking lot. After the silent treatment on the drive over he figured Dietz's allegations had scared the hell out of her. Now he knew this woman had plenty of hell left inside her. Along with some spit, venom and whatever hormones made her so damn sexy.

She didn't push, scream or do any of the typical hysterical woman things he'd expected. Not that Annie qualified as typical. Not at all. Her calm demeanor meant he could settle down and eat.

"You can tell me about the kid now," she said between sips.

So much for the she-doesn't-care theory.

"Nothing to tell," he said, lying to her for the first time.

"Yeah, we all have a dead kid in our backgrounds," she said in a dry tone. "I was thinking just the other day, 'Gee, it's a shame I killed that kid' and then—"

"Dietz is a dick." Kane felt the tension roll right back into his shoulders.

"I don't disagree." She winced when a song blared

over the diner speakers. "The question is whether he's a lying dick."

Spilling his guts never came easy for Kane. The public aspects of his job—the forfeiting of his zone of privacy and opening up his life to scrutiny—grated against his nerves. While with the DEA, he blended in. Doing otherwise could have gotten him killed. Certainly would have made him ineffective. Instead, he excelled himself right out of one job only to land in the middle of a police career mess.

But, if he wanted her to trust him with secrets, he had to tell a few of his own. "Ask me what you want to ask me."

Annie leaned back in her seat, holding her mug with a death grip. "There's the most obvious question."

"Which is?"

"Don't be dense." She cut off when the hostess walked a party of four by their table. When Annie started talking again, she sat forward, elbows on the table and whispered, "Did you kill a kid?"

He didn't bother to whisper. Not as if this part of his life was a secret. "Yeah."

Her facial expression didn't change. She didn't condemn or encourage. Didn't get anxious or scared. She just sat there.

He turned back to the menu and scanned the left side. "Did you see the specials?"

"Kane—"

He kept his nose buried in the sandwich section. "What are you getting?"

"Annoyed."

He flipped to the back cover. "I don't see that one on mine."

She reached over and knocked his menu to the table. "Come on, Kane. There's more to this kid story than the fact he or she is dead."

"He, and he didn't fall asleep at the wheel or drink himself stupid."

Those cases were bad enough. Parents angry with their kids for not coming home on time turned hysterical as the hours wore on and those kids didn't reappear. Then the dread settled in. The realization that something awful had happened. Something inconceivable.

Kane had walked that path in his own life when his wife's car jumped over a guardrail and plunged off the Pali Highway on Oahu to the canyon bottom two hundred feet below. Every time he watched a rescue unit pry a kid out of tons of twisted metal, that ache moved through him, grabbing his stomach in a clench he couldn't shake. He remembered feeling that useless. Powerless.

"Tell me how he died," Annie said in a voice so low he had to strain to hear her.

Kane knew then that Dietz had hit his mark. Annie wasn't going to let this subject drop until she got some answers, and he really couldn't blame her. This wasn't the type of information he'd ignore if he were on her side of the table.

"The circumstances won't change it, Annie. He was seventeen, and he's never going to see eighteen. End of story."

"If that were true, Dietz wouldn't have been so hot to tell me about it."

"Don't kid yourself. Dietz would say anything to discredit me. Our feud started long before this incident." And would continue long after.

Dietz lost someone on the Pali Highway that night. His sister. Then he lost the police chief job to Kane. Faced tough criticism in the press for not uncovering the preppy drug ring and having to depend on Kane and the DEA to do it for him.

Kane reached for the menu again. "The club sandwich is usually good."

She held it against the table. "You're pretty desperate to change the subject."

"You have the basics. The how and why don't matter."

Her lips screwed up in a frown. Disgust couldn't be far behind, so he waited. He'd heard it all before. Hell, Sam's mother attacked him at the police station the night Sam died. Pounded on his chest until she fell on the floor in an exhausted heap. Kane let her hit and scream because, well, the woman earned the right to mourn. He'd done enough mourning in his life to recognize when a deep, blinding pain held someone else.

Annie finally said something.

Just not what he expected.

"Give me a break," she said.

"Excuse me?"

"You need to drop the macho bullshit act."

"Did I forget to tell you I carry a gun?"

She ignored his joke. "Of course the how matters. How is the difference between having a conscience and not. Serial killers kill. Cops sometimes have to kill. Those groups aren't equal."

The couple at the table next to them started arguing over which song to punch into the table jukebox. Annie shushed them, and the woman scowled back, even sneered a bit, which was hard to miss since her purple nose ring bounced around in response.

Kane lowered his voice. "Maybe you missed the part where the kid was seventeen? At seventeen someone should have shot my smug ass, but they didn't. Sam didn't get the same second chance."

Her frown deepened. "The way I figure it, you had a reason to do what you did."

He'd known her less than one day. From that short time together, she'd granted him more blind faith than the mayor and Police Commissioner who'd hired him. Never mind that he was a hometown boy. That he'd grown up on Kauai and returned after college. Never mind that one of his oldest friends, the same one who'd convinced him to leave the DEA and serve as Police Chief, cast the first vote against him on the Commission.

Mike Furtado ran the Commission and convinced him a voluntary vacation would look better than an imposed leave. Then Mike stopped talking and turned the file over to Dietz. That hit had stunned Kane the most.

"What makes you think I care about what happens to one kid or another?" Kane asked more to hear her response than anything else.

The couple finally chose a song, then started on a discussion about the cost. A whole dime. The money debate was even louder than the music disagreement.

"Well, tough guy, chalk it up to instinct. There are bad guys out there. Trust me, I know."

Finally an opening. "You ready to tell me who?"

"No. My point is that you're not one of them, Kane. You rescued me and never took advantage, though God knows you had the chance."

After spending his life as the rescuer and getting nothing but crapped on in response, Kane wondered if there was another life out there for him. "Only because you were pretending to be unconscious."

"I'll have you know I was plotting my escape in case you turned out to be a nut." She tapped her nails against the table. "I'm still not sure you aren't."

"That's sweet."

"I'm not saying we're best buds or anything. I'm just saying you don't strike me as a guy who would shoot a kid for kicks. If you shot the kid, there's a reason. Don't get cocky about it. It's a pretty low morality bar."

The waitress came over and took their orders, leaving a new basket of sugar packets. As she walked away, Kane stared blankly at a spot on the wall above her head.

"She your type?" Annie asked.

"Huh?"

Annie nodded in the direction of the counter. "The waitress. You're staring at her ass."

He wished he could think about another woman's ass. The only one on his mind was Annie's. "Staring into space. Nothing sexual."

She flipped the music screens on the jukebox and looked at the song titles. "Sure."

"If I were staring, I'd tell you."

"Right."

He put his hand over hers. "Your radar is off. In fact, you proved last night that you can't tell when I'm really seducing a woman or not."

"Did it ever dawn on you that I might not be interested in you?"

He dropped his hand and chuckled. "No."

"Arrogant."

"Tease."

She winced.

"Don't tell me I offended you." Since he'd said worse things to her, he doubted that was the case.

"Hardly." She shifted in her seat and winced again. "My knee is throbbing. That pivot move you did in the parking lot this morning didn't exactly promote healing."

"Damn. Sorry about that."

"I'll make you pay later. Right now I need aspirin."

"Put your leg up." He patted his lap.

"Why?"

"So I can rub it." Touching her would destroy his control, but he owed her.

She closed one eye and peeked at him through the other. "Is this another seduction?"

"I'll let you know when I switch to seduction mode. Maybe after we eat."

She slipped her ten-dollar sneaker onto his lap. "It hurts, so not too hard."

"Give me some credit. I'm a professional." Using only his fingertips, he massaged the area around her knee with slow, gentle circles.

"Do you have a certificate in massage?"

"You wish."

"Yeah, I kind of do. You can't blame a girl for trying." Her head fell back against the top of the booth. "If I fall asleep, get the food wrapped up to go."

The touch of his fingers against her warm flesh and sleek muscles made his cock push against his fly. One move and those fingers could trace a line up her sleek leg and under the band of her shorts. Then those grumbling sounds at the back of her throat would morph into a moan. He'd probably take her on the table.

"I didn't forget, you know," she said.

The sound of her soft voice made him jump. "About what?"

"The boy." Her eyes stayed closed.

Damn. "I thought we were done with that conversation."

"No, we aren't." Her sleepy eyes opened. "Talk or I call Dietz and ask for his version."

That threat worked. Dietz's version included lies, embellishments and incorrect information.

"He was dealing ice."

Annie blinked a few times. "Do you mean crystal meth?"

"Yeah."

"Here?"

"Why not here?"

She grabbed up a stack of sugar packets and began building a wall. "But, this is Hawaii. Paradise."

"Hawaii has its share of crime."

"Why in the world would any kid lucky enough to live on this beautiful island turn to drugs?"

Her reaction was naïve but not unusual. Tourists saw only the lush, exotic part of Hawaii. The perfect weather. The sandy beaches. He knew about the other part. About the dissatisfaction that frequently led kids away from productive lives to lives based on getting high.

"Happens all the time. Ice is a huge problem. You take a bunch of bored kids, put them in a confined space, add in economic pressure, high prices and typical stupid teenage insecurities, and you get a disaster." Kane had seen it a hundred times. The pattern never changed. Neither did the addiction or its destructive aftermath.

With every word, her eyes grew wider. "But why?"

"The lure of euphoria and promise of escape hook a lot of kids around here."

"I had no idea."

"The wild stories of days of non-stop sex are an incentive, too."

Her fingers moved faster, piling packet upon packet until the stack toppled over. "That part I can understand. Boys like sex. They talk big."

His hands froze. "Is that right?"

She knocked against the table. "Hey, don't stop."

Demanding little thing. "Talking or touching?"

"Both."

Since the night of the shooting, Kane had pushed the memory of Sam's murder scene to the back of his mind and had to fight to keep it there. This time, he let it out. Concentrating on what had happened helped him ignore the feel of her skin under his hands. Not the easiest thing to do since the ball of her foot kept rubbing against his fly.

"The kid—"

"What's his name?" she asked.

The words stuck in his throat. Always did. "Sam Watson. He and his private prep school buddies ran the drug ring. To cut down on a lot of unnecessary details, there was a joint operation between the police and DEA. A sting. The kid had a gun, kept firing and wouldn't drop it."

The lazy look disappeared from her eyes. "Oh, God."

"So, I shot him."

Kane decided to leave out most all of the details. The shot Sam rammed into Kane's shoulder. Sam pointing a gun at Josh's head. The blood. The grilling in the newspapers as the Watson family portrayed their kid as a saint and Kane as the vicious cop. The racial overtones of a rich white kid being shot by a local boy. All of it.

Then there was the aftermath. The mole he couldn't find. The connections he couldn't close. The adult at the head of the operation who let the kids swing rather than go down. The death threats. The punch to the gut when the people he served rushed to believe someone with a bigger wallet.

Sam knew who ran the ring. Sam couldn't talk. Sam couldn't do anything anymore.

But Kane couldn't share any of that. The DEA sting continued, but the focus had switched from the kids to the unknown leader. Josh kept hunting, convinced a wealthy member of society was to blame. Until they identified the head of the organization, Kane needed to stay out of the picture.

"Did Sam die right away?" Again, no judgment from her. Just a question.

That was the kicker. The kid could be sitting in a juvenile home or, with his family's money, been shuffled off to a military school somewhere. Kane wondered for the thousandth time what he could have done to make Sam put the gun down. What would have happened if they had arrived at the hospital in time.

He wouldn't have to wonder long. When Dietz finished his investigation, he'd tell everyone. Put it in the newspapers and post it on the Internet. Kane knew he'd have to fight to get his badge back.

"First time, I shot him in the upper leg. The damn kid kept firing. My second shot clipped his neck."

"Kane . . ."

"He bled out before we could get him to the hospital. We were too late."

For a few minutes she just sat there, arranging sugar packets in a circle around her mug. When she looked up, he thought he saw a twinge of sadness behind that intense green.

"I don't have to tell you that you're not at fault, right? You were doing your job. The kid didn't deserve to die, of course, but he was responsible for the situation he put himself in."

"I'm not wallowing in self-pity or looking for absolution Annie."

She hit him with one of those flirty smiles. The kind that telegraphed a message to his lower half and made his brain shut off. "Good, because I'm not much into confessions."

Her snotty attitude lifted the mood. "You sure? You and me in a little box? Think about it."

She rolled her eyes. "Get back to Sam."

He shrugged, trying to pretend the story didn't matter even though it did. "The incident stays with me, and not just because of Dietz and his warped agenda."

That last part pissed him off. Jealousy and bitterness

motivated Dietz's hatred, not any feelings of compassion for Sam or his family.

"It should," she said as she reached for her mug again.

As usual, she said something he didn't expect. "Not the sensitive type, are you?"

"Keep massaging my knee."

He didn't realize he had stopped. "Yes, ma'am."

"If taking another person's life didn't change you, then you wouldn't have a conscience. Sam's death is a part of you. It's damaged you. And you know what?"

Seemed to Kane that this woman knew a lot about killing. "No."

"That's the way it should be. It shouldn't be easy, and you shouldn't get to forget it."

Derek trusted Kane's judgment and had never questioned his motives in the shooting. Josh had walked the same road, had stood there in Sam's sights, so he knew what had happened even if Dietz refused to listen. Now, Annie understood.

Kane didn't know why or what had happened in her past to give her the knowledge. Before they went much further, he needed to know the answers to those questions.

With the utmost care, he moved her foot to the floor. "We should eat fast and then go."

"Sharing time over?"

"My part." He drained his coffee cup. "You have yet to tell me anything other than your name, and I had to figure that part out myself."

"I'm still angry about that, by the way. Sneaky bastard."

He flashed her his best grin. "That's Chief Sneaky Bastard to you."

"Where next?"

"Some calls, then a trip to police headquarters."

She snorted. "Are you looking for trouble?"

"Don't have to look. Trouble generally finds me without much effort."

"So, why are you borrowing more?"

"We need to see what the police pulled off the yacht." He watched her face for signs of panic. Except for a raised eyebrow, she didn't show any emotion.

"Any particular reason?"

"Because you were on that yacht and because you refuse to tell me why or what happened. If you won't fill in the gaps, I'll have to hunt down the information myself." This woman knew something. He planned to find out what.

She exhaled and her shoulders slumped. "You're kidding."

"I told you I don't have a sense of humor."

"Or a great sense of timing." She motioned for the waitress. "And you certainly know how to ruin a good meal."

"If it makes you feel any better, the food here isn't that good anyway."

Chapter 10

"I'd like to go on record as voting against this plan."
Annie stood in the empty parking lot at the back door of what was quite possibly the least impressive structure she'd ever seen.

Good food or not, she couldn't figure out why she'd rushed through her lunch for this. Half a sandwich sat on her plate. She thought about driving right back to the diner to finish it.

"So noted," Kane said, though it was obvious he was ignoring her lecture.

Heat bounced off the pavement, boiling her on the spot. The bandage around her knee made her skin itch. She wondered if the humidity could melt the cotton wrap.

"Really, Kane. This is a terrible idea."

"Still noted."

Kane sat on the hood of his pickup, looking all smooth and tanned and in charge. He talked to her, but his hand stayed on his cell phone. His eyes focused on the slight ramp leading up to the glass door.

Her gaze followed his. Then she cringed. The single-level beige building blended in with the other state office buildings grouped together off the main road. Lihue, the county seat, housed quaint shops, cute cottage homes, chickens and impressive scenery lined with mountains in the distance and fresh greenery and fragrant flowers all around. If everything went as she planned with Howard, maybe she could come back and photograph the area.

But not this part of Lihue. There wasn't any greenery back here. Except for a small strip of park between the front of the building and the road, the area consisted mostly of parking meters and macadam. The only visible water was the puddle under the fire hydrant by the next building.

"Are you sure this is police headquarters?" she asked.

"Last I checked."

"It's claustrophobic." Windows were spaced every eight or so feet apart around the building. She guessed each one marked an office. "Shouldn't there be police cars and activity?"

"Not here. There are about twenty-five officers in the investigative bureau and another ten who work patrol. We have smaller outposts around the island, and some of the administrative stuff is done elsewhere."

A chicken came right up to her foot. The little bugger moved on only when she rubbed the bottom of her sneaker against the pavement, making a crunching sound against the pebbles and rocks there.

"The size of the police department doesn't tell me why none of them are actually here right now."

He exhaled in the universal male sign for disgust over being questioned. "It's Sunday afternoon. This is a pretty quiet time around here."

"Nice of the criminals to take the day off."

"Yep. Crime is a Monday through Friday activity here. Frees up time for surfing and hula dancing," he said in his best smart-ass voice.

She fought the urge to knock those sunglasses off his nose. "There are two cars in the parking lot, and one of them is yours. That was my only point."

"Which is why we're here now instead of on a work-day." He slid off the hood.

"Oh, right. You're on a leave of absence."

"Vacation."

She tried to fill in the holes to his story. "Is there a difference?"

"There is to me."

"Because of Sam?"

His jaw tightened. "Among other things."

"You know, the closer you get to the office, the more coplike you become. Those short, sharp responses. That demanding attitude. No eye contact. Do they teach you that in police school?"

"Very first day."

"It's really annoying. I can't even see your eyes."

Kane hesitated for a second, then took off his glasses. "This better?"

"A charm lesson wouldn't be a bad use of your money."

"This is as good as I'm going to get. Too old to change now."

Said the guy with zero body fat and the tight butt. "I guess we know why you've never been married."

Kane slipped his glasses back on. "Who said that I haven't?"

A haze settled in her brain. "You've—"

His phone buzzed. "Here we go."

She wasn't ready to move off the previous conversation. "The fact you have a wife is basic information. The kind of stuff you should share."

"Like why you're on the island? Some people might consider that pretty basic intel."

"Are you still married?" The question came out as a squeal.

"Have you seen a wife?" He took off for the door.

She followed quickly at his heels. "Is that an answer?"

He smiled at her over his shoulder just as the glass door opened and a dark head peeked out. Dark hair, sharp green eyes with a relaxed stance and friendly smile. The guy looked to be thirty-something and part Asian, part something else. By the polo shirt and dress slacks, she guessed he ranked higher than the nervous officer she'd met earlier.

" 'Bout time, Greene," Kane said.

"Sorry, Chief. Dietz hung around for hours. He only drove off a short time ago. We wanted to make sure he was gone."

The officer ushered them into a small lobby. The only decorations were a few chairs, racks of pamphlets and a security desk. A set of double doors blocked the view into the main room except for a small window in the middle.

"Ted Greene, this is Annie." Kane continued after the other man nodded his hello. "Ted heads my investigative team. He's running point on the trouble at the marina."

By trouble she assumed Kane meant her.

Kane turned back to Ted. "Who else is here?"

"Wallace, Clark and Simmons. The evening patrol just started its shift, but anyone who comes in and out should be friendly. The major problem left." Ted handed Kane an envelope.

Kane unhooked the clasp and looked inside. "Good. Let's get to it."

Happy *they* knew what was going on. "Not to be dense, gentlemen, but what's the 'it' we're doing?"

Ted started at her. "Ma'am?"

"You can call her Annie."

At least Kane had stopped calling her Fern. If he could stop barking out orders, they'd really be making progress.

He could also take ten seconds and explain that wife

comment. She shouldn't care, of course, but since the conversation kept replaying in her mind, Annie knew she did.

"I can speak for myself," she grumbled at Kane, then flashed Ted a wide smile. "Please call me Annie."

The corner of Ted's mouth kicked up in a grin. "Okay, Annie."

She put the marriage question on hold and focused on the task in front of them. Being in this building was bad enough. She'd bet there was a jail in the building, too.

Yeah, this wasn't good. She knew—deep down in her gut knew—something they pulled off the boat implicated her. People could point fingers at her, but not for a missing boat. That sin belonged to someone else. She had enough of her own without taking on more.

"Where are we going?" she asked.

"You can have a seat in the waiting room," Ted said.

"I'm coming along."

Ted shot Kane a questioning look.

"It's okay. She's with me."

The way Kane said that made something flutter in the bottom of her stomach. Her insides generally didn't move and wiggle. Well, they had for a second or two when she first got on the yacht, but that had to do with motion and nerves, not a man. This time felt more like attraction than nausea.

Truth was she'd rather be sick. Vomiting she could handle. Take a pill, lie down, drink a little seltzer and, miracle of miracles, a few hours later all better. To handle Kane, she'd need a vaccine.

"Chief—"

"Don't worry, Ted."

"But Dietz could come back at any time."

Kane tapped the envelope against his thigh. "She knows about my vacation. Saw Dietz in action. She won't say anything about you helping me out, will you, Annie?"

"No." Never mind the fact she had no idea whom she knew to tell.

"And she won't touch anything either." Kane cleared his throat. "She'll stand there and behave."

Annie felt a headache coming on. "Should *she* roll over and play dead? Maybe fetch your slippers?"

Maybe that belly thing was the stomach flu after all.

"She could start practicing staying quiet," Kane suggested.

"If you refer to me as 'she' one more time, I'll kick you."

Ted coughed into his fist in a lame attempt to cover a laugh.

"Yeah, she's hysterical," Kane muttered. "Let's go."

They walked through the double doors and into an open area. The building was small enough for her to see past the counter and through to the double doors at the other end of the room. Except for two glassed-in offices to her left and a kitchen area to her right, only desks, chairs and paperwork littered the room.

Kane exchanged a few words with two men. One wore a uniform, and the other the same casual attire that most men in Kauai wore to work, khaki pants and a short-sleeve shirt.

The tour was a bit of a letdown. Nothing like the squad rooms on television. Messy, yes, but no action. No guys in handcuffs. No screaming. No gunfire. Kind of boring and normal.

"Where do you interrogate people?" She was dying to take a photo of that. She could see a feature about jails in a place where visitors rarely thought about crime.

Both men turned to look at her. They wore matching

frowns. If this were a contest, Kane would hold a slim lead.

Words finally popped out of Ted's open mouth. "Excuse me, ma'am?"

"You know, the two-way mirror. You sit in there and ask a suspect a bunch of questions until he cracks. The good-cop-bad-cop thing." Her gaze went back and forth between their blank stares. "Don't you guys do that?"

"We prefer to beat up suspects and throw them in the torture chamber downstairs. We can't starve them up here where anyone could walk in and see," Kane said.

"That's not funny."

"Who said I was kidding?" Kane kept a straight face when he said that.

Would it kill the guy to answer a question? "Forget it."

"This way." Ted pushed open a door to a stairwell and walked through.

Annie had the sneaky suspicion Ted was laughing at her, not with her. "Where are we going?"

Kane answered with a soft whisper next to her ear. "Downstairs. To the special room."

She elbowed him and felt a measure of satisfaction when she heard an "ompf" in response. He might be armed with a licensed weapon, but she had enough attitude for both of them. Her mouth versus his gun . . . yeah, she'd win that battle. No problem.

They walked in a line down the stairs, with Ted in the lead. He opened the gray metal door at the bottom and shut it behind them, locking them inside.

The underbelly of the building made the top half look like a palace. Without the windows, the walls seemed to close in on the long, narrow hallway. A musty smell killed off the soft scent of flowers that hovered over every other part of the island.

There wasn't anything open about this area, just a series of closed doors on either side. Buzzing fluorescent lights lined the ceiling. A desk sat in front of a heavy locked door about halfway down the hall.

"What's that?"

Ted looked where she pointed. "Lockup."

"A jail?"

Kane's husky voice buzzed by her ear again. "Want to stop in for a visit? Pick a bed?"

She threw another elbow in the direction of his midsection. "You're in my personal space."

"Yeah," he snorted. "I wonder why."

Ted slipped a key in the door marked "Evidence Room" but glanced up at them before turning the knob. "Something wrong?"

"Inside joke." Kane slid past her and pushed the door open for them to follow.

They walked into a room lined with shelves, lockers and filing cabinets. Except for the boxes stacked on the long table, nothing else was visible in the room.

"This is everything you collected off the *Samantha Ray*?"

Ted braced his palms against the table and watched Kane sort through the envelopes. "Except for fluids and some other items that were sent to the lab. We roped off the yacht and surrounding area in case we need to take another look."

"Then, what's in the envelope you have?" she asked Kane.

Kane flashed an unreadable look at Ted. "The preliminary police report and copies of the notes."

"Should you have that?" she asked Kane, wondering if he was borrowing more trouble.

Ted stayed quiet. He looked down at his feet, probably trying to blend into the floor.

Kane smiled. "Since the police gave it to me, I don't think it's a problem."

"Probably not," she mumbled as she looked around at the other envelopes. Her hands itched to flip through everything to look for the journals and papers she hadn't left at the hotel. She inhaled to calm her nerves and keep her heart from racing.

"Describe the scene for me." Kane read through a file.

She admired his multitasking abilities. All she wanted to do was dive in with both hands. With everything in different-sized marked envelopes, she couldn't see a thing. Peeking over Kane's shoulder was out of the question. Not because she wouldn't do it, but because he was too damn tall for her to see anything.

That didn't stop her from moving closer. She shifted until she stood right at Kane's left elbow. If he would lower the file she could . . .

"There are four staterooms and staff quarters on the yacht. All but two bedrooms—"

When Ted started talking, she jumped a foot. So much for her covert skills.

"Something wrong?" Kane asked.

"No, I'm just feeling a bit—" Anxious, scared, worried. All those things. "Just tired. Something kept bugging me when I tried to fall asleep last night."

"I hear sleeping outside helps that problem."

Ted reached for something. For a split second Annie worried that thing was a gun. When he pulled out his car keys, she chalked the irrational thinking up to the exhaustion of the last two nights.

"I could take Annie home and circle back around and help you here."

Kane didn't even lift his head. "She stays."

Ted glanced at her but didn't say anything.

"Go on with the story." Kane dropped the file and opened an envelope.

"Two bedrooms were in good condition. By the clothing and personal effects, we think Chester Manning was in one of those. Someone wrecked the two suites along with the family room."

"And the other bedroom?"

"A woman." Ted dragged a box toward him. "These are the items from that room. Not much, but interesting."

Annie felt her lunch churn in her stomach and regretted getting mayo on her turkey club. She'd taken one small bag and her camera bag on the yacht with her. Everything else she'd left in the room at the hotel.

That didn't explain why everything she brought with her to Kauai, the stuff from the boat and from the hotel, seemed to be gone. The box held, maybe, five envelopes. No camera. No papers. No clothes, or if they were there, someone folded them into tiny squares.

Something was very, very wrong.

"What's in the envelopes?" she asked.

Ted waited until Kane nodded his okay to answer. "A negligee, underwear. Nothing much really. The woman, whoever she was, was there for a booty—"

"A what?" Shock made her voice lift an octave.

Ted cleared his throat. "As a guest of Sterling Howard."

Her cheeks burned. "Only underwear? That's it?"

"Yeah. Some of it went to the lab to check for fluids."

"Fluids?" This time she choked on the word.

Kane smiled again. "He means from sex."

"Yeah. Thanks. I got that part," she grumbled out.

"We got this pair out of the drawer." Ted pawed through

the envelopes and pulled one out. He broke the seal and dumped the contents on the table.

There they were. Panties. White, lace thigh-high panties. Make that white and very transparent and very skimpy lace panties. Hers.

"Looks like someone has some explaining to do," Kane said.

The smile in his voice made her look up again. She waited for a physical reaction. Why she bothered, she'd never know. His gaze never left the underwear. He'd worn that same stupid grin when he saw her half naked and chained to his bed.

"First we have to find the lady," Ted pointed out without taking his gaze off her panties.

If either of them made one move, inched even a little pinky toward the underwear, gun or not she'd kick them. Even without moving she seriously considered banging their empty heads together. Had they never seen women's underwear before?

"As far as we know, Howard didn't have a mistress, but she could have been new. The guy views women as disposable." Ted leaned in for a closer examination of the underwear. "But I'd say those belong to someone young and hot with good taste in lingerie."

A scream raced up her throat and fought to get out. The idea of sleeping with Sterling Howard made her physically ill. The guy was garbage. Sure, she'd come to Kauai to find him, but not for that. No, when she had discovered his identity, she tracked him down and followed him to Kauai for one reason only. The same reason that put her on the opposite side of the law from Kane.

She'd come to kill Sterling Howard. Make him squirm, let him know he was going to die, maybe even give him a chance to beg. Then kill him anyway.

"Find any paperwork on the mystery woman?" Kane's gaze still hadn't moved. Unlike Ted, he kept a respectful distance from the panties.

Ted shook his head. "We're hoping the lab finds something. If not, tracking her down will be tough."

"Yeah." This time Kane raised his head and stared right into her eyes. "I wonder where we'll find her and what story she'll come up with to explain this."

Well, as soon as *she* invented a feasible story, she'd let him know.

Chapter 11

Sterling Howard's mistress.

A few hours after their visit to the police station, Kane still couldn't get the thought out of his head. He sat on the edge of his bed, turning the possibility over in his brain. No matter how hard he tried, the information refused to fit into the picture he'd put together of Annie.

Still, the idea made his back teeth slam together. Howard touching Annie, kissing her . . . The thought of Annie having sex with Howard, with any man, made everything inside him tense.

The damn woman sure knew how to ruin a perfectly boring vacation.

And she was taking her sweet time in the shower. He would have worried if the room had a window or other obvious escape. It didn't. The only way out was through him.

The woman wasn't going anywhere until he confirmed she was the owner of the underwear. Then he needed a believable answer about her underwear showing up at a crime scene. That was if he could tolerate talking about her panties without actually pulling them off of her, which he doubted.

The memory of the little white scrap flashed in his

mind all evening. She wouldn't talk, and he couldn't concentrate on anything else.

One cold shower later he sat a few feet from the bathroom door, dressed only in a pair of shorts and a tee, and waited for the knob to turn. Annie had stepped in there almost forty minutes ago. The water stopped running ten minutes after that. Unless she'd squeezed down the drain, she was in there.

She didn't strike him as someone who hid. No, from his experience, she came out guns blazing and mouth running. The quiet, introspective Annie was new and likely only a ploy.

As the minutes ticked by, he wondered about the size of that drain.

"Annie?" When she didn't respond, he walked over and banged on the door with the side of his fist. "Open up, sunshine. It's time for bed."

"Go away," she said in a muffled voice.

He leaned in close and listened for movement. "What are you doing?"

"Nothing."

Then silence.

He rattled the knob. "Annie?"

"Leave me alone."

"This happens to be my house."

"How could I forget?"

He heard a crash and a yelp.

"That's it. I'm coming in." With one shoulder aimed at the door, he backed up a bit and hit his target at a jog. His weight combined with the age of the house resulted in the wood shredding right by the doorknob. The shot also kicked in the door until it bounced off the inner wall and flew back toward his head.

He caught the edge, preventing the inevitable concussion, and focused on Annie. She sat on the toilet with one ankle crossed over her other knee. She wore one of his long T-shirts, but thanks to her pretzellike sitting position, the material hiked up high on her thighs.

Just the tee and bright pink painted toenails.

All the blood in his head rushed to his shorts. The effects of the cold shower vanished at the sight of all that naked flesh. His lower body went from interested to rock hard as soon as he crossed the threshold to the bathroom.

She frowned up at him. "I guess you didn't know I unlocked it."

He was so busy staring at her toned legs that her words took an extra second or two to sink in. Even then he had to swallow twice to get his simple question out.

"When?"

"Right before you did your little macho act and broke it down. That was impressive, by the way. Very cop-like." She wrapped and unwrapped gauze around her hand in what he assumed was a nervous gesture.

"You didn't answer me."

"I wanted privacy."

The gauze wasn't just around her hands. Rolls were scattered all over the floor. So were pieces of tape, two pair of scissors and a stack of crumpled tissues. Apparently she'd used the forty minutes alone to practice her surgery skills.

"What are you doing?"

"For a guy who claims to have been married, you don't know much about women."

"Right at this minute, I can't disagree with you." He saw wet towels balled up in the sink. "Tell me what's going on."

"Nothing."

"Do you plan to clean up all this nothing before bed?" He reached over and turned off the sink faucet. How the dripping sound didn't drive her mad, he'd never know.

"I'm not your maid."

"Thanks for clearing that up."

"If you must know, my knee is killing me. Since Derek isn't here to help me, I was trying to wrap it myself. Happy?"

"Ecstatic." Kane kneeled down and gathered up the remnants of what once was the contents of his first aid kit and now was garbage. "Any reason you didn't ask me for help?"

"Damn it!" She muttered and swore a few more times as she wound the stretchy bandage around her leg. Maybe because she pulled the band tight enough to cut off all circulation to the bottom half of her leg.

"Give me that." He grabbed the wrap and undid the mess she'd made.

"Hey! That took me forever." She slapped at his hands.

"Your calf is turning purple."

She bent down to get a closer look. When her head dipped, her hair fell forward and brushed against his face. "Oh."

As gently as he could, he straightened her shoulders until she sat up again. "I can't see with your hair in my face."

And he needed some space or he'd be all over her.

He unraveled about ten feet of bandages. Ten feet, and almost none of it secured over her actual injury. "I'm guessing you never took a first aid class."

"I did about fifteen years ago."

He sat on the floor at her feet. The view from below was pretty damn impressive. The light above her head highlighted the blondish streaks in her red hair. Her green eyes contrasted with the peach of her skin, giving her a young, almost vulnerable, look.

No wonder Derek had taken so long to wrap her leg the last time. The kid was probably mesmerized by her.

Annie wasn't the type to visit the island in a tiny bikini and throw litter on the beach. Nor the type he grew up with who reflected his dark hair and dark eyes. No, Annie's beauty started with an earthy glow and exotic coloring so distinct and new that a guy could forget everything else. Like the trouble that seemed to follow her.

When Derek had helped, she wore clothing. Kane had a bigger challenge. A nearly naked Annie. His fingers touched smooth bare skin, and that was all he could see. A man could exert only so much restraint before his control broke.

Fresh from her shower, the scent of vanilla still lingered in the air and on her skin. He regretted putting shower gel on the list of items she needed from the store. He had a hard enough time resisting her when she smelled like guy soap. Having her smell all sweet and feminine promised to make this a very long night.

Then there was the glimpse of yellow underwear between her thighs. Right in his line of sight. This pair wouldn't be of the silky, lacy type sitting in the evidence lockup. This would be whatever type Derek had thrown in the shopping cart without looking. His money was on cotton grandma panties. That distinction should make a difference but didn't. She'd look sexy in men's boxer shorts. Better without anything.

But right now she needed his help.

With her ankle balanced on his knee and her leg slightly elevated, Kane wrapped the injury. The swelling continued to worsen, and bruising had started to show.

She'd hidden her pain well during the day. He made a mental note to keep an eye on her tomorrow. As if that would be a hardship. Watching her was his only job at the moment.

"Better?"

"No."

He assumed from the way the color flooded back into her cheeks and the muscles around her eyes relaxed that she was lying. No surprise there. The woman seemed to excel at evading the truth.

"Ready to talk about the underwear Ted found?"

"I didn't say they were mine." She winced when he lowered her foot to the floor.

"You didn't deny it either."

This time she sighed. "I'm sore and tired. Is there any way we can table this until tomorrow?"

The officer in him wanted to say no. The man knew the answer would be yes. Maybe they both needed to take a break until morning. "Let's go to bed."

"You go ahead." She stood up, leaving him on the floor next to her bare feet.

"We both go."

"Until the knee stops thumping, I won't be able to do much other than toss and turn." She tried to take a step but limped instead.

He jumped to his feet and put his hand on her elbow. "We're going to bed, Annie."

She shook off his hold. "I get it, I'm still a hostage. You think I'm going to run."

He hadn't until she put the idea in his head. Now he'd have to worry about that, too. "The thought had occurred to me."

"Well, I've got news for you, genius. I can barely walk, and I don't have anywhere to go. Right now you're stuck with me."

"Then we'll do it this way." He scooped her up into his arms and felt some relief when her arms wound around his neck in response. Hitting the light switch with his elbow, he marched out of the bathroom and into the adjoining bedroom.

"I can walk, you know," she said.

He noticed she wasn't fighting him or demanding to

get down. That could mean only one thing: her knee hurt a hell of a lot more than she was letting on.

"Indulge me and stay quiet for a second," he said.

"Or what, you'll use a gag as well as the handcuffs?"

"Don't tempt me."

"This attitude of yours is why I didn't invite you into the bathroom."

He thought about dumping her on the bed, letting her bounce a time or two, then walking away. No matter how tempting, he decided against it. Whatever crap came out of her mouth and whatever she thought of him, he would help her.

Unless they killed each other first.

"A little gratitude wouldn't be a bad idea," he said.

She blinked several times, as if the comment actually shocked her. "For what?"

"Rescuing you. Feeding you. Not turning you in to Ted. Not throwing you in jail. Pick any of those."

He stopped making a list. Once he started he'd never stop. The goal was to make her comfortable, convince her to trust him and get some answers. Not antagonize her.

"Are you ever going to put me down?" she asked in a chilly voice.

Comfortable. Not antagonizing. He repeated those places in his head.

Yeah, great in theory. Impossible in practice.

Chapter 12

Kane hadn't counted on how good Annie would feel snuggled in his arms. How sexy she would look curled up against his chest and hanging on to him.

Comfort hell. That he could walk was a small miracle. So was her willingness to ignore the erection poking into her hip.

"I told you that I can't sleep with the pain." Her fingers slipped into his hair.

He doubted she even noticed the intimate gesture. "Did you take some aspirin?"

"Of course," she snapped back.

"You are not the best patient in the world."

"I've had a hard couple of days."

"Might help to share. Let me hear the story and then see what I can do for you."

She made a face. "Nice try."

He eased her onto the mattress and fluffed up the pillows behind her. That type of thing worked on television. The sensitive hero always did something totally unbelievable like patting a pillow. Looked ridiculous, but he was willing to try anything to help her relax.

He blew out a tense breath. "Move over a bit."

"Why?"

"I'm going to massage your leg." He gave her a gentle push until she shifted to the middle of the mattress. "I'd prefer not to fall off the bed and on my ass while I do it."

"I'm fine." She clamped her lips together. Her thighs followed, so did a sharp intake of breath.

"Yeah, I can see that."

"What does that mean?"

He pointed at her lips. "Those tiny lines around the corners of your mouth suggest you're in pain."

Her gasp—this time from indignation, not pain—nearly knocked him over. "I don't have lines."

"I only meant—"

"I'm too young for wrinkles."

The conversation had taken a turn he didn't understand. "When did I say wrinkles?"

"That's what you meant."

This was why a life without women suited him just fine. They were all nuts. "If I had meant wrinkles, I would have said that."

She scoffed, and those lips pressed together again.

He tried blowing out a second breath. Then a third. Nothing seemed to calm him down. "Okay, let's try this. You lie back. I'll massage your leg. If it hurts, I stop."

After a slight hesitation, she leaned back all stiff with her hands plastered to her sides. "If it hurts, I'll kick you."

"Now there's something to look forward to," he grumbled as he moved to the bottom of the bed and started to part her legs.

Her body sprang right back up again into a sitting position. She grabbed the edge of the tee and stretched it toward her knees. The move pulled the neck edge down, flashing him with a view of the tops of her pale breasts.

"Where do you think you're going?" She actually squealed.

"Your knee is down here. You know, toward the bottom of the bed."

"Your head needs to stay up here." She smacked the pillow.

Rather than argue, he let his hands speak for him. With slow certain squeezes, he massaged the ball of her foot. Kneading with his thumbs and soothing with his palms.

"Holy . . . You're amazing at that." With a groan, she flopped back against the pillows.

"I aim to please." He sat against her outer thigh and reached across her legs to continue his ministrations.

"You do."

Gently rubbing but never applying too much pressure, his hands moved up her leg. He tended to her calf, then to the area surrounding her knee.

"Mmmm . . . you could charge for this service."

Her husky voice sent a wave of heat coursing through his body and straight to his groin. "Just relax and stay quiet."

He caressed and touched, stroking his fingertips over her bare skin until her eyelids slipped shut. With the stiffness gone, her thighs fell open in a welcoming gesture. The arch in her back eased, and her arms dropped open at her sides as if her bones had turned to mush.

With each pass of his hands, he eased closer to her. As his fingers glided to the top of her knee, his body settled into the vee between her legs. She shifted to make room for him, so that one leg lay behind his back and the other across his knees.

"Damn, Kane."

Yeah, damn. Shit. Hell. All of those.

The more relaxed she became, the harder he got.

Comforting her and wanting her blended together. Her, here in his bed. Him, ready and in need of release.

Just then she tilted her head back and exposed miles of glorious neck. Flowing copper hair spilled over his white pillowcase.

Any smart-ass comment she might have made dissolved on her tongue. Instead, her mouth fell open in a tiny "o."

The comfort part of the program had been accomplished. Well enough that his shorts felt two sizes too small.

Before he could think through all the ramifications, his hands eased higher. Past her knee and up to her middle thigh. The tiny whimpers at the back of her throat drove him to reach even higher. His palms massaged her warm skin as his fingertips dipped under the edge of her shirt.

If she yelled, screamed or followed through with that promised kick, he'd deal with it. Hell, he probably deserved a shot or two for changing a therapeutic massage into foreplay.

He'd definitely regret this in the morning. Or when he had to haul her off to jail for kidnapping and murder.

A humming groan escaped her lips. When her hips lifted off the mattress, his hands pushed deeper under her shirt. Then his mouth followed their path. Breathing in the mixture of vanilla and sweet excitement on her bare skin, he kissed his way from the top of her knee, up her leg, to the top of her thigh. When his fingertips traced the elastic band of her bikini underwear, he sent silent thanks to Derek for his good taste.

He stepped over the line from protector to something else. He didn't trust her or believe her, but he couldn't stop wanting her. All of her.

He waited for her to push him away. Instead, her

thighs fell wide open until he could see the dark patch under the thin yellow panties. Smell the hot scent of her sex.

She wanted him. The message connected in his brain. He wasn't alone in this cross to the dark side.

Slowly at first, then with increasing firmness, he rubbed his thumbs over the base of her underwear. Pressing and circling until her head fell deeper into the pillows and her hips lifted against his palm. The cotton dampened under his fingers.

He needed to see her.

Shifting his body, he turned onto his stomach and settled deeper into the space between her legs. He slipped his open hands under her panties and up to the waistband. The warmth of her skin seeped into his fingers.

She whispered his name through shuddering breaths.

"Relax, baby." Feel. Enjoy.

He wanted to prolong the seduction. Watch need wash over her. See all that attitude and strength transformed into desire and frenzied craving. But, having her come, hearing her scream her satisfaction, trumped all that.

With his hands under her panties, he plunged a finger deep inside her. A second joined the first. Pumping and moving. Internal muscles clenched and pulsed around him as her hips rocked back and forth. Pressing in and out, his speed matched the steady thumping in his chest.

Unable to stand another second of a barrier between them, he stripped the cotton down her legs and threw it across the room. Tomorrow he'd find the panties and remember. Right now, he wanted to shut out every memory. Forget every woman who came before her. Just to sneak a taste of her.

He pulled out, then slid his forefinger through her short red hair as his mouth settled over her sex. He licked and sucked. His tongue swept inside her wet body, alternating between short darts and long strokes.

Her back was arched, her breathing shallow. Sheets were clenched in her fists. Kane could see her hovering at the edge of reason. Could sense her orgasm rumbling through her.

He felt her desire in the tensing of her thighs. Saw the changes in her body as a deep flush spread over her pale skin. Heard the deep, drawn-out groan emanating from her throat.

When his fingers joined his tongue inside her, she came. Not on a soft pant and a sigh. No, she yelled her satisfaction. That tough and sassy exterior gave way to a primal orgasm. One so feminine and sexy that he had to bite down to keep from burying his body deep inside hers.

He wanted completion. To fuck her. But that wasn't going to happen. Not yet.

That meant he needed another shower.

What the hell was that?

Annie asked the silent question a dozen times as she lay there, arms outstretched, half naked and totally confused in Kane's king-sized bed. Sure, she had experienced a wild orgasm. She let go, listened to her body and found satisfaction like she'd never known.

Then he walked away, favoring a shower to the release of her body.

Yeah, making love with him would have been a mistake.

Yeah, she didn't have time.

Yeah, he'd hate her, possibly arrest her, if he figured out her plans for Sterling Howard.

Yeah, yeah, yeah.

None of that explained how an interested, healthy

guy walked away from a sure thing. The erection pressing against her side had not been her imagination. She'd heard the hitch in his breathing when he touched her and found her wet and ready. The guy wasn't gay. He certainly seemed capable. He knew how to please a woman, that was for sure.

She hadn't been with hundreds of guys, more like three. Exactly like three, but she could identify a skilled lover when he touched her. She could sense an emotional void when she fell right into it.

The void in question clicked off the lights in the bathroom, then stalked to the bed and slid between the sheets. The bedroom lights blinked off next. She waited for him to wrap her in his arms, maybe offer an explanation for his sudden celibacy preference.

He turned on his side away from her, blocking her out both physically and mentally. Now that she wanted attention, he wanted space.

Tough.

Time to explore the one issue she could think of to account for his sudden strange behavior. "Tell me about your wife."

"Now?"

"Why not now?"

"This isn't the time."

"You are divorced, right?"

"No."

This was far worse than she figured. Being the other woman was not on her agenda. Ever.

She tugged at his sleeve until he rolled onto his back with a moan. "Kane!"

"What now?"

The darkness made it difficult to read his expression. Hovering over his prone form, she let loose. "What do you mean, what? Start explaining or I will find your gun."

"Keep your hands off my gun." He lifted his arms above his head.

When he tried to cover his eyes, she pushed his arm away. She needed to see his reaction. "I'm serious, Kane."

"Why?"

"Because you . . . we . . . you had your—"

He placed his fingers over her mouth. "You're stuttering."

"I'm trying to understand what the big secret is," she mumbled behind his hand.

"We're not cheating." He dropped his arm back on the bed. "She's dead."

Dead, not killed. This time he didn't play verbal gymnastics or take all the blame.

"How?"

"Car accident."

That was it. Whatever information she wanted, she'd have to drag it out of him. "When?"

"About three years ago."

"What did—"

"We're ending twenty questions with two. Go to sleep. We have a big day tomorrow, and your knee needs some rest."

She let him change the direction for now. She had the most important information. She'd gather the rest later.

After a tick or two of silence, she started talking again. "What's so big about tomorrow?"

"I thought we were sleeping."

"Not until you answer me." She hated being kept in the dark. Her life ran at a simple level of control. Growing up with a mother who needed pills to wake up and took pills to sleep had taught her to stay focused.

When he didn't say anything else, she shoved him again. "Kane, I want—"

He swore into his pillow. "You're sleeping outside from now on."

"Tell me about tomorrow."

"If you must know—"

"I must." He sure was taking his good ol' time providing the agenda.

"We're going to commit a felony."

She rubbed her hands together. "Now you're talking."

He yawned and sank deeper under the covers. "Thought you'd like that idea."

She noticed he also sounded pretty serious.

"Wait, you're not kidding?" she asked.

"Breaking the law isn't something I joke about."

For some reason the idea of being his sidekick in crime excited her. "Any felony in particular?"

"It's a surprise."

She curled up next to his side with a hand on his chest. "You sure know how to show a girl a good time."

His hand covered hers. "And you know how to screw up a guy's vacation."

Chapter 13

When Kane said tomorrow, he forgot to mention he actually meant the early hours of the same day. As in just a few hours after they went to sleep.

As in before sunrise.

As in four o'clock in the damn morning.

Yeah, that was the kind of information that would have been helpful to know *before* she'd decided to skip his offer of toast a half hour ago. The hunger pangs were taking over. In a few more minutes she'd wrestle anyone to the death over a bran flake.

Standing there in the marina parking lot wearing one of the only two outfits she now owned, Annie shivered from head to foot. Kane had warned her about the early morning trade winds and the chill off the ocean. If he had suggested she change instead of ordering her to do so, she would have listened.

Soon she'd have to deal with his over-the-top bossiness. Unless she starved to death first.

The lights of the marina bounced off the metal trim on the boats and reflected on the water. The shine guided their steps across the deserted lot to the docks. Sailboats, fishing boats and speedboats of all sizes floated on their moorings.

The closer they got to the lapping water, the cooler

the breeze felt against her bare legs. The more the smell of fish and salt overshadowed the fragrant scent of plumeria in the night air. By day the view over the vast ocean filled her with awe. At night, like this, the endless darkness sent her stomach flopping.

"There she is." Kane pointed off to the right, squarely behind the clubhouse, where heavy ropes tied the *Samantha Ray* to a dock far away from the other boats. The private dock sat behind a locked gate.

Yellow police tape marked the area, warning passersby to keep out. She assumed they planned to ignore that legal mandate.

Part of her feared what they might find once on board, but the rational side of her brain knew Kane stood as her only connection to, and hope for, catching Sterling Howard.

"Do policemen always get up this early?"

"Only when there's something they need to do." He shortened his long strides after she stumbled trying to keep up.

"Yeah, well, you no longer get to set our daily agenda. My preference is for late morning activities. Nothing before ten."

"For a career criminal, you do a lot of complaining." Kane grabbed a key ring out of his back jeans pocket as soon as they reached the gate.

"I'm not a criminal."

"Uh-huh." He handed her the flashlight. "Hold this."

"This scheme was your idea. You're the one breaking into the marina, not me."

He fit the key into the lock. "Am I breaking anything?"

"Where did you get that?"

"I have my ways."

"I guess that means Ted gave it to you."

He shrugged. "Roy actually, but I'm sure he had Ted's approval."

"Roy is the young guy we met the last time we were at the marina, right? He struck me as too scared to do anything."

Kane opened the lock and slid the heavy chain off the gate, dropping it to the pavement. "He's old enough to hold keys."

"Since you have them now, I'm not so sure."

No one who worked for Kane seemed to understand that he wasn't supposed to be involved with police work right now. They all helped him without question. She wondered how it felt to be on the receiving end of that sort of blind loyalty. For people to believe so deeply they ignore whatever awful information they hear.

She had no idea. She'd never experienced that kind of devotion. Her father died before she left kindergarten. She had committed her mother to an institution more than a year ago. Emotionally her mother had died long before that. A darkness, a deep, sucking hole that spiraled down and consumed her mother's life, started the day she met Sterling Howard.

Sure, he went by a different name then. Cliff Radnor. Exciting guy. Fake life. Con artist, thief and murderer. He'd conducted his search and destroy mission, saddling Annie with the job of cleaning up his mess.

"Let's go." Kane took the flashlight back. With a palm against her lower back, he guided her to the yacht and helped her step on board.

"Why are we here?" she whispered.

"To check out the scene and see if my officers missed anything." He shined the flashlight around the deck.

"Shouldn't you be whispering?"

"Are you afraid someone's sleeping? Speaking of that, where was your bedroom?"

The question knocked the chill right out of her bones. "I never said I'd slept on the yacht."

"Give me a break, Annie. Which one?"

"I don't—"

"Look, I haven't turned you over to Ted or exposed any secrets. Right now, we're in this together. I'm all you've got, so you need to be straight with me."

The truth of the words hit her full force. "Down the steps. Second on the left."

He lowered the light to the floor. "Lead the way."

She hesitated, unsure what to do next. The last time she walked along this hallway, she left over the side. Her memories of the place weren't exactly good.

"Is your knee bothering you?"

"No." That qualified as a lie since her knee hadn't stopped thumping since she woke up this morning. Which, unfortunately, was far too close to the time she went to sleep.

A "yes" would have meant an early trip back to the cottage. Not practical but very tempting since the only time she forgot about the pain had come last night when the orgasm ripped through her. Without Kane licking and touching her, the pain came roaring back with a vengeance.

She wondered if he ever planned to talk about it or if he'd continue on without emotion and ignoring his body's needs. He had this ability to shut his mind off, compartmentalizing his life into neat, no-nonsense boxes. Being put into one of those boxes and locked out of his feelings ticked her off.

Nothing about Kane Travers seemed easy to understand.

She walked down the stairs, leaning on the arm rail for balance. Better to get this over with and get back to somewhere a little less creepy. If any piece of evidence existed to lead her back to Sterling, Kane would find it, and she'd know about it.

The first door led to a small extra bedroom. Kane pushed it open and walked in. "Was anyone in here?"

She leaned in. The double bed looked untouched. She had searched the room on her last visit. Nothing had changed. The place still looked abandoned. "No. Mine's next."

The door stood open, but Josh's assessment was right on about her room. Nothing in the drawers, closet or bathroom. The floral room smelled lemony sterile. Looked as if no one had stayed there in years, when in reality she'd unpacked her things just a few days earlier.

"I had a bag and some clothes. Everything is gone."

"Why did you get off the boat?" Kane checked under the bed and behind the curtains as he asked the question.

"I didn't. Someone threw me off."

He stilled with the mattress in his hands and in midair. "Who?"

"I don't know. People, two I think, grabbed me from behind, and in I went."

"Naked." He dropped the mattress.

"I was changing clothes at the time." Together they turned over and looked under everything that could be turned over and looked under. "Want to check the other rooms?"

"You're done sharing information?" he asked.

"Pretty much."

"Figures," he muttered as he stepped back into the hallway and aimed the flashlight's beam at the other doors. "What else is on this floor?"

"Bedrooms and a family room area."

"Where did Howard sleep?" No eye contact. Just a curt tone.

"Not with me, if that's what you're asking."

This time Kane aimed the light right at her stomach. She guessed the idea was to shine close enough to her face to see her reaction without also blinding her.

"Correct me if I'm wrong, but I'm thinking those panties at the station are going to lead back to you." .

"Probably." She gave the king of short answers the receiving end for a change.

"Not exactly the underwear one takes to a business meeting. Unless the woman in question is in a certain type of business, which you're not from what I can tell."

That probably qualified as a compliment to Kane. "You look at a lot of women's skivvies during meetings, do you?"

"You know what I'm asking."

She thought about slapping him. Matching her with that, that creature Howard . . . the idea made her sick. "Those cop instincts of yours are getting rusty during your vacation. You know the answer and don't need me to spell it out for you."

"You didn't sleep with Howard." Kane said it as a statement, not a question.

"Exactly."

"Run out of time?"

Maybe slapping wouldn't be enough. "No interest."

"Tell me what he is to you."

She saw something move behind those intense dark eyes, an emotion she couldn't name. This time she responded to the question Kane didn't ask. "Not what Ted thinks. You're the only man I've slept with on the island."

Kane stared at her for a few seconds. Just long enough to make her squirm. When he broke eye contact to open the door across the hall, relief rushed through her. An in-depth conversation about her life and motivations could wait. Twenty minutes after forever worked for her.

Kane took a step into the next room. When his head snapped back, she thought something must have hit him.

"Kane, are you okay?"

"Looks as if my officers missed something." He blocked the doorway. "Though it's hard to imagine how."

She wiggled her way between his arm and the doorjamb. Peeking into the room, she expected to see something odd. Maybe an animal or food.

Not a dead body.

"Oh, my God . . . is that . . . ?"

"The publisher. Chester Manning." Kane slipped the flashlight into her numb fingers and pushed her back into the hall. "Stay right here. Do not move and do not look."

Last thing in the world she wanted to do was look, but she couldn't stop.

Kane kneeled down next to Chester's lifeless body and felt for a pulse. Somehow Kane maintained control. Didn't even retch over the blood. He checked around the area looking for something.

She could see only Chester. A once fit and handsome fiftyish man with gray hair and a dignified way about him. A guy with a designer suit for every occasion, and a photo in the paper for every charity event he hosted.

She'd met him only a few times. Those communications had come mostly in the form of memos about contract photo jobs. She negotiated with his staff, but he signed the paperwork.

Many viewed him as a legend in publishing. A rich kid who turned an interest in Hawaii into a specialty book business and eventually a successful international magazine on island living. He symbolized the new wealth pouring into the island.

Now Chester lay sprawled next to the guest bed with a gash on his head and a huge bloodstain on the beige carpet beneath him. He faced the wall away from her, so she didn't have to look into his eyes. She saw the back of his head. That was enough.

"Is he—"

"Dead." Kane stood up. "Very."

"How?"

"My guess is blunt force trauma. The body isn't bloated. Doesn't smell. There are no outward signs of decomposition. Probably happened a few hours ago. Not even twenty-four hours."

"Here?"

"Right here."

"Where has he been for the last few days?" If she could figure that out, she'd likely know Howard's whereabouts.

"I'm more concerned with this."

She shined the light on Kane's hand. He held out a dark leather binder. Newspaper clippings. Notes. Photos. She recognized the album without even opening it.

"Where was that?"

"Next to the body. There's a piece of paper clenched in Chester's fist, too."

Bile raced up the back of her throat. She got dumped into the ocean. Now one of her fellow passengers turned up dead with her property planted around his body. She wondered if someone had resorted to Plan B. Expose and get rid of her. The most likely candidate was Howard. They'd never met before a few days ago, but he must have known who she really was.

"Take this." Kane handed her the folder.

Her fingers clenched on to it like a life line. "What are you doing?"

"Seeing what this other piece of paper is."

He knelt down next to the body again and wrestled the paper out of the dead man's grip and looked at it. "I think we have a problem. Maybe I should say a new problem."

"What now?"

Kane held up the crinkled paper. "A photo of you."

Even in the darkness she recognized the photo. A self-portrait she'd taken while playing around with her camera. She liked the shot, so she carried it. Now a dead man had it.

"We'll talk about this later." Kane shoved the wrinkled photo into his front pocket and returned to his feet. Taking her elbow, he pushed her into the hall.

Annie wasn't ready to budge. "Why?"

"Until I know why Manning had it, it comes with us. We'll go home and regroup." With a bit of force, Kane propelled her toward the stairs.

"There could be something else in here that implicates me." She dug in her heels and spun back around.

"Like the dead body?"

"Stop pushing me, Kane. This is my life we're talking about. I didn't do anything."

"For the first time in my life I've messed with a crime scene, so excuse me if I'm not in the mood for a lecture." Anger strained his voice.

The gesture humbled her. "Sorry."

His shoulders relaxed as he visibly fought for calm. "Look, we don't know where the killer is. We need to get out of here now. While we still can."

"You think I did this." The thought paralyzed her. She'd never given Kane a reason to trust her, but she expected trust anyway.

"Think, Annie. I know exactly where you've been for the last two days. With me. Unless you snuck off while I was in the shower, killed a guy and then dropped your stuff by the body on the way out, I'd say someone is trying to send a message."

He believed her. Well, on this he did. That realization got her moving. After one last visual scan, she let him take her up the stairs and back out to the dock. They got two steps before a blinding light shined in their faces.

She tried to block the beam with her hand. Kane's instincts took him another way. He reached behind his back for his gun. She'd seen it earlier and ignored it. Now she wished she hadn't lost hers.

"Not one more move, Travers."

They both froze at the sound of Dietz's voice. Kane let loose with a string of profanities, some combinations she'd never heard before. She would have been impressed if she weren't so damn scared.

"Put your hands up." Dietz shouted his command. "Both of you."

"I'm with the fucking police, you idiot," Kane yelled back.

The light lowered. In the shadows she could see Dietz, his gun and the huge grin on his face.

"I've been waiting for you to screw up. To do something you can't talk your way out of with your damn local boy charm."

"You aren't a detective. You're a desk jockey." Kane settled his hands on his hips. "Get back in your car and go home."

She could only imagine how Kane's fingers must itch to pull out his own gun in response to Dietz's. Hell, right now she considered grabbing the weapon herself.

Dietz didn't back off. If anything, his chest puffed up

with pride. "You're under arrest for interfering with an active police investigation and trespassing."

She noticed he didn't mention murder. Must be no one knew about Chester yet. Dietz was too busy being impressed with his ingenuity to ask why they were at the marina. Once he knew about the murder he could pin on Kane, he'd be downright giddy.

Kane shook his head. "As usual, you don't know what you're doing."

"I'm taking away your badge. Consider it a public service."

"Call Ted." Kane's clipped tone made her tremble. His voice turned icy when Dietz came around, which seemed to be all the time.

"I'm in charge this time. Not one of your buddies." Dietz managed to grab his handcuffs and hold the gun on Kane at the same time.

"This is ridiculous," she muttered.

"I warned you he was no good." The gun barrel jerked to the side. Now the thing aimed at her. "Can't say I didn't try."

"Call Ted." Kane repeated his order, and the gun swung right back in his direction.

Even in the dark, she could see Dietz's face flush red with anger. He sputtered. "I said—"

"And the coroner. Better wake him up while you're at it," Kane added.

Confusion showed on Dietz's face. "What in the hell are you talking about?"

Kane exhaled loud enough for her to hear. "A dead body. The bad news for you is that it's not mine."

Chapter 14

Kane used his one call from police headquarters to contact Josh. After some inventive grumbling about having to leave the hot blond waitress underneath him, Josh promised to be there in a few minutes.

Which was good because if Kane had to spend much more one-on-one alone time with Dietz, he could add assaulting a police officer to his list of alleged crimes. Looking at Dietz's smug smile across the interrogation room table bugged Kane more than Dietz's wild accusations and baseless threats.

Being separated from Annie was the worst part. Not seeing her, knowing Dietz locked her in the jail cell, tormented him.

And Dietz knew it.

"Where's Annie?" Kane asked.

"Your girlfriend is fine where she is. I'll get to her in due time." Dietz's voice took on a sleazy quality.

"Don't touch her." Blood pulsed in Kane's veins as the muscles across his shoulders tensed for a fight.

He dug his fingernails into his palm to keep from losing his cool. One or two well-placed words and he knew he'd lunge across the table to take Dietz out. He'd been waiting for years to do just that.

"It's not like you to let a woman get under your skin." Dietz chuckled, enjoying the scene far too much.

"You don't know anything about me."

"Thought you gave up women for good when you realized none of them had any longevity where you were concerned."

Kane let the words roll off him. Same as he had for years. "Let her out. Now."

"The concern for your newest bed partner is touching, but you're the one with a problem." Dietz opened the manila case file in front of him and started flipping through the attached photos.

Kane could read the label. Sam Watson's file. Dietz had made the kid's case into a full-time job. Forget that Josh backed up the story about the shooting. That the kid's fingerprints were on the gun. The truth didn't matter.

Dietz shook his head in mock disappointment. "Kane, Kane, Kane. You watched your sister die. You couldn't save your precious wife from her drunken rages. You killed an innocent kid. Now you've killed a public figure. Yeah, your officers found the body."

"I didn't kill anyone."

"Maybe all of those years sniffing out drugs turned your mind soft."

"The only thing soft around here is you."

Dietz's mocking tone disappeared. "Who gave you the key to the dock?"

No way. Kane decided if he was going down, he was going down alone. "No one. I took it."

"You expect me to believe that?"

"I don't give a shit what you believe."

Dietz closed the file and leaned down on his elbows. "Do you have any idea what happens to a dirty cop in prison? You'd be smart to talk to me. Things might go easier on you if you cooperate."

"Find me a real cop and I'll talk."

"I'm the only person standing between you and serious time. Your career's over, but you can salvage some part of your life if you talk now."

Even if any of that were true, Dietz was the last guy he'd confide in. The man operated on revenge. Pure and simple, he thrived on hate.

In Dietz's world, Kane took everything. Dietz lost his sister in the fiery crash that took Leilani. A crash Dietz believed Kane could have stopped had he recognized Leilani's drinking problem in time. Dietz also lost his job as acting police chief when Kane came on the scene, did the work better and won the Commission's approval.

Kane understood Dietz's rage, his sense of impotence. Kane didn't like Dietz's irrational behavior, but he understood it. But, it was time for Dietz to move on.

"Ted is in charge of this investigation." Kane hoped pointing out the obvious might stop Dietz from going any further with this. "Did you bother calling him, or is this just part of your plan to frame me at any cost?"

"We'll see how arrogant you are after a few days in jail."

"That would require evidence, Dietz." Josh wandered in with his hair sticking out in every direction, a T-shirt hanging over his sweatpants and his running shoes untied. "You got any of that?"

Dietz stood up to block Josh's path to the table. "You're not needed here. This isn't a federal investigation."

"Ted let me in." Josh pointed at the two-way mirror parallel to where the men faced off. "Wave to Ted."

Dietz's obnoxious smile flat lined. "How did he—"

"Yeah, about that. He wants to see you. Seems in all the excitement you forgot to call the lead investigator and let him know what was going on."

"An oversight, I'm sure," Kane mumbled.

"I'm not going anywhere," Dietz insisted.

Josh didn't let up. "Ted said something about calling Mike Furtado over at the Commission to check on the scope of your appointment."

"Mike values his sleep, so I'd leave," Kane said.

"We're not done here." Dietz growled his warning.

Kane smiled for the first time in hours. "I don't know about that. It feels like we're done."

Dietz threw open the door and marched out. Kane assumed he was off to throw his weight around with Ted. Kane didn't envy his lead officer's next few minutes but did respect the hell out of him for taking on Dietz.

"Did Ted really call Mike?" Kane asked even though he knew the answer.

"You're not the only one around here who hates Dietz."

"I don't hate him." Kane glanced at the mirror.

"Don't worry. Ted turned off the intercom." Josh flipped a chair around backwards and sat down across from him. "You okay?"

"I've had better evenings."

"You've had better years."

"Sorry about dragging you away from your waitress."

Josh waved him off. "You gave me a good excuse to kick her out. We were done anyway. An hour earlier, now, I really would have been pissed then."

Kane felt the tension constricting his chest ease. "Not the future Mrs. Windsor?"

"Not even second date potential." Josh rubbed a hand across the stubble on his chin. "Manning's dead?"

"Yeah. We stumbled on the body while checking out the scene."

"We?"

"Annie."

"Somehow I knew she'd be at the bottom of this,"

Josh muttered. "Look, I'm happy to know your dick is working, but you need to stop thinking with it."

"It's not like that."

"Red's got your head spinning. You want to take a ride or two between the sheets, fine. I'm all for your gettin' some."

Hearing his friend brush Annie off like a one-night stand made his temperature spike. "Get to the point."

"This lady's trouble. Her story doesn't fit together. Her showing up like that near your house. It's all too convenient."

"You didn't see her. She nearly froze to death in that water."

"Think about it." The chair scraped against the floor as Josh leaned forward. "We're looking into Howard's business dealings. She's connected to him. She winds up on your doorstep. That kind of thing can't be a coincidence."

A heaviness settled in Kane's lungs again. The mysteries surrounding Annie frustrated him more than Dietz's vendetta.

For that moment, he decided to act like the police chief instead of a lovesick schoolboy. "What did you find out about her?"

Josh picked up Dietz's pen and started tapping it against the metal desk. "More questions than answers."

"Not a surprise. That seems to be the modus operandi with Annie."

"You don't know the half of it."

"Tell me." Kane was in the business of information. In this case, he waffled between wanting to hear it and wanting to ignore it.

"Annie Parks is her real name. She's a freelance nature photographer. She does picture spreads for calendars and books. Some work for organizations."

All good so far.

Josh continued. "She's single and lives alone in a rented house on Bainbridge Island, outside of Seattle."

The basics checked out. "Why is she here?"

Josh drummed the pen against the table. "No idea. Her agency doesn't know anything about an assignment in Hawaii. They think she's on vacation in the Caribbean."

"Sounds like she vacations the same way I do."

"If you mean not at all, then yes." Josh stared at the ceiling for a second before giving Kane eye contact again. "You know and I know that Red's looking for something. What that is, is the question."

Kane knew Josh well enough to figure out biographical information wasn't the only information he had. "What else?"

"Before she got here, she spent a few months cleaning out a savings account by paying a private investigator." Josh kept tapping that damn pen.

"For what?"

"Can't tell you. Tracked down the bank records, but so far the investigator is nowhere to be found."

Investigators. Made-up work assignments. Lying to work about her vacation. More pieces and no answers.

"Is it possible this guy is on vacation, too?" Kane asked.

"I have some people checking on the PI. We should have the information in a few days." Josh tapped faster and louder. "Until then is the problem."

Back when they worked together every day, Kane had seen Josh twirl pens a thousand times. The more tense and agitated Josh became, the more he'd work on those drumming skills. Kane had lost every single pen from his desk until he stopped working in the same office with Josh.

Because of that, Kane saw the lecture coming and decided to stop it before it began. "I can handle her."

The minute he said the words, he wondered if they were true. Annie always edged one step ahead of him, ready with an excuse or an explanation. She turned up everywhere she shouldn't have been. Underwear here. A journal there.

Dietz had cuffed him but let Annie get in the car without being bound. Kane knew she'd taken the opportunity to slip the journal into the back waistband of her shorts. The damn thing could be anywhere by now. Some of the answers he needed were in there. Years of experience and common sense told him that.

"She was on the yacht," Josh said.

"I know."

"Everyone else on that trip is either gone or dead. Do you know that, too? What does that tell you?"

"Her luck sucks." The pieces didn't fit together. Not the way Josh wanted. Nothing about Annie turned out to be that simple.

"Come on, Kane. Open your eyes."

For some reason, Kane needed his friend to believe in Annie. "She weighs a little more than a hundred pounds. There's no way she could've disposed of Howard and four staff members without someone making a noise or trying to stop her."

"You're looking for excuses. Maybe you should look for accomplices instead."

"I'm trying to be rational." Kane hesitated. "And I know she didn't kill Chester. She was with me."

"She could have—"

"In *bed* with me." Kane let the words sit there. Never one to boast or talk about sexual conquests, not since he was a teenager with nothing much to boast about, but he needed to draw a line for Josh.

"You're leading with the head in your pants."

"I can handle her," Kane repeated.

"Can you handle the idea of being out of a job, possibly in jail?"

"I can only control what I can control." Kane lowered his voice. "Someone killed Chester. Someone is going to a lot of trouble to make it look as if Howard is missing, too. Someone tried to kill Annie by throwing her off the yacht. All of this could be related to the meth sting. I don't know."

"I can't find a tie."

"We have work to do because we need to find it before anyone else gets hurt."

Josh stood up and took the pen with him. "Then I better break you out of here."

"And Annie."

"You're a matched set now?"

"Where she goes, I go."

Kane realized that for the first time in a long time, the thought didn't scare him.

Chapter 15

Annie stewed and bitched and complained. Since no one was around to listen, she finally slumped back down on the bench in her dank cell. The small area smelled like mildew. The stale air added to the foul atmosphere. The thumping around her knee didn't help her disposition either.

She could tolerate all of that if she could see Kane. Make sure he was okay. Dietz had separated them as soon as they walked into the lobby of the police station. He'd handed her off to a young man and stalked off with Kane, handcuffs still hooked behind his back.

No one took her journal. Dietz's obsession focused on Kane. Being out of the spotlight allowed her to hide the folder. Right now, it doubled as a seat cushion.

When she heard keys jingle, she hoped in vain Kane had gotten out and come to take her home. Instead, Josh walked in dressed in what looked like a mismatched set of pajamas.

"You look like you rolled out of bed and into your car," she said.

"I did." Josh wrapped his fingers around the bars. "That's my life. Kane calls and I come running."

Sounded good to her. She wondered who would run

for her. "You've known each other for a long time, I guess."

"We started together at DEA. Worked our way up the ranks fighting the bureaucratic bullshit."

Been through a shooting together. She knew that part from Kane but didn't share. With his flip attitude, Josh didn't strike her as an emotional guy. No need to make him uncomfortable.

"Where is he?" She rubbed her knee one last time, then stood up and faced Josh through the gate.

"Upstairs filling out some paperwork."

"He didn't do it." No matter what else happened, she had to make Josh believe that.

"I know."

"He would never—"

"I know." Josh's knuckles turned white. "What I don't know is why you're here. Why Kane?"

His anger drove her backward. "He found me."

"And ever since then he's been running around getting himself deeper and deeper into trouble. He's had enough issues with women, Annie. Don't drag him into your shit."

Loyalty was one thing. Being insulted was another. "Wait just a minute. His wife died. I know that, but it doesn't have anything to do with me."

Josh's eyes widened. "Kane told you about Leilani?"

No choice now but to fake it. At least Josh gave her a name. "About the car accident a few years ago, yeah."

"Did he also tell you why Dietz wants his ass so bad?"

"Yes."

"Why?"

She silently cursed Kane for his secretive ways. Never mind that she had her own private tales. Right now she could use a tidbit or two for cover.

"Okay, fine. No."

"Then, Red, you don't know everything about Leilani or Kane." Josh opened the door to the cell. "Let's go find your superhero and get out of here."

She couldn't let that cryptic remark be the last word on Kane's wife. "Tell me the rest."

"Not my story to tell." Josh hitched his chin toward the bench. "That belong to you?"

"Yeah." She hurried over and scooped up the journal. "Dietz is letting us go?"

"Ted is. He's in charge."

She followed Josh down the long hallway. From the back he reminded her of Kane. Broad shoulders and long, lean body. They sure shared the same ability to tick her off. But what Kane could do for her the way he could make her forget everything else . . . yeah, that had to do with more than an awesome set of shoulders and fine ass.

Since meeting Kane, she thought about what might happen the day after she found Howard. The daydreaming was silly, really. Nothing serious could ever bloom with Kane. Once he found out her intentions, the cop part of him would kick in, and he'd stop her. All those plans she'd made as she bided her time waiting for Howard to surface would go to waste.

Couldn't happen. Sterling Howard had to die. He'd scammed enough innocent women. The authorities didn't care, so she'd be the one to end his streak.

She watched Josh's stiff form ascend the stairs. His lazy, disinterested demeanor covered up a serious guy. Right now, a very angry guy.

"Why do you hate me so much?" she asked.

Josh stopped but didn't turn around. "I don't hate you."

"It's no secret you don't like me very much."

"I don't trust you. There's a difference."

She took one more step until she stood one stair below him. The move put her close to his back.

"I'm not going to hurt him," she said in a low voice.

When Josh started walking again, she figured he didn't plan to answer.

A few steps later he did. "I'm more worried you'll get him killed."

She didn't have an answer to that, so she followed the rest of the way in silence. When they entered the squad room, Ted and Kane sat there talking. Ted balanced his chair on the back two legs with his arms crossed behind his neck. Kane leaned against the desk, looking far too relaxed for a man who just got arrested.

"Here they are." The front legs of Ted's chair fell to the floor with a thud.

"Hey there." The roughness around Kane's eyes softened when he glanced at her.

Her heart did a little tumble in response. Damn traitorous thing. When Kane pressed his hand against the small of her back and pulled her close to his side, she gave in to the urge and relaxed against his strong body. Just for a second. Because of her knee, of course.

"What did you think of our cell?" Kane asked with a smile.

"Not exactly four-star accommodations."

Ted stood up and motioned for her to take his seat, but she declined. "Sorry about the last few hours downstairs, Annie. Dietz sometimes lets—"

She finished the thought. "His hatred of Kane rule his common sense?"

Ted chuckled. "That's about right."

"The guy's a jackass," Josh muttered.

"A pissed-off jackass." Kane's smile grew wider. "He didn't take it too well when Ted kicked him out of here."

"He's lucky he's not in jail." Without thinking, she rested the back of her hand against Kane's chest. Touching him warmed her from the inside out.

"Yeah, well, I'd bet he's not gone." Ted bent down and locked his desk drawer.

Annie felt Kane's body stiffen in reaction. The more she knew about Dietz, the more she suffered the same reaction to hearing his name. The guy brought out the worst in all of them.

"What do you mean?" Kane asked.

"I'd bet he's waiting in the parking lot for another shot at you. That's his style. Covert and underhanded."

At Ted's comment, Josh rested his hand on his gun. "Let him try."

"Easy, tiger," Annie said. "We're not going to have a shoot-out in the parking lot. Kane and I are going home—" She broke off in mid-sentence and bit down on her lip. Home. That sounded so domestic. So committed.

When she glanced around the room to see if anyone caught her misstep, only Josh stared at her. His blue eyes didn't miss a thing.

"No need to worry. Josh and I will escort you. But from the way the chief's holding you, I doubt he'll let anything happen."

With that reminder, she dropped her hand from Kane's chest. From Josh's smile, she guessed he caught that move, too. But if Kane thought her sudden shift away from him was odd, he didn't show it. His hand stayed firmly on her back, which was good since little else was holding her upright at that point.

"We'll go home, get some sleep and be back," Kane said.

She twisted around under his arm. "Back?"

"Ted needs a statement from you."

For a man who'd spent the last few hours heaven knew

where, Kane seemed pretty damn calm. And looked unbelievably hot. His straight black hair showed tracks from his fingers, but that was the only hint of fatigue. After only a few hours of sleep, his tan skin glowed, and his eyes sparkled with mischief. Not the typical ex-con reaction.

"We need to get these two home before they embarrass me," Josh said.

Kane blinked, breaking their eye contact. "Right. Let's get out of here."

With Ted in front of them and Josh behind, they walked out the back door of the station. She thought the armed-guard escort was a bit much. Until she got outside.

Despite the early hour, drizzling rain and a stray chicken or two waddling around, three men stood in the parking lot. They glanced up in concert when the door opened.

One idiot she could name. Dietz. The other two stood about ten feet apart. One, kind of pudgy and balding, shifted from foot to foot, kicking a pebble around and staring at the ground. The other man was older, maybe around fifty. That one clenched his fists at his sides the second his gaze connected with Kane's.

"Fuck me," Josh whispered behind them.

"This is what I imagine the welcome party in hell must look like." Kane gave her arm a squeeze. "Let's get this over with. Josh, you watch Annie."

"Watch me do what?"

"Are you kidding, she could probably take all three of them with one knee tied behind her back," Josh said.

Kane ignored both of them. "Ted, come with me. I may need someone with an active badge to clear the way."

"Sure."

They started down the steps, marching as if the next

stop were war. A few more minutes and they'd be able to stage a scene out of the Old West.

"Hey," she called out to the two boneheads, who obliged by looking back at her. "The macho crap is cute and all, but make this quick. I'm tired, and I've had about all I can take of Dietz."

Kane winked at her, then bounded down the last two steps. In a few strides, Kane bridged the gap between the two groups. How they could stand there without tripping over all that testosterone, she'd never know.

"We're not actually going to stand up here and miss the action, are we?" she asked her bodyguard.

"You know, Annie. I'm starting to like you."

"I grow on people."

Josh cracked a smile. "A little like mold."

"Only without the helpful medicinal qualities." Just then the clenched-fist guy took a threatening step toward Kane. "Uh-oh. Looks like a rumble."

"Hank Watson isn't known for his level head."

Sounded as if Kane had been dipping into her bad luck pool. "Any relation to Sam?"

"How do you . . . never mind." Josh nodded. "Yeah, his dad."

Of course it was. "Could this day get any worse?"

"Probably. It's only eight in the morning."

Chapter 16

The parking lot looked like a pep rally for the we-hate-Kane club. Dietz. Hank Watson. Former friend Mike Furtado. If the kid he crushed into third base in seventh grade and a few of the guys he arrested over the years showed up, Kane figured they could hold a parade.

"Nice morning for a meeting. Raining, but that might be appropriate for this get-together," Kane said to the angry crowd.

"Gentlemen, let's break this up." Ted delivered the order from behind the darkest sunglasses Kane had ever seen.

Hank stepped forward, but Dietz grabbed his arm and pulled him back. In a flash Kane felt Annie press against his back and Josh hover off to his left side. Flanked on all sides by people ready to defend him. Yeah, no doubt about it—the Cavalry had arrived.

Kane appreciated the gesture, but the show of force wasn't necessary. He could handle Dietz. Been doing it for years. Mike's change stumped him, but Kane refused to dissect that right now.

"How many guys did you call, Dietz?" Kane didn't know when Dietz managed to gather reinforcements. They'd been together ever since they left the marina, except for a minute or two when Dietz let him use the john.

"He doesn't have to call me. I make it my business to know where you are at all times." Hank practically spit when he spoke.

Nothing new there. Hank funneled most of his anger at Kane. He figured he should be used to it by now. He wasn't.

"And you?" Kane asked Mike. Kane would have stared him down if Mike had the balls to look him in the eye. That hadn't happened since Mike set Dietz on his ass and washed his hands of their friendship.

"Ted called. I came to make sure everything was under control," Mike explained.

"Bit late for that, don't you think?" Josh asked.

"Hours too late," Annie said, making no attempt to lower her voice.

Nope, not his Annie. She saw a fight and jumped right in, arms swinging and mouth motoring. Kane found the characteristic pretty damn sexy.

Dietz stepped forward this time. Chest out and chin held high, he walked right into Kane's personal space. Anyone else would have noticed the breach. Dietz just blundered through.

"You always have someone around to fight your battles. First the broad. Now Mr. DEA."

"Did you just call me a broad?"

Dietz talked right over her. "This time I got you. Caught you coming right out of the crime scene with blood on your pants and no alibi."

Kane looked down. Saw the streaks of red on his oldest pair of jeans. "Well, damn."

"Killing my son was only the start." Hank's voice trembled.

"That's just about enough drama for one morning." Annie didn't try to hide the disgust in her voice.

"And you!" Hank's anger found a new target. "You're sleeping with this animal."

Annie looked at the men on her side of the fight. "Does everyone on the island know about our sleeping arrangements?"

"I didn't, if that makes you feel any better," Ted said.

"Are you blind?" Josh asked.

Kane almost laughed at the open-mouthed, appalled look on Annie's face.

Hank whipped around and went after Mike. "Do your fucking job. Get this murdering bastard off the force and in prison where he belongs."

"He killed his wife and my sister. Now Manning." Dietz joined in the pile-on. "How many dead bodies do you need?"

Kane refused to go down this road again. Not with Annie standing right there listening. She'd jump on this information and not let go until he told her everything.

"For the last time, I didn't kill any of them. Your sister died years ago. Let this go."

"Unlike you, I can't just walk away. My sister is dead."

Kane gave in to a shout. "From a car accident!"

"Stop." Mike's low, even voice cut through all the arguing. "Dietz, you're done here."

"Well, well, well. Look who grew a pair," Josh muttered.

Kane thought the same thing. About time Mike stood up and acted like the decent man he was.

"You assigned me to do a job," Dietz pointed out. "Let me do it."

"The Commission appointed you to investigate Mr. Watson's charges regarding his son. Not to shadow Kane's every step. Not to team up with the complainant, and certainly not to settle old scores. You've overstepped your bounds and your mandate."

"One paid official protecting another. I knew you wouldn't do your job." Hank started grumbling and shaking his head.

Kane knew Hank needed to find an outlet for all that grief. Kane once tried to have a rational conversation, talk man-to-man and explain what happened with Sam. Kane took responsibility for his actions and wanted to give Hank closure.

Hank decked him. Kane didn't defend the punch. Seemed only fair the guy should land one free one in the name of his dead son. The problem was Hank wanted a lifetime of revenge, not one punch or one fight. Kane took it, but when the anger spread to innocents like Annie and Josh, well, that was when Kane had to step in. Tolerance was a fine line, and Hank kept crossing it.

Dietz pointed to the center of Kane's chest. "He is the one in trouble here, not me. Him and his girlfriend."

"I guess that's better than broad," Annie said.

Free shots didn't include Annie as a target. "Step back, Dietz. This is your last warning."

"Or what, you'll kill him, too?" Hank shouted out his question, unraveling and losing more control by the minute.

"You deserve everything that's coming to you. People think death follows you, but the truth is that you cause it." Dietz scowled over Kane's shoulder at Annie. "That's what you're tying yourself to. A guy with a history of death. Is that what you want? Is the raunchy sex worth it?"

"One more word and I knock you on your ass," Kane warned.

"I said stop." Mike repeated his command, louder this time.

Josh crowded in closer, pushing Annie behind him. "Good choice on the neutral investigator, Mike. No fairness issues here."

"Shut up." Mike answered Josh, but his gaze stayed on Dietz. "You, go."

Dietz didn't move. He didn't talk either. A silent war waged between Mike and Dietz. One Kane had no interest in joining. Mike was more of a business guy than a fists guy, but he held the power position in the relationship. He could fire Dietz at any time.

Dietz caved. "Fine, but I'll be back."

"Call first," Ted said to Dietz's retreating back.

Dietz stomped off to his sedan. Hank stayed put.

"You, too, Hank." Ted edged forward. "We've had enough excitement for one day. Go home to your wife."

"You won't get away with this one, Travers. I'll go to the press."

"Nothing new there. You ran to the newspaper with your story about me last time."

"His false story," Josh added.

"Hank. Now," Ted ordered.

Hank held his ground for a few more seconds, then gave in. "You won this time, but you won't the next. Your days here are numbered."

"You threatening me, Hank?"

Over the months, Hank had fallen apart, changed until only a shell of a man remained. Kane could see the hard days take their toll and age Hank before his eyes. Every time they met, Hank deteriorated a bit more. Unkempt. Dirty clothes. The rumor was that the board of directors at his company had voted him out. When Sam died, so had the best part of Hank.

When the fury welled up inside of Kane, he tried to remember Hank's loss.

"You're a dead man." Hank lunged.

Kane deflected. He didn't want to hurt the guy, just slow him down. Ted and Josh had other ideas. Josh knocked Hank to the ground and held him there with a knee to his back. Ted slapped on the cuffs.

When Kane stepped forward to help, Annie grabbed

his T-shirt and started pulling. If he tried to move forward, she'd accidentally strangle him. At least he thought it would be an accident. Maybe not.

"Annie, let go," he said. "They have him."

"Damn it," Mike hissed under his breath. "None of this was supposed to happen."

Josh looked up, easily handling Hank with one knee and a hand. "What the hell did you think would be the result of this witch hunt?"

Kane decided the time had come to lessen the tension and go home. "Josh, it's okay."

"No, it isn't." Josh stood up and handed Hank off to Ted. One shove later, Mike landed on his ass on the pavement.

"How many people am I going to have to arrest today?" Ted asked.

"You can count me out," Annie said.

"No one is getting arrested." Kane held a hand out to Mike to help him up, then tried to hide his surprise when he took it. "Ted, take the cuffs off Hank and get him home."

"Chief, he threatened you."

"I know." The adrenaline rush cooled down, leaving only fatigue behind. "We're done here. Let him go."

The older man grumbled about not wanting to owe Kane anything. Somehow Ted wrestled him into the back of his squad car and drove off.

"Letting him go was a mistake," Josh said.

"Yeah, well, what's one more." Kane glanced over at Annie. "You okay?"

"Suffering from a bit of testosterone overload, but otherwise okay."

"I'll be going, too," Mike said.

"Good idea," Josh shot back, but Mike had already broken from the group and started for his car.

Kane called out to him. "Mike?"

"Yeah?"

"Thanks for putting the leash on Dietz."

"Just be careful." With his head down, Mike climbed into his Mercedes.

"I don't get that guy," Josh said.

"Me either."

"I think you're all a bit strange," Annie said.

"It's the heat." Kane tucked a silky strand of hair back behind her ear. Truth is, her hair looked fine. He just wanted to touch her. "Scrambles the brain."

Josh rolled his eyes. "Unless you need me to pay more bail, I'm out of here."

"Thanks."

"Yeah, you owe me."

Kane watched Josh amble to his car, all cocky and superior. A gruff demeanor on the outside, but a different guy underneath.

"I got a question for you, island boy." Annie clutched her journal to her chest.

"Hit me."

"Does anyone on this island like you?"

That one was easy. "Not as far as I can tell."

"Maybe I need to find another island tour guide."

"You act as if anyone else would be able to stand you."

Chapter 17

"We really appreciate the lift back to the marina," Annie said from the backseat of Roy's patrol car a half hour later.

Kane had wanted to get home immediately. Then he remembered he didn't have his truck. Dietz had been too busy playing super cop and throwing his weight around to let them drive to the police station on their own. Where Dietz thought he'd run to, Kane had no idea.

Roy peeked at her in the rearview mirror, then ducked his head again. "My pleasure."

Kane gazed out the window to keep from laughing in his sergeant's face. The poor bastard had a crush on Annie. Roy barely combed his hair most days. This morning he'd arrived hours before his scheduled shift with his hair slicked back and his navy pants pressed to perfection.

Yeah, poor bastard.

Kane could sympathize. Annie tormented him, too. From her shiny hair to the sexy way her green eyes sparkled when she joked, to the trim body that moved with a catlike grace. He couldn't breathe without wanting to plunge deep inside her.

Even after hours locked in a cell, she retained her spunk. She didn't back down from Dietz. No, she defended Kane's integrity despite all the talk of him being a murderer.

If only he could trust her.

Kane turned in his seat and watched her stare at the passing scenery. The surprise shower didn't dampen her spirits, which was good since the rainy season had descended. Some moisture ranging from sprinkles to a downpour arrived every afternoon, even if only for a half hour.

"You've spent a lot of time behind bars today," he said.

She frowned at him. "I notice you didn't offer to sit back here."

"People will have enough to talk about without seeing me in Roy's backseat. No need to add to the rumors."

"You okay back there, Annie?" Roy asked.

A sweet smile returned to her lips. A smile meant for Roy alone. "I'm fine. Thanks."

"Roy?" Kane hated to break up this love fest, but the sergeant was so busy staring at Annie in the mirror that the cruiser was inches away from missing the turn and, instead, plowing into an embankment.

"Yeah, Chief?"

"Watch what you're doing."

"Huh? Oh!" They almost missed the parking lot. The tires squealed as they rounded the corner and edged in. "That was close."

"Kane?" Annie stared past him through the front window. "What happened to your car?"

"My . . ." Kane spun back around and stared out the window at what used to be his truck. Now it looked more like a smoking pile of junk. "What the hell?"

"It didn't look like that a few hours ago," she said.

"Did Chester Manning get killed in your vehicle or something? It looks like shit . . . Oh, excuse me, Annie."

"No need to apologize. We have bigger problems at the moment."

Kane blocked them both out. He wished he could block out the scene in front of him, but his vision worked just fine.

"It's destroyed." That was it. Kane couldn't say anything else because no words stuck in his brain long enough to translate into a comprehensible sentence. Pressure built in his chest and a mixture of rage and frustration balled up inside of him.

"What should we do?" Roy stumbled over his words but managed to force out the question.

"Other than try to keep Kane from killing someone?" Annie talked slow and soft, as if she feared he would blow at any minute. "I'm thinking that will be a full-time job."

Kane jumped out before the police car came to a stop. He ran to the smoldering truck but stopped about five feet away. If there were flames, and there must have been at some point, they were gone now. All that was left was a burnt-out shell where his prized truck used to be.

"Engine failure, sir?"

For a second Kane debated taking out his anger on Roy for asking such a dumb-ass question. Somehow Kane controlled the impulse. Barely. "Trucks don't implode without some help."

"Then, what's the explanation?" Annie asked.

These two were having some trouble grasping the obvious. "Someone set it on fire."

Roy whistled. "That sucks."

"What?" Annie pushed her way between the two men and stared at the blackened metal. "In broad daylight? In a public space?"

"This probably happened hours ago. Before daylight. We moved the car after the chief's arrest since this lot is overflow and out of the way of the crime scene. And, it's raining, so no one is around," Roy explained as he circled the former vehicle.

Kane still couldn't find his voice. If he tried to talk, he knew he'd yell. Probably tear the marina apart with his bare hands until he found the idiot who did this.

"Shouldn't you cops be around here somewhere making sure this kind of stuff doesn't happen?"

Roy shrugged at Annie's question. "We don't have officers assigned here. Most are out at the crime scene or on rounds. I would have passed by, but not for another few hours."

"The police were too busy arresting us to watch over my truck." Kane added this to the list of reasons he wanted to forget last night ever happened.

"Dietz at work again," she said.

Kane gave Roy a stiff nod. "Call it in."

"What now?" She whispered the question, but Kane heard her just fine.

"We go home and regroup." He'd probably punch in a wall while he was at it.

For some reason, having Annie with him was a comfort. Women usually meant trouble. He'd lost a mother and sister at young ages to breast cancer. A wife in a drunken car accident. Dietz got it right when he said the women in his life lacked longevity.

Kane found if you didn't let them hang around long, death didn't become an issue. That thought led him back to Annie. What in the hell was he going to do with her? She was in the missing yacht scandal up to her beautiful eyeballs. She had an agenda that could land her in jail or worse. But letting her go was not an option.

"Do you have any idea who could have done this?" she asked.

"As you said, the list of people who hate me seems

to be damn long and growing. But, some of the obvious suspects are out."

"Dietz?"

"Yeah. Hard for him to set my truck on fire when he was sitting across a table looking at me. He drove us to the police station and never left. Had to be someone else."

Someone who hated him. Wanted him to get a message. That meant Hank, or some unknown enemy. The latter worried him more than the former. Better the devil he knew than the one aching to sneak up and destroy him.

Hell, he'd fought the drug war for years at the DEA. Never had anyone torch his property before. Threats, yeah, those came with the job. Usually handed out by guys about to serve a good bit of time in one of the federal prisons in another state. He always thought the plan of shipping hardened criminals off Kauai and thousands of miles away to the South and other regions outside of Hawaii was a good one. Now he knew why. The island was too damn small to have this many enemies lurking around.

A population of approximately sixty-some thousand people should allow a guy to blend in. Enjoy a vacation, even a forced one. Nope.

Maybe if he were the only potential target in the mix. When his sister died, he took in Derek and gave him a home. Made sure the kid always felt welcome. Derek lived with him for so many years that the small house felt even smaller when Derek went away to school.

Now Annie. A woman who carried around her own danger like a two-ton weight. She didn't need to borrow some of his.

Kane sensed on some fundamental level that the time would come to protect her, and he'd mess up. He'd lose one more person to tragedy. Like Leilani. Like with Sam. He'd be that one second too late.

"Did you have anything important in there, Chief?"

"Like what?" Annie asked.

"Some folks keep important papers in their cars."

At least he didn't have to worry about that problem, Kane thought. "Not smart people."

"I need to stay here and secure the scene—"

"No offense, Roy, but it's a little late for that, isn't it?" Annie glanced around the parking lot. "I mean, there's nothing here but rubble."

"Don't remind me," Kane muttered.

"When I called it in, Ted told me to wait. He's coming over with another officer to do a canvass. Check if a groundskeeper or anyone else saw anything unusual."

Annie laughed. "Like, maybe, a truck on fire in the middle of the parking lot?"

Kane decided Roy didn't get the joke. Since it was on Kane, he didn't find it all that funny either.

"I wonder if we'll get blamed for this crime, too," Annie asked as she moved burnt pieces of something around with her shoe.

"My guess is that people will care less about the destruction of my truck—" He broke off to keep from chewing through his cheek.

"Than the murder of a wealthy businessman? Yeah, you're right." She clicked her tongue against her teeth. "It just seems . . ."

He hated to ask but did anyway. "What?"

"Never mind."

He exhaled as loud as he could. The day had been hard enough without a guessing game. "What?"

"To borrow your phrase, it's all too coincidental."

Kane had no idea when he used that phrase before, but he took her word for it. "How so?"

"Manning's murder. Dietz shows up at exactly the

right time. At an unholy hour of the morning, Sam's dad shows up—"

"You show up on my beach."

"—and now your truck catches on fire."

Not his favorite subject. "Let's not talk about that last item. I haven't recovered."

"Seems to me that someone is trying to send you a pretty clear message."

He thought so, too. A nasty message. "Wish I could read the language it's written in."

He really wished he could stop staring at her. Through the knocks of the last few hours, her smile and sharp wit kept him sane.

"You're in the way. Maybe something you're investigating is blowing up."

"I'm on vacation."

She smiled "So you keep saying. Did you bother to tell the bad guys that?"

Her theory made sense. The Watson case still had a lot of open holes. He knew an adult had planned the drug operation. No kid could pull that scheme off. He just didn't know who. No one had stepped forward with any information, and all the leads dried up.

The only change he'd make to Annie's observation was to add her life into the mix. Everything changed when she washed up on his beach. His life collapsed on top of him. So had his well-made plans for a solitary life.

She'd breezed in and turned everything upside down with her lies. Danger settled around her. Despite all that, he couldn't let her go or hand her off.

The drizzle turned into a downpour again. Appropriate timing. The rainy season had picked that moment to live up to its name.

She stopped watching Roy scurry around looking for his keys after dropping them a second time and started staring at Kane. "For a guy who's not working, you sure are spending a lot of time at the police station and at crime scenes."

"It's a small island." Kane noticed how her hair darkened as it got wet, taking on a richer and deeper hue against her flawless skin.

"Everyone here has some sort of problem with you," she pointed out.

"Except you."

"Except me." She pushed that damp hair behind her ears. "But, remember. I'm just an annoying tourist."

"Don't be so hard on yourself." Kane saw Ted's car pull into the lot.

"Is that a compliment?"

"Sure. You're really more of a guest than a tourist."

Chapter 18

Annie decided to wait until they arrived back at Kane's house before peppering him with questions. Between being handcuffed and threatened, she figured he'd had a hard enough morning without her joining in the bashing.

Heck, she could be sensitive when needed. And Kane said no one else would like her on Kauai. She'd remind him of her consideration and make him take back his words later.

The leave-Kane-alone-then-get-answers-later theory would have worked, too, if Derek hadn't been sitting on the front porch with his feet up on the railing and a carton of orange juice resting at his side. While the rain pounded on the sand, Derek polished of a thick sandwich. Oh, to have the metabolism of an athletic twenty-something male.

"Where's your truck?" Derek called out through the munching.

"Burnt to a crisp." She stuttered a bit when Kane growled. Actually growled. "What? It is."

"Crisp?"

"You're going to have to deal with it sooner or later, Kane."

"I choose later. Much later."

Derek tried to follow the conversation. "Your truck?"

"Don't ask." Kane stepped up onto the porch.

In case Derek missed the hint, she gave him a slight shake of her head to signal a change of subject. Just about any subject would work. Woodworking. The flight of the bald eagle. A good bout of pancreatitis. Anything.

"What are you doing here?" Kane rapped his knuckles against Derek's sneakers.

Derek lowered his legs and removed his earphones. "I live here."

"You know what I mean. You've got classes. You don't need to baby-sit me."

Annie jogged the rest of the way up the steps and huddled next to Kane under the short roof. It was either that or stand out in the rain. She'd been soaked enough for a lifetime, thank you very much.

"Where are these classes exactly? Are we talking Portland or around here somewhere?" She rubbed her arms, trying to ward off a chill.

Derek wore that same satisfied half grin she'd seen so many times on Kane's face. The one that telegraphed self-assurance and a hint of healthy ego. "I'm a grad student at the University of Hawaii. Over in Manoa."

"It's on Oahu," Kane mumbled.

"I'm familiar with the geography of the islands. Thanks." She tried not to let Kane's condescending attitude bug her.

Derek's grin turned into a full-fledged smile. Only a kid could find this episode so amusing.

"Oahu is a twenty-minute island commute hop away, right? That doesn't sound like such a big deal." She looked to Kane for confirmation.

His eyes bugged out at her insight. "It is a big deal. He has priorities."

"It's not every day you get arrested." She hesitated. "Or, is it?"

That seemed like another piece of information she should know. Kane's criminal record ranked up there on the scale of importance. Right after she got the scoop on his marriage, his dead wife, his suspension and his fight with both Mike and Dietz, she'd get to the criminal history question.

Good thing she had a one-way airline ticket. Unraveling Kane's secrets could take some time.

"I wanted to come to the station, but Josh insisted I stay here and wait." Derek shrugged. "Something about making sure Ted wasn't going to hold you overnight."

"There's no evidence to tie me to Manning's death."

"Since he didn't do it," she added for clarity.

"That's comforting," Derek said.

"You don't need to stay. I'm fine."

She watched the byplay, trying to get a sense of their relationship. "Sure, you count Kane being threatened as okay, then, yeah, he's great."

"Annie," Kane warned. That growl of his was starting to become a habit.

"Threatened?" Derek straightened in his chair.

Kane waved it off as if undergoing a police interrogation happened every day. "Just Dietz."

"Actually no. Don't forget Hank Watson," she added more to make Derek understand the danger than anything else.

Kane didn't appreciate her efforts. He shot her a look hot enough to boil milk. "You're not helping."

"Hank was there?" Derek's confused gaze traveled between them. "That doesn't make any sense."

"Dietz thinks this is his opportunity to take me down. Hank joined in. No big deal. Nothing new."

"Never mind that some poor guy is dead. The important thing is that Dietz be allowed to do and say whatever he wants." She didn't realize she'd used such a mocking tone until both men stared at her. "What did I say?"

"You're a bit punchy." Kane grabbed on to her elbow in a familiar gesture that also was quickly becoming a habit for him.

"So?"

"You need to rest."

She looked to her wrist out of habit, then remembered her watch was just one more item lost somewhere on Kauai. "It's not even lunchtime."

A corner of Kane's mouth kicked up. "Of course, if you're not tired, we could use the time to talk. Maybe get to the bottom of your connection to Sterling Howard. Read through that journal you have tucked under your arm."

She lifted her arm. "This?"

"Yeah, that."

Well, damn. She walked right into that trap. "On second thought, I could use a nap."

"Thought so."

Kane opened the front door and guided her inside, then called out to Derek. "This will take some time. You okay out here?"

"I'll be fine."

"Smart boy." Kane didn't stop leading her around until they were in the dead center of his bedroom with the door closed behind them.

"I can nap by myself." Not that she wanted to.

He sat down on the edge of the bed. "You look wide awake."

"Adrenaline." And she wasn't lying. She feared her body would soon crash from the sustained and exhausting activity of the last few days.

"You can sleep later. Now it's time for show-and-tell."

"Is this your idea of foreplay?" The words tumbled out before she could stop them. Didn't matter, though. Kane didn't appear inclined to budge from his chosen topic.

"Tell me how you know Sterling Howard."

There it was. The question—in this case, really more of an order—she dreaded. The thought of lying to Kane started a nervous churning in her chest. She couldn't exactly admit she'd come to Hawaii with the plan of getting Howard to confess to his financial scams, then kill him. That was the kind of information a police chief, even one on vacation or on suspension, couldn't let slide.

"I'm on a photo assignment. Howard was the subject."

Kane leaned back, balancing his palms on the mattress behind him. "Funny, but he doesn't look like a tree."

Not exactly the response she expected. "Should I know what that remark means?"

"You're a nature photographer. I've seen your portfolio. Not a human photo in it."

The policeman had done his homework. "My portfolio is in Seattle."

"With your agency. The same agency that will e-mail the contents to anyone who calls claiming to have a potential job."

"No."

"I'm afraid so."

She knew he was telling the truth. Wait until she got hold of the agency receptionist. "They're supposed to check those leads first."

"I'm sure they did. Josh can be very persuasive."

"But, how—"

"Police chief and DEA. We're a hard combination to ignore."

Air whooshed out of her lungs, followed by a swift flow of indignation. "How dare you?"

Kane held up a hand. "Save it."

That indignation exploded. "I'm not one of your officers. I don't have to stop talking just because you tell me to stop."

"Outside this house is one thing. Inside operates by my rules."

"That's ridiculous."

"You could always leave."

His comment, delivered in a raspy hard voice, knocked the wind right out of her. Leaving was the one thing she did not want to do. She needed him. His strength. His knowledge.

Standing there hovering over his bed, watching his shallow breathing and seeing the soft smile hidden behind his penetrating dark eyes, she wanted him. Not just for what he could do *for* her. For what he would do *to* her. Where he would take her if she let go long enough to enjoy.

"Thought I was a prisoner," she said, softer this time.

"I hoped you were staying because you wanted to stay."

If she'd wanted to run, she would have. If she'd wanted to get him in trouble, she would have used that card and called Dietz. Instead, she traveled with him. Slept with him. Let him touch and kiss her.

Without any warning he sat up and slipped the journal out from under her arm. "I'll take this."

"Hey!"

"Daydreaming?"

"More like a nightmare." She reached for the leather binder, but he held it back and away from her. "Give me that."

"I don't think so."

At this rate, she'd have to tackle him with one good knee. Maybe wrestle a pillow over his head. Find those handcuffs of his. That last possibility intrigued her more than she expected.

"What's in here? What will I find if I read it?" he asked in a deceptually calm voice.

She dropped down onto his lap, straddling his thighs with her knees and reached for her book. Careful not to put any weight on her injury, she leaned against his chest. She strained and stretched with one hand out and the other wrapped around his neck for balance. When she grabbed onto his forearm and tried to pull the arm with her journal closer, she almost fell face first onto the mattress and on top of him.

"You're going to hurt yourself." He evaded all of her attempts without even a heavy breath.

Somewhere along the line, he also developed elastic arms and superhuman strength because no matter how hard she tried, she couldn't reach the journal.

"Kane!"

"Annie," he repeated back to her in a high-pitched mocking voice.

"This is ridiculous." She took one more swipe and lost her balance, landing hard against his broad chest with a thump.

"Couldn't agree more." He put a hand on her hips and eased her knees back onto the bed. Even in a fight, he watched out for her injury.

She slumped back down onto his lap. "You win."

"Does that really surprise you? I outweigh you by about a hundred pounds." He looped an arm around her back. The other hand, the one with the journal, stayed behind him.

"But I have superior brainpower."

He chuckled "Then why do I still have the journal?"

With her hands on the waistband of his jeans, she relaxed against him. "Dealing with you is exhausting."

"*Hard* might be the word you're looking for."

Parts of him were stiffening by the second. His erection pushed up against her inner thigh, distracting her from her task. Retrieval of the journal should be her only goal. Her lower body ignored that fact.

"Can we get up now?" she asked.

"I like you right where you are." He shifted his thigh, bringing his erection in direct contact with her very center. "And, I'm still waiting for that explanation."

She decided to say something while she could still talk. The English language could be beyond her in a very short period of time.

"Fine." She exhaled, making the dark hair on his forehead shift. "Manning's office contracted with me to take Howard's photo for a magazine spread. Something about his infinity pool with a waterfall."

She'd begged for the job. Pulled every string she could find to yank. Even then, she had to call in a favor and ask a colleague to step aside and recommend her instead. Her friend hadn't understood her interest in the piddling shoot either.

Then again, like Kane, he hadn't known about how the then Cliff Radnor had wined and dined her mother, earned her trust, then stole all her money. Her weak, limited mother who before Radnor arrived on the scene had survived only by taking a handful of daily drugs to ease her depression and pain. The same woman born into privilege, who'd never worried about money a day in her life.

After Radnor left, her mother had nothing to live for except those pills. Certainly not her daughter and only child.

Annie's mother tried to end her life with dramatic flair, including a vial of pills, a frantic call for help and a note begging Annie to avenge her. The attempt had failed, leaving her mother broken and incoherent in a mental health facility in Washington State overlooking Puget Sound. She spent her days rocking back and forth and calling out Cliff's name. In her twisted mind Cliff existed.

The doctors pointed to the little amount of time Annie and her mother had spent together in recent years as the explanation. Annie wasn't around when her mother's drug use increased, when Cliff Radnor or whatever his real name was arrived on the scene, or when her mother tried to end it all at the bottom of a bottle. Annie had run years before and never looked back. Now, all she did was look.

Cliff Radnor didn't suffer from that problem or any guilt. He'd ridden off to the tropics, changed his name and started a new scheme. According to Annie's private investigator, Radnor had surfaced on Kauai as Sterling Howard with some brewing land deal. Lucrative and as phony as the names he kept choosing for his license and life.

The Seattle police weren't interested. They couldn't find other victims. Worse, they knew about her mother's instability. Said this was just the last raving of a mad-woman before she dove over the edge.

That left only Annie, so she'd made a decision. If the law wasn't going to help her, then she wouldn't follow the law.

"Why doesn't your agency know you're here?" Kane asked.

"I didn't tell them."

"Because?"

"It's a personal project."

"Uh-huh." He shook the journal at her. "There anything in this about that project?"

The biding-the-time portion of the program ended.

She poised for battle. "If you want to read it, you have to get through me first."

Pushing off from her knees, she lunged. Hands open and arms in front of her, screaming all the way. Not in battle. In pain.

"My knee!"

He caught her in midair and flipped her onto her back. With his elbows close to her ears, he leaned over her. "You are a menace."

"You aren't exactly a picnic in the park yourself." Her back teeth snapped together.

"Is your knee okay?"

"Like you care." The pain eased but her attitude stayed intact.

"I asked, didn't I?"

When he brushed his knuckles down the side of her face and across her chin, her nerve endings jumped to life. The air in the room changed as if a shot of electricity vibrated around them.

His thumb traced her lips. "Ready for that nap now?"

"I'm not sleepy."

He lowered his head until his mouth brushed against hers. "I was hoping you'd say that."

Chapter 19

Annie tried to make a mental note of where the journal had landed when Kane swept it from the bed to the floor. Since her brain synapses kept misfiring, she doubted she'd remember anything other than the feel of him over her.

He kissed her then. Deep and hot and long as his hands raked through her hair.

His thighs balanced over hers. His erection pressed tight against the dampening vee between her legs. Theirs wasn't a gentle mating. No, this was about pulsing need and frantic caresses.

"You have too many clothes on," he whispered against her wet lips when they finally came up for air.

"It's the tropical heat."

"More like the heat off your skin." He dropped a line of kisses across her exposed collarbone. "You taste like fresh peaches. So alive and sweet."

She dropped her head back to give him greater access to her neck. Teeth nibbled against the base of her throat as his fingers tunneled under the stretchy camisole covering her breasts.

"You are so beautiful." His breathing turned harsh. His movements less controlled.

With one jerk, he pulled the camisole down, freeing her breasts to his view. He didn't wait. His lips traveled over the fleshy tops of her breast. Around in a circle, igniting the heat beneath her tender skin, until he finally landed on her nipple. Drawing the nub deep into his mouth, he caressed her with his hot tongue.

A shot of pure need rained down her spine to the top of her legs. She grew wet as her nerves tingled and swelled. Every inch of her prepared to take him.

Silky hair passed between her fingers as she cupped the back of his head and drew him even closer. She loved the feel of him. The balance of hard and soft. The musky scent of his neck drove her wild. His firm shoulders, firm chest, firm butt . . . firm everything.

"This is a mistake," she said as she yanked the T-shirt out of his jeans and over his head. The material drifted to the floor.

"Definitely." He treated her other breast to the same intensive lovemaking as the first.

She wanted to watch him. To see his eyes as he touched her, but her eyelids slipped shut on a rumbling groan. She'd never survive this. Her body was too sensitive, too primed for foreplay.

"Take your pants off," she said as she placed a kiss against his hair.

He returned the touch with an identical one. "You first."

Before he finished the phrase, his fingers fumbled with the snap of her shorts. Then her zipper. The clicking sound echoed in the quiet room as the teeth slipped apart.

"Kane—"

Whatever she was going to say died on her lips when his hand found her wetness. With gentle strokes he fingered her clit. Around the hard tip. Back and forth until her hips followed his hand.

Soon the tension clamped down inside her, spiraling until her body shook with need. "Now, Kane. Now."

He stripped her shorts and panties down her legs, and her shirt off her shoulders. Before she could blink, she lay there naked and open, with her thighs spread wide on either side of his knees.

Through her haze, getting his pants off seemed to take forever. Her patience snapped. Reaching up, she unbuttoned one button, then another, then another, until his fly lay open and his member brushed against her hand.

She didn't hesitate. Couldn't. She took him in her palm. Sliding her fingers along his length, squeezing and pressing, as he grew and expanded against her hand.

"Damn." The word hissed out between his teeth.

"All the way off, Kane. I want you naked."

He broke away and stripped down to his bare skin. Naked and proud, he stood there, threw open the nightstand drawer and rummaged around for something.

Just looking at him made her desperate to touch him again. His tanned skin covered miles of lean corded muscles. Firm with broad shoulders and a trim waist. He was long and thick and ready for her.

He shifted back with a small packet between his teeth. At least one of them had the sense to use protection. Safety was the last thing on her mind.

After ripping open the foil, he kneeled between her thighs and lifted her legs. Balancing her calves on his biceps, he pressed his body against her entrance. He nudged, slipping just inside her. Letting her adjust to his size before pressing forward.

Having her legs in the air made her vulnerable to his needs. From this position, he set the pace. Slowly slipping inside her inch by inch, filling her full. With each thrust, he plunged deeper. His length slid against her sensitive inner muscles, making her fever spike and her shoulders press deep into the pillows.

His breathing sped up with the timing of rotating hips. More urgent and less focused, he moved in and out of her until that clenching between her legs grabbed her whole body.

"Kane . . ."

"Yes, baby."

With one last push, all of her muscles tightened; inside and outside she clenched and stiffened. A final surge of his body against hers forced her hips off the bed. A flush of heat and her lower body let go, convulsing and pulsing as a wave of dizziness hit her.

Her breath rushed in and out of her lungs, thumping against her chest walls until her shoulders shook. When her eyes dropped open again, she saw him stiffen above her. His jaw tensed, and the muscles in his neck pulled tight from the force of his orgasm.

With a shout of satisfaction his head whipped back as his body bucked. When his body stopped moving, his head dropped forward against her.

Soft hair tickled her breasts. She gave in to the desire to run her fingers through all that black silk.

"I don't think of Travers as a Hawaiian name," she said, distracted by the heavy scent of sex in the air.

He rolled off of her and lay on his side with a warm palm on her bare stomach. One arm stretched under the pillow, and his thigh rested between her legs as he faced her with his eyes closed.

"I see you don't know your Hawaiian history." He sounded breathless.

She loved that. "Travers is a famous Hawaiian name?"

He opened one eye and peeked at her. "Are you always this chatty after sex?"

"Be happy I'm not singing."

"Oh, I don't know. I like the idea of having a woman break into song right after an orgasm."

She fought a smile, then gave in. Punched him on the shoulder, too. "Get back to the story."

"Yes, ma'am." He rolled to his back with his arms folded above his head. "Native Hawaiians are people who can trace some portion of their ancestry to inhabitants of the islands at the time Captain Cook arrived—"

She yawned. "So, this is going to be a long story."

"—in the late seventeen hundreds and stop interrupting."

"In seventeen seventy-eight, to be exact." She enjoyed his shock. Guess he thought he was the only one in the room who went to high school.

"I can see I'm not dealing with a novice," he said with a measure of respect. "Fine, I'll skip to the abridged version. The bottom line is if your ancestors can't be traced back to before Cook's landing, you're not native Hawaiian, or so the theory of some goes."

She could listen to Kane's deep voice all day. Hearing him talk with such authority on a culture about which she admittedly knew very little excited her in a way that went deeper than sex.

"Only part of the ancestry has to predate Cook. With intermarriage and centuries of mixing, the European names continued. For me, the name was Travers."

"You don't look European." She ran her fingertips over his lips. "You're dark with dark skin and dark eyes and sharp features. Very exotic. Very Hawaiian."

His cheeks reddened a bit under his tan. "About twenty percent of the population can lay claim to the Native Hawaiian title. If a resident can trace back only to missionaries or can't find an ancestor before Cook, then, technically, they aren't Native Hawaiian."

"That's a rough standard. I can't imagine people kept a lot of records about this stuff."

"You'd be surprised." He stretched, lengthening that lean body before curling next to her again. "It's a strong culture. Some people have traditional Hawaiian names, using the Hawaiian alphabet. Others have Anglo names thanks to European settlers."

"So it's not just a matter of residing in Hawaii."

"Some people try to argue yes, but, really, it's a historical issue. Folks have lived here for decades; their families go back more than a century. That's not the key. Think of it the same way you think of Native Americans and Indian tribes. In fact, there's a similiar push for sovereignty for Native Hawaiians. To give Native Hawaiians back their land. For self-rule. It's a growing issue."

"Go back to the alphabet thing."

"Only five vowels and seven consonants. Never two consonants together. Look at the street names. You'll see it. That's why outsiders find them so hard to pronounce."

She slipped her arm over his chest and let her hand fall across the bulge of his bicep. A body toned by hours outside, running and working in the sun and surf. So strong and tough. So gentle in his touch yet insistent in his lovemaking.

"Anything else you want to teach me?" she asked as she nuzzled her nose against the side of his neck.

"I can think of a thing or two."

"Should I get a pen? Take some notes?"

He dragged her thigh over his stomach to the other side of his body. The move brought her sex over his. The man was ready, willing and certainly able to teach a lesson.

"First"—his fingers traveled up her thigh—"we'll try a live demonstration."

She pressed a hard kiss on his mouth before letting him talk again.

"And, if you need further instruction—"

She finished his story. "Then we'll do it again."

Chapter 20

Kane's plans to sleep in the next morning ended with an insistent poking in his side from Annie. After two more rounds of hot and wild sex the previous afternoon, including an inventive pairing over the rim of his bathtub with her in front and him behind, he figured she'd be worn out.

When that wasn't the case, he'd tried feeding her dinner with a dessert of after-meal sex. They'd spent the rest of the night into morning touching, kissing and hunting down more condoms. Hell, even he was sore. And tired. Damn tired.

He finally had drifted off to sleep early in the morning when the annoying poking started. One rounded fingernail jammed right into his ribs. Over and over again.

The woman needed a lesson in the lost art of cuddling. Usually not his favorite part of the process. He was an action man, but he needed to recharge. Damn woman needed to understand he wasn't twenty.

When she ended up demanding, not sex, but breakfast and coffee, he figured her batteries needed a jump, too. A different type than the kind they'd been enjoying.

Later, with the breakfast dishes cleared, they sat down

in the family room with Derek, who had arrived just as the food hit the table. Derek and Annie talked and argued, even fought over the television remote. Within minutes, Kane's eyes slipped shut. Not normally a nap guy. But, not normally the type to get arrested and sleep with a suspect either.

An insistent knocking came later. He had no idea how much later. Or which was worse, the earlier poking or the current knocking.

The banging grew louder. So did Annie's arguing with Derek.

"Anyone going to get that?" Kane grumbled into the pillow tucked under him on the sofa.

Having just gotten comfortable stretched out on his stomach, Kane wasn't about to abandon his position without a fight. He thought his hard tone would clear up any confusion about his position on the issue. Someone, that someone not being him, should answer the door.

"You go ahead." Annie turned her head away from the argument long enough to say the phrase. Then she went back to debating her point with Derek. Didn't even try to get the door. Too busy trying to prove her point about some indigenous flower. As if that were more important than sleep.

"No, really, it's fair that the guy who pays the mortgage also has to answer the door." Kane pushed up off the couch and stalked to the front door. With each step he grumbled about the benefits of owning a studio condo.

Annie finally glanced up. "Is he always this grumpy after a nap?"

"Don't know. Never seen him nap before." Derek delivered the comment with a bit of awe in his voice.

"Is he an alien or something?" she asked, and then came up with a few more insulting questions all centering on Kane.

Kane thought about throwing them both out on the

porch. Let them sit in the rain for an hour or two, then see how eager they were to open a door. He ignored them instead.

"Hey." Kane opened the door and motioned Josh inside. "Doesn't anyone sleep in anymore?"

"What's wrong with you?"

"Nothing." Kane massaged the back of his neck, trying to work out the kinks. "What are you doing here? Shouldn't you be on top of some not-so-innocent woman right now?"

"Yeah, I should. We can talk about what you owe me for this later."

"What are we talking about?"

"I need a second of your time. Alone."

"So, it's about Annie." Kane couldn't come up with another explanation for Josh's covert spy act. "I'll probably need coffee for this. Let's go."

With a wave to Annie and Derek from Josh, Kane escorted his friend into the kitchen. They barely crossed the threshold before Josh started in on Annie. "I see she's still here. Guess that explains why no one else disappeared during the night."

When Josh sat down at the table and grabbed the notepad out of the pocket of his oxford shirt, Kane could sense this was going to be a tense conversation.

"Can I have that cup of coffee first?" Kane asked, knowing he'd need the whole pot to handle this conversation.

"You might want to make it a beer."

"It's not even"—Kane glanced at the clock—"noon. Hell, when did it get to be noon?"

He grabbed two mugs. Didn't bother to dilute the strength with milk or sugar. He needed it straight up. Dropping into an empty chair, one that would block Josh's view of the family room and Annie, Kane slid a mug in Josh's direction.

The noise from the family room interrupted them. Annie's voice grew louder, even though the subject matter hardly called for excitement.

"What is she yelling about?" Josh asked.

"She's arguing." One of her strengths, in Kane's view. "Something about the state's restrictions on the importation of fruit and plants."

"Sounds boring as hell. Did they talk about everything interesting and now they're stuck with that topic?"

"Derek said something about his marine biology program and a fish nearing extinction. That led to a big debate about the fragile ecosystem. I'm guessing they've worked their way around to plants." That was right about the time he drifted off to sleep.

Josh saluted the doorway with his mug. "Worse than boring. If Derek keeps this up, he'll never get a woman."

Since Kane knew about Derek's success with the ladies, he let that comment slide. The kid possessed a mixture of brains, looks and charm that women found irresistible. The gig as a research assistant put him in the classroom with undergrads, so that he had his pick of both fellow grad students and younger coeds.

Yeah, Derek did just fine. Kane had the near empty condom box to prove it.

"The best part was when Annie whined about having to fill out that agriculture declaration form on the plane," Kane said.

"It takes two seconds."

"That was Derek's point." Derek said a bunch of other stuff, too, but none of it warranted repeating. Too boring.

Kane complained, but, really, he enjoyed the verbal sparring. Watching Annie bluster, listening to her talk with a respect and knowledge of the land, eased the tension that had been running through him since the confrontation at the police station.

And Derek. The kid matured every single day, growing into the kind of man who would make his mother proud. Kaia had valued education, even though a surprise pregnancy at seventeen had stopped hers short. Derek's father had split early, and cancer had taken Kaia while Derek was still in his teens. That left Kane in charge. Possibly the least qualified man on the planet to play the role of father. Somehow Derek had managed to thrive despite all of Kane's mistakes.

A smirk formed on Josh's lips as he flipped through the pages of his notepad. "You join in this scintillating conversation between Derek and Red?"

"Hell no." Not exactly a lie. Kane had listened until he fell asleep.

"Too busy staring at Red, huh?"

Time to change the conversation off his private life. Last thing Kane needed was a safe-sex lecture from Josh. "What do you have for me?"

"Information on the private investigator Annie hired." Josh stopped there.

Kane wasn't in the mood for a dramatic pause. "And?"

"Gone."

"Still?" Kane yelled the word.

"No, this time really gone. The authorities are starting to worry his disappearance is permanent."

"What?" Kane really needed to ask Annie why everyone's lives changed around her, and not for the better.

"There was a fire," Josh said.

Kane's brain immediately clicked on the scene in the marina parking lot. If flames did that to his truck, he could only imagine what happened to a body.

"His office caught fire two nights ago." Josh stirred the coffee, then clanked his spoon on the side of the mug. "Everything is gone. No paperwork. No files. No Jed Richards."

"Jed is?"

"The PI. Married guy with a teenage son. The fire investigator is working on the case."

"Any witnesses? Anyone else around?"

"No. The wife says Richards got a late-night call to meet a client. In his line of work, that wasn't unusual."

"We could follow that lead."

"No one knows who the client was. This person wasn't listed on the computer calendar the wife kept at home." Josh flipped the pages of his notepad. "Richards smoked. The theory of the day is that he fell asleep with a cigarette in his hand."

"And then vanished into thin air? I don't buy it."

"The only connection I see in all of this is your new girlfriend."

Kane didn't bother to correct his friend. "She's been in Hawaii for several days."

"True." Josh took a long sip of his coffee, draining the cup. "She could have a partner."

"A partner in what? What exactly is it you think she's doing?"

"The investigator's wife kept more than a calendar at home."

Dread crawled up Kane's spine. Josh wasn't the type to engage in histrionics. His instincts had saved both of their asses more than once. But, Kane refused to believe Annie could murder anyone. Couldn't see it. She had a secret. That wasn't it.

"Tell me." Kane said the words but didn't mean them.

"Richards tracked a man named Cliff Radnor for Annie. A real loser. Con man who beat the system and eluded the cops. Preyed on very wealthy women with known psychological problems, so no one looked too closely when they cracked. And they did. He broke them and left with their money. Traveled around. Used various names. Never caught."

"Sounds like a guy someone should follow and lock up." Or shoot.

Josh closed his notepad and folded his hands on top of the table. "The guy had Annie's interest."

The dread morphed into a sharp pain in his stomach. "Why?"

"I don't know yet. The wife said Annie wanted to know everything about this guy. Annie rode the investigator until he tracked Radnor down."

"Is the wife being protected?"

"That's under control. Unfortunately she only had limited intel on the home computer, but we should be getting whatever's on there soon."

"Anything else?"

"Sure." Josh continued to dole the information out in small bits.

"Of course there is." Kane raked a hand through his hair. "Go ahead."

"Whatever the investigator told Annie caused her to book a flight and head to Hawaii."

"Let me guess. To Kauai."

Josh didn't stall this time. "Right again."

"Fuck me." Kane stood up and paced the room. "Whatever she's looking for has to do with Radnor. Never heard of the guy."

"She didn't come here for a legitimate photo assignment. She came here for another reason. One she's not sharing. Now the investigator is missing. Two plus two equals four here."

The information didn't compute that easily for Kane. He turned the pieces around in his mind, trying to finish off the puzzle. He couldn't get there.

Confronting Annie with the limited amount he knew wouldn't work. She would evade or lie. Hell, he might not even know which she was doing. The journal was the only answer. He wanted her to come to him. To open up and be honest and show him the journal, but they didn't have time for that. He'd have to take the information. Not wait to receive it.

"Take Derek out of the house for a few hours. I need to get her alone." Kane heard the rough edge to his voice but ignored it.

Josh frowned. "Why?"

"I think I know how to get some of the details we need and figure out what she's hiding."

Josh shook his head. "Look, man, I'm not knocking your skills in the sack, but—"

"You're not the only one with a notepad." Kane dumped his mug in the sink.

"She wrote something down? You think she'll give it to you?"

"No. I'm going to have to take it." Then she'd hate him.

"This sounds like a bad idea." Josh tucked his notepad away. "Do you have a plan?"

"Yeah."

"Are you going to fill me in on what it is?"

"No." One guilty party was enough. Kane didn't need to drag someone else into his scheme.

"You're going to hate yourself in the morning."

"Long before then." In fact, he already did.

Chapter 21

An hour after Josh and Derek left on a mysterious errand, Annie wondered exactly what bit of news Josh had given to Kane during their kitchen discussion. Kane had spent every minute since moving around the house and wasting a significant amount of time doing nothing.

The mundane task of the minute included a screwdriver, the kitchen window over the sink and a new screen. She could describe every step Kane took in this project—actually, in every project of the day—because she'd watched him nonstop since his company left.

For an unemotional guy, some pretty deep feelings bubbled right under his surface.

She tried to break away and look for her journal. That didn't work. Kane found a home improvement task wherever she went. He repaired a broken curtain hook. Fixed a clothing rod in the bedroom. Even went through magazines in the family room and threw away some sports magazines that looked decades old. And smelled it, too.

Yeah, he was running from something or, worse, planning something.

"Could you hand me that dowel?" He asked the question as if she knew what the thing was.

She peeked in the toolbox on the table. "What does it look like?"

"A dowel."

"Believe it or not, that's not helpful."

Standing behind her, his musky scent filling her head, he reached under her arm and grabbed up a pin-looking thing. "This is it."

She plucked it off his palm and held it between two fingers. "That doesn't look like anything."

He didn't move away, which was a good thing since she wanted him right there. To keep him from pulling back, she leaned against him, letting his chest brush against her. Only two thin strips of cloth separated them.

"It holds the screen in place." He cleared his throat, but his voice stayed husky and deep. "The winds off the water can get strong."

"Uh-huh." Winds. Rain. Whatever.

That old hurricane could take another run at the island, and she wouldn't notice. All that mattered was the feel of his warm body against hers.

She closed her eyes and concentrated on the puffs of air caressing her neck when he spoke. The firm contours of his upper body fit against hers. Even the rough scratch of denim along her bare legs felt right.

The dowel rolled into her palm as his hand closed over her fist. His fingers laced between hers, trapping the wooden piece between them.

A hot stream of air blew against her ear. "I've been meaning to do this chore."

"Afraid the chickens will get in?"

The plastic end of the screwdriver thunked against the wooden table where he dropped it. Seconds later his free hand slipped up her thigh and landed on the button to her shorts. The position wrapped her deep into his arms, cheek to cheek, with his soft hair brushing her forehead.

"Chickens?" His voice sounded unsteady.

He might be tough and hard on the outside, but he had a soft, squishy side. A part of him she could connect to on a level separate from want and sex. But, getting there, to that place, seemed impossible.

Their relationship was fractured from the start. She lied. He bossed her around. Nothing about her time on Kauai went according to plan. The boat disappeared. Chester Manning turned up dead. Most confusing, she met a guy who made her think of something other than guilt and revenge.

She didn't know how to repay that kind of gift. Except . . .

"Kane?" Her head fell back against his shoulder.

He dropped a soft, lingering kiss on her open mouth. "Yeah?"

"Why are we talking about chickens and windows?"

His rumbling laugh vibrated against her lips. "I have no fucking idea."

She turned and folded her arms over his shoulders. "I like part of that sentence."

"Why, Ms. Parks, are you feeling naughty?" Hot palms slid over her butt and pressed her lower body tight to his.

"It has been almost"—she looked at the clock and pretended to calculate the time—"four hours since we got naked and climbed all over each other."

"Five."

She pulled back and stared into his eyes. "Five?"

"Five hours and thirty-seven minutes, but who the hell is counting?"

This man, this tall, dark, handsome island man, mixed strength and charm better than any man she'd ever known. The look in his eyes was both intelligent and heated. He wanted her and didn't try to hide it. Despite everything that had passed between them, she could trust this.

She kissed the stubble under his chin, then rubbed her cheek against the rough patch. Every part of him intrigued her. His smell. His body. His loyalty to friends and ties to his past. A past that didn't include her, and a future that might never be opened to her.

And none of that mattered in this moment. Right now, all she wanted was the touch of his hand and wet press of his lips on her body.

As if she spoke her desire out loud, he bent down and captured her mouth in a searing kiss that wiped out all of her lingering doubts. His fingers trailed up her back, following the path of the deep groove between her shoulder blades.

Faster. She needed this to happen faster.

While her mouth tasted his, her fingers went to work on his belt. The back of her hand grazed the bulge below his waist. When his body bucked in response, she swept her knuckles across his body a second time.

He broke the kiss and pressed his forehead against hers. "Damn, woman. Your touch will kill me."

She cupped him, pressing and molding him in her palm. At first, with a light and teasing touch, then with increasing pressure and pace.

"Tell me exactly what my touch does to you." She whispered the order against his chin.

"You can see. Feel it." His hand covered hers and pressed her fingers tight against his fly. "I get hard. Stay hard."

The waistband of her shorts loosened. The khakis fell to the floor around her ankles. She lifted one leg, then the other, leaning on him the entire time and trying not to lose her balance as she disrobed. Standing there, resting her butt against the edge of the table, she wore only a white shirt and aqua panties.

"Nice underwear." The compliment rumbled against her neck as he placed a line of kisses down her throat to her shoulder.

"I have them in every size."

He lifted his head and grinned down at her. "What did Derek do?"

"He brought me six packs of underwear ranging in size from something a preteen would wear to something a four-hundred-pound man might wear." Kane's belt slipped open, and she started working on his zipper. "I think he's afraid of women's underwear."

"I think he's more accustomed to taking them off than buying them."

"I hope you mean taking them off women."

"Yeah, and for the record, if he's wearing women's underwear, I don't want to know."

She eased the zipper down and over Kane's erection and slid her palm inside his jeans. "I guess Derek gets his stud qualities from his uncle."

"Since I'm the only one in the room, let's concentrate on me instead of Derek."

With his hands on her hips, Kane lifted her onto the kitchen table and stepped between her thighs.

"Here?" she asked, more excited by the idea than she expected.

"Standing up. Sitting down. I don't care. We just need to get to it now."

Not the most romantic come-on she'd ever heard, but urgency pulsed off of him. She couldn't think of a more fundamental and feminine feeling of strength than that. To have an attractive, virile man want her without questions or explanations. The power associated with having all of that intensity turn and focus on her shook her. Left her feeling weak and strong at the same time.

He dropped his jeans to the floor. A condom appeared out of nowhere. She guessed he kept a spare in his jeans for moments like this. They'd christened every other room in the small house. The kitchen deserved a spin.

"Are these the only pair that fit?" His thumb pressed against her growing wetness.

Her chest rose and fell faster than she could breathe in. "Of what?"

"Is this the only pair of underwear you have?"

"No . . . no." The thread of the conversation moved farther away from her every time his thumb passed along her slit.

"Good."

She felt a tug. Heard the rip. Saw a flash of aqua in his hand right before it dropped to the floor.

"Did you—"

"Yes. No more waiting." His jockeys followed her underwear to the floor.

She wrapped her thighs around his trim waist and fitted her body against his. Fingers dug into his T-shirt, wrinkling the thin material and balling it in her fists.

Poised above her, his body prepared to enter hers. With one strong surge, he filled her, pressing deep and strong inside her. The friction of his size against her softness made her stomach dip and flatten.

With a sudden urgency, he grabbed the fleshy underside of her legs and tightened her hold around him. He moved in and out in a steady beat that knocked the legs of the table against the floor with a smack. The harder he pushed, the louder the wood cracked against the tile.

He buried his mouth in her neck. "God, yes."

She ran her fingers through his hair, tugging his head close for a kiss. Their mouths fused together as the tension built below. With thrust after thrust her body tightened, and her legs clenched harder to his waist.

Heat rose around them. Sounds of deep breathing and heavy pants rose to fill the silence in between the scrapes of the table against the floor.

He groaned and shifted his body one last time, driving high and strong inside her. With a shudder, his body released. His hips bucked as a low rumble sounded in her ear. The final plunge sent an orgasm crashing over her. Ripples seized her. Her arms and legs squeezed his bare flesh just as his damp body slumped against her. She threw back her head and tried to gulp in enough air. Despite her thundering heartbeat and rough gasps, her skin and muscles sparked with life. She rode out the orgasm, reveling in the closeness of their heated flesh.

When she finally came down from her sex-driven high, she heard the loud ticking of the clock on the wall. She'd never noticed that before. That wasn't all that was new. Kane had lifted her off the table. She didn't even notice until he started walking down the hall, each step pushing him hard inside her.

His cock stayed semihard even after their sexual activity. She could barely move, and he was ready to go another round.

"How can you walk?" She asked the question with her cheek resting on his shoulder and her lips pressed against his hot neck.

"Can't."

She smiled at his clipped tone. Need did funny things to a man's voice. Funny, sexy things.

His voice touched off something inside of her. "What are we doing?"

"Getting to the bedroom." He turned down the hall.

"Sounds so traditional."

"Practical. It's where I keep the extra condoms."

Chapter 22

Kane rolled Annie off his arm and, making as little noise as possible, slipped out from under the sheets. Bare feet fell against the bedroom carpet as he rounded the bed. Bending over, he slid Annie's journal from its hiding place between the mattress and box spring, watching her sleeping face the entire time.

After successive bouts of lovemaking and hours of tasting and entering her, his muscle strength hovered at an all-time low. Exhaustion pulled at him, luring him back to his pillow and to her soft skin.

Hell, he doubted he could lift the coffee pot. But he had to move.

Wearing her out not only satisfied his body's needs, it served his purpose. He had to have her out of the way while he read through her journal. Since sleep seemed to be the one time he could trust her, this was the perfect solution. Tire her out, then conduct an investigation.

He scooped his jeans and underwear off the kitchen floor and quickly dressed. By the time he sat in the hard chair with the binder open in front of him, he was wide awake.

Page after page, her secrets came to life. Articles about her mother, a frail-looking woman from a wealthy

California family. About her father, the hard-driving executive who worked hard and died before Annie left the playground. Society Page features on the glory couple and their beautiful red-haired little girl. The family photos mirrored the distance between the parents and the coldness behind her mother's eyes.

He couldn't imagine that life. His parents split and his dad remarried and followed a military career all over the United States, but his mother stuck around. Though little money, no child support and a series of dead-end jobs, she always smiled. Always had food on the table. Always insisted on a clean home. She lived only ten more years after her marriage ended. She got married at eighteen, gave birth to Kane at nineteen and died right before turning forty. She lived to see her grandson born. Holding Derek filled her with great pride. Kane viewed it as a blessing that his mother never had to watch his sister suffer a slow death from the disease that appeared to claim the women in his family.

Annie had the benefit of a mother, but they didn't appear close. There were huge gaps in the journal's timeline. No photos of graduations or birthdays past the teen years. The pages picked up again much later, less than two years ago, with articles about Cliff Radnor. The Society Page linked this Radnor guy with Annie's mother. No photos, just blurbs about where they'd been and gone.

Still no Annie.

He flipped another page and came face-to-face with Sterling Howard. The caption identified him as Cliff Radnor, but it was Howard. Howard looking pissed about having his photo taken. Sure, different hair. A different look. The same guy.

He scanned the article. An engagement announcement for Radnor and Annie's mom. The thing didn't even mention Annie. Just referred to the new couple and how each lost a spouse early in their previous marriages. It was as if Annie didn't exist in her mother's life.

"That couldn't be good," he said to the quiet room.

Then the journal pages changed. The articles told about the exploits of several men. Showed a timeline. Marked out the men on a map. "What the hell?"

"They're all the same guy." Annie spoke from the doorway.

"Annie."

"They're all Sterling Howard, or Cliff Radnor, or Mitch Conwell or whatever name he used at the time. Same guy."

Her even voice scared the hell out of him. He never heard her coming. Never saw her face look so drawn and pale.

"Annie—"

"I wondered why you ran from the bed so fast."

She had to be kidding. He couldn't run to the truck . . . if he still had one. "You fell asleep."

"You thought I did. I saw you sneak out and felt the mattress tip." She shoved away from the wall and walked into the kitchen.

"Got up. There was no sneaking involved."

She hitched her chin in the direction of the journal. "A very clever hiding place, by the way."

So much for his undercover skills. The days of covertly looking for leads appeared to be over. He couldn't even fool a woman knocked into a dead sleep by sex.

"You knew I had the journal, and that I intended to read it. This isn't a surprise," he said.

She sat in the chair across from him and reached for the sugar packets. "Why the con?"

"I haven't lied to you." He hadn't confided in her either, but that was different.

"Then why add sex into the mix?"

"Separate issues." He slid the journal closer to him in case she tried to take it.

"Only a man would think so."

"Is it that strange that a man would want to know more about the woman he's sleeping with?" The argument seemed rational to him.

She didn't think so. She put the most negative spin on it possible and used a surly tone that matched her words. "It's the use of sex to get to the journal that bugs the hell out of me, and you know it."

"The last few days, the two of us in bed together, were inevitable. That would have happened with or without the journal. One didn't follow the other."

"Look at the clock, Kane. That's exactly what happened. You jumped out of bed with me to stick your nose in my journal. In my business."

He clenched the sides of the journal as his anger rose to match hers. "You wouldn't tell me the truth. You didn't give me a choice but to hunt it down."

"So, it's my fault you stole my property."

"Give me a break. You've been lying and hiding ever since we met. You're ticked now because you got caught, not because I'm doing anything wrong."

She shot him a sad smile. "And now you think you know how I feel."

"The one thing I know about you is how you feel. I've spent hours figuring out exactly how every part of you feels."

A charged silence filled the small room. Other than the hum of the appliances, there was no sound.

She met his gaze, held it for a second or two, then glanced away, clearly uncomfortable with the intimacy of his comment. When she spoke again, her voice returned with steady control.

"Sterling Howard is a fraud. He gets his jollies out of conning rich widows out of their fortunes."

The stiffness across his shoulders eased. This conversation, this topic, he could handle. "Bastard."

She continued to build her tiny pink packet wall and tell her story. The design reminded him of the one she made in the diner.

"He's used a number of aliases over the years. Howard is the newest. From what I could figure out, he cut a path from Florida to Chicago, to San Francisco to Seattle and now to Kauai."

"A world traveler."

"A disgusting con man."

Her body never stopped moving. Her hands. Her feet. As she talked about Howard and his history, a weariness crept back into her voice, and a new sadness shadowed her eyes.

His first thought was to provide comfort. Offer a shoulder to cry on. But she needed to get the story out. No con. No scam. Just let it out.

He'd tagged Howard for a drug dealer. Josh couldn't find a history on him before Kauai. Not one that stood up. A clean record and a few tracks, but none of it looked real. Their inclination was to look at Howard as Sam's contact. Now Kane wondered if Howard's network went in a different direction.

"What did he do?" Kane tried to keep his voice as soothing as possible.

"He doesn't work. Doesn't have to. Apparently there's a long line of dumb women willing to fall for him and turn over their assets in blind lust."

There it was. The anger and desperation. The very personal ache.

"Including your mother." Kane whispered the conclusion.

"Yes."

He flipped another page. The next photo, grainy and black-and-white, showed Annie walking into an imposing building. The way her skin pulled taut against her cheeks and tension radiated off her body in the article mirrored her face and body now. Kane decided that discussing this topic must mentally drag Annie back to that same place.

"Read the caption." The strain in her voice intensified.

Kane suspected he wouldn't like what he was about to read. "Annie Parks visits her mother, Victoria Redfield Parks of Kirkland, at Western State Hospital. The tragic case of love and fortunes lost continues to baffle close friends."

He stopped reading and glanced up at her. "If you bite any harder, you'll go right through your lip."

"My mother and her current home," Annie said as if lost in another world.

"What happened?"

"Radnor, or Howard, whatever you want to call him, destroyed her. Took everything. Left her."

As with most things about Annie, the story didn't fit together. Pieces were missing. "I get that Howard scammed her. How did she get—"

"He *destroyed* her. What he did went beyond a scam. He preyed on weak women. My mother fit the profile. He killed her mind and left her broken."

It was what she didn't say that told him the most. "What did you think of Radnor when you met him?"

She got up and walked to the sink. Her back stayed toward him as she stared out the window and across the scaling mountains behind his property.

"Never did."

More pieces. "I don't know my Seattle geography

real well, but isn't where you live near this Kirkland suburb and near this hospital?"

When she turned back around, her skin had blanched to the color of chalk. She leaned against the edge of the sink and grabbed the counter behind her. "Yes."

"So?"

"My mother and I lost touch. By the time I found out about the upcoming wedding and got to her, Radnor was gone. So was her money."

Money. Kane turned the idea over in his head, then discounted it. Annie didn't care about the money. Nothing about their time together suggested a pecuniary motive. No, she cared about revenge. For what sin, he wasn't quite sure, but Annie had a mission. A purpose. And all roads led to Sterling Howard.

Kane hated Howard before. He loathed Howard now. A guy who used women for their money, maybe children as cover for his drug trade, and hid behind the recluse label. No one on Kauai asked questions so long as Howard threw his money around and gave to the right charities. Locals viewed him as an outsider, but a decent one. Money bought him acceptance. Other people's money.

The history explained Howard's tendency to back out of photo opportunities. Unlike many other wealthy residents, Howard never wanted the fame that went along with the money. No wonder. People thought his absence showed his desire to stay private and give for the sake of giving. The real answer had to do with Howard's need to hide his face.

Annie's knuckles turned white from the force of her hold on the linoleum. "Do you feel better now that you know the truth about me? My mother is insane and Howard caused it. That's it."

That wasn't it. Last he checked, being poor didn't

usually drive people insane. He could understand how losing everything might break someone who never had to work for a living, but there was more to this story. Annie's strained relationship predated Howard's actions.

"Better? No." That was the truth. He felt something, but not better. Frustrated. Concerned. Definitely not better. "There's something else."

"I've told you—"

"The investigator you hired is missing."

"You knew—" Color rushed into her face. "You knew about all of this and made me tell you anyway? All of that talk about me having secrets. How dare—"

"Whoa." He rose from the chair to stand in front of her. "Josh found out about the investigator when he found out your name and basic information. Everything else remained a mystery."

The steam behind her renewed outrage dissipated a bit. "Where's Jed now?"

"Missing means no one knows. Someone burned down his office and all his files. Like your stuff, there's nothing left."

Her hands dropped from the counter. "What?"

"Josh has some people looking for him." The idea of sparing her flashed in his head. He shoved the thought aside as soon as it came. She deserved better than that. "We suspect Jed's dead."

She shook her head so fast he was surprised she didn't make herself dizzy. "No. You're wrong. That can't be true. No."

Kane grabbed her shoulders to steady her. "When did you last talk to him?"

"Before I got here . . . Wait. You don't think that I had something to do with Jed disappearing, do you?"

Not for a moment. "No."

"I would never—"

The woman never listened. "I said, no."

"But you think he's dead. Like Manning."

Kane crowded her back against the counter and trapped her there between his arms. "Right, but not by your hand."

"Two deaths and both connected to me. I find it hard to believe you're not looking at me for this." Rather than touch him, she folded her arms across her chest.

He tried not to be offended by the slight. "You sound as if you want me to believe the worst. I can have Ted interrogate you if that will make it feel more official."

"What a lovely offer."

"Look, no one is blaming you for Manning's death. Dietz wants me, not you."

"Just wait until he finds out about my history."

Since she was willing to talk, he decided to take advantage of the opportunity. Eventually she would shut down, and he'd be stuck again. "Were you really on board the *Samantha Ray* for a photo shoot?"

"Yes. Manning hired me. I arranged to be available and made sure I was his only option, but he didn't know that part. He thought everything was legitimate. I didn't share any of my concerns about Howard."

"Clever." And cold-hearted. This warm woman lost her glow, even her spunk, when talking about Howard and her vow to find him.

"That's why killing Manning doesn't make any sense."

"Killing for sport rarely makes sense." Kane wanted to say it never happened, but it did. Too often.

All emotion disappeared from her face. Her lips, everything, went flat. Kane couldn't figure out what he'd said to cause that reaction, but something was going on in that mind of hers.

"The itinerary included a cruise out to the Napali Coast. It's on the northwest side of the island," she explained.

Interesting how tourists always tried to tell locals about the sites. "Yes, my haole friend, I know where Napali is."

"Haole?"

"Basically means white person in Hawaiian."

"Why do I think it's a slam?"

He tried to swallow his smile. "It's a legitimate word, but some folks do use it in a less than respectful way."

"Gee, thanks for that."

"My only point was in keeping with the Hawaiian saying, 'I grew here; you flew here,' which means I know all about the island. I was born and raised here. Have hiked Napali several times. You don't need to give me a geography lesson."

"Well, I didn't know about the area. I looked it up on a map and couldn't imagine why Howard wanted to go to a wilderness area that could only be reached by water and air. He's not exactly known for welcoming hardship."

"And hiking."

"What?"

"You can hike there, too. Hike, air or water."

If she frowned any harder, her forehead would be at her chin. "It's supposed to be a twenty-mile hike. I checked because I thought the sunsets and views might make a good shoot. Don't tell me hiking that distance is your idea of fun."

He'd hiked more miles than that at a time, but they'd wandered way too far off topic already. "Eleven miles and, yes, it's one of the most scenic areas in Hawaii. Twenty-plus acres of rocky, unspoiled coast. There isn't a bad shot from there."

Her eyebrows lifted. "Could we get in with a camera? Maybe by helicopter. Get some—"

Way too far off topic. "Finish your story. Sterling Howard."

"Right. Well, I wanted to find Howard's paperwork

and see if there was anything in his files to incriminate him."

The way she described her plan, with such a calm disposition, made Kane even angrier. She had no idea what kind of risk she was taking by getting that close to Howard. The guy was a heartless bastard. She needed to run as far and as fast as she could in the other direction. Let the professionals take over.

"Are you fucking crazy?"

Her eyes went wide at his reaction. "What's wrong with you now? How did I offend your Hawaiian sensibility this time?"

"You could have gotten yourself killed." All sorts of horrors flashed through his mind. Her in a ditch. Her sprawled in a yacht stateroom in a puddle of her own blood.

"I got myself thrown overboard, so I came close."

Her flippant attitude sent his temperature soaring. "This isn't funny, Annie. There are people who do this work. Professionals. You may have heard of them; they're called police."

"I tried that. The Seattle PD wouldn't listen and Howard got away. It took me months and months to find him again. Even then, I had to spend a small fortune on an investigator to do the tracking. Now that *professional* is missing."

"You're here. On Kauai. My island."

"So?" She rubbed the bottom of one sneaker over the laces of the other.

"You're in my house and my bed. Eating my food. Damn it, you're sleeping with the police chief." The words choked off before he asked one question too many. He refused to ask. Wouldn't beg.

He pulled back from her, putting a few feet of air between their bodies. Blowing up at her wouldn't accomplish anything.

"Kane—"

Nope, didn't work. He had to ask the question. "Why not come to me? Let me help?"

There it was. At the bottom of everything he couldn't understand that simple flaw in her plan. All the resources of the DEA and police department were at her disposal, and she chose secrecy.

She lifted her head and looked straight into his eyes. "Why would I?"

Her words packed a punch. Hit him right in the gut, out of the blue and with such force, he was surprised he didn't stumble under the assault.

"I could help you. It's my job to help."

"All you've ever done is threaten me with jail time." She waved her hand in the air in a nervous gesture. "You've provided security and sex. I appreciated both."

"Appreciated?" He didn't think he could get angrier. He was wrong. Everything inside him turned cold.

"It's not as if you're involved with me or my life." She shook her head. When he took a step, she held up her hand to keep him from coming any closer. "The minute you figure out where Howard is hiding and who killed Chester Manning, you'll put me back on the beach and wave goodbye."

"What the hell are you talking about?"

"You're detached."

Not the first time he'd heard that from a woman, but with Annie things were different. He didn't understand why or how, but they were.

"You're not making sense," he said when he couldn't think of any other response.

"You've never shared anything with me, but I'm supposed to open up to you, tell you my life and put everything on the line." She scoffed. "No thanks."

"You're supposed to be smart enough to know when

a situation is dangerous. Blustering your way onto Howard's yacht isn't the answer. You don't know if your mother showed him a photo of you. He could have recognized you."

"She didn't."

She was the most stubborn woman he'd ever known. Bull-headed and frustrating enough to make him want to put his fist through a wall. "Listen, you don't know. You hadn't seen your mom—"

"We didn't speak. I didn't exist for her. Okay? Happy? Are you satisfied now?" With each question her voice increased in volume until she screamed the last one.

Something about her response, and the desperation behind her rage, deflated his anger. "If you were estranged, why fly around the country trying to avenge her?"

"She's my mother. I owe her." The fury left her voice, leaving behind only resignation.

She didn't need to explain. Guilt, he understood. Kane remembered how lost he felt when his mother died from breast cancer. Being poor and sick in America sucked whether or not you lived in paradise.

He couldn't seek revenge from a disease. Couldn't put a bullet through it or punch it out. But, if someone had screwed his mom, he didn't know what he would have done. Tracking the bastard down would have been the start, but likely not the end.

More pieces fell into place. "What were you going to do when you found him?"

Her mouth dropped open, then closed again. "Confront him."

"And?"

"Bring in the police."

Back to lying. He recognized the signs now. Her inability to meet his gaze. The way she clenched her fists against her stomach. "Right. Because you have such a great love for the men in blue. Why don't I believe you?"

"You never do."

"That's because, as far as I can tell, you rarely tell the truth."

Chapter 23

Annie walked the waterline in front of Kane's house. The rain had stopped, but not before soaking the sand and whipping the waves into a frenzy. The white-caps curled and crashed against the beach, blocking out all sound except the running dialogue in her head.

Any other time, she would have framed the scene in her mind, looking for the best angle for a shot. Not this time.

An hour had passed since Kane declared they needed to take a break. One of his patented pull-back-and-regroup discussions. Almost sixty minutes later, the break wasn't working. She didn't feel regrouped or better. Lost and confused, yeah, those were more like it.

Only an idiot would have spilled all that personal information after realizing Kane had used sex in exchange for getting a few minutes alone with the journal. Not just any idiot, no, the biggest idiot.

Actually, the more she thought about it, the more she believed that title belonged to Kane. She should have knocked him on his ass for the journal stunt.

She sat down on the beach, just out of reach of the incoming waves. Kane's sweats blocked the chill from reaching her skin. If the sand stained them, who cared.

The fact that he never lied to her danced through her

brain, but she shoved it out. No matter how hard she tried to block it, reality wandered back in again. He didn't lie. Kane had made his intentions clear from that first night with the handcuffs. He was keeping her close until he knew her story.

Shame on her for thinking making love with him might change the rules. This was just another example of Kane's ability to compartmentalize and stick her in a little box somewhere at the end of his priority list. And her inability to tolerate that box.

His attitude and easy dismissal of their time together still ticked her off. Would it be that tough for the guy to show some connection? Yeah, she would leave the island soon. Yeah, she would track down Howard and kill him, no matter what anyone else said. Yeah, she might go to prison. All that was true, and it all sucked.

The plan had seemed much easier back in Seattle.

She wrapped her arms around her legs and dropped her forehead to her knees. The time had come for a new strategy. Her gun had disappeared along with Howard. Her welcome with Kane was wearing thin.

Without any money or resources, this revenge stuff wasn't so easy. It certainly didn't help that her last paying boss rested on a slab at the morgue. And she thought she had problems. At least no one had succeeded in killing her yet.

At the crunch of shoes against the hard sand, her head popped up. Expecting to see Kane, a crush of disappointment hit her when she recognized the anti-Kane.

"Mind if I sit?" Dietz asked two seconds after he actually sat down next to her on the beach.

"I'm really not in the mood for a Kane-is-a-killer speech today."

"I'm just enjoying the scenery. Travers has a hell of a view out here." Dietz stared out over the ocean, watching the waves roll onto the shore.

"You expect me to believe that you just happened to be driving by Kane's house and just happened to feel like a bit of fresh air? I don't think so." She glanced over her shoulder at the house to check for signs of Kane in case she needed reinforcements. For the first time since she met him, Kane was leaving her alone. Great timing on the chief's part.

"That's how things work sometimes."

"Uh-huh. What do you want?"

Dietz smiled at her. For being the human reincarnation of Satan, he pulled off the grin pretty well. She gave him credit for his impression of a normal person.

His gaze searched her face. "You're not very trusting, are you, Annie?"

Every man on the island seemed concerned with her trust and honesty issues all of a sudden. A female visitor didn't stand a chance with this group.

"I've had a rough few days. Finding Chester Manning's body didn't help. My vacations usually don't include corpses."

"Are you still providing Travers with an alibi for that?"

"I thought I said no killing talk." She picked up a piece of driftwood and drew a picture of a house in the sand. Not one she'd ever known, but a happy house with trees and a chimney.

"Did he tell you how his wife died?"

"Car accident." She pretended not to care when, really, all she wanted to do was pepper Dietz with questions and get the whole story.

"A drunken car accident," he said.

She added stick people to the front lawn. Then a fence.

"She killed two other innocent people." Dietz stressed the word *killed,* which wasn't a surprise to Annie since that seemed to be his favorite word.

"The 'she' being Leilani?" Annie tried to remember if she ever saw Kane take a drink.

"She drank to excess. Travers knew it. He stayed away from the house rather than deal with it. Purposely signed up for DEA assignments that took him away from home, so the rest of us got stuck with his responsibility. He abandoned her." Dietz's gaze returned to the ocean and stared as if lost in his thoughts.

The last thing she could imagine was Kane slacking on his responsibilities. If anything, he took them too seriously. He'd taken in Derek. He'd taken her in and helped her. He insisted on doing his job, no matter the personal cost, even when on suspension.

Bossy, demanding and a tad too controlling, yeah. All of those fit. But, no, the Kane that Dietz described wasn't the Kane she knew.

"What should he have done?"

"Stopped her." When Dietz turned back, his eyes glowed with hatred. "I warned him, and he ignored me. Because of Travers, my sister is dead."

"See, that's where you lose me." She scratched out her happy beach family and their small house.

"They fought, and Leilani went to Oahu." Dietz cleared his throat. "Oahu is one of the other—"

Good grief. "Stop."

"What?"

"Stop right now. What is it with people from Hawaii assuming no one else knows about the multiple islands?" She dropped the stick and wiped the sand from her hands. "We're not all dumb tourists, you know."

Dietz's gaze darted from her to the ocean, as if he were looking for an easy escape. "Most people get confused with the idea of Oahu and the Big Island. That's all."

"Yeah, well, not me."

"Okay."

"Fine." She waved her hand in the air. "Go on with the story."

"Leilani went to a baby shower and convinced my sister to go with her. Leilani got drunk, as usual. She always did. Everyone knew. She ran her car right off a cliff."

He finished his explanation, then looked at her with an air of anticipation. Satisfaction showed in his eyes and on the curve of his mouth.

"When was this?"

"Five years ago."

That qualified as holding a grudge and refusing to move on. "Is that it? That's why you hate Kane after all this time?"

Dietz's head shot forward, invading her space and her comfort zone. "Isn't that enough? All three women in the car died instantly."

"It's enough for you to be mad at Leilani. Not Kane. He didn't do anything."

"You don't get it." Dietz shook his head in disgust.

One of them didn't get it, but she suspected she wasn't the problem. "You both lost someone in that accident."

"His wife was young and spoiled, much younger than him. He ignored her. He had his pretty bride. That's all he needed. Like with everything else in Kane's life, he took what he needed for himself and the hell with everyone else. Only he can win, which means others only lose."

She had the sneaky suspicion they were no longer talking about Dietz's sister. "What else happened between you two?"

After a hesitation, Dietz answered. "He took my job."

"DEA or police?"

"Police Chief." Dietz picked up her drawing stick and broke it into small pieces. "Convinced the Police Commission I wasn't qualified for the position, then stepped into it himself."

"You mean that the Commission voted him in."

"The Commission led by Kane's friend."

"Mike? The guy I met in the police parking lot hardly seemed like a good friend to Kane." She switched topics before Dietz started arguing with her about Mike. "You were the chief?"

"Acting." Dietz threw the pieces of wood toward the water and watched them ride the tide. "My predecessor lost his job due to incompetence and fraud. I stepped in. Travers pushed me out."

She got it now. Dietz blamed Kane for everything that went wrong in his life. If Dietz lost something, then Kane must have caused it. She couldn't imagine living like that.

Except she did. Her whole life worked like that. Her mother had failed, and that failure defined her life. Made her run from home and stay away. Made her come back and play the role of martyr.

"Annie?" Dietz touched her elbow. "You okay?"

She heard his voice, but it took her a second to focus. "Fine."

That hand slipped to her back, not in an inappropriate way. More like how a big brother would comfort an upset baby sister. "Do you finally get it?"

"I think I do." Not the point Dietz wanted her to get, but a more important point.

"Then I have a proposition for you." He folded his arms over his knees, mimicking her sitting position.

"I'm listening."

"It has to do with Kane."

Now there was a surprise. "I'm still listening."

Chapter 24

Annie walked back into the house, barefoot and holding her sneakers, just as Kane picked his police shield up off the coffee table.

"You planning on shooting someone?" she asked.

"Maybe." He secured his sidearm.

"Anyone I know?"

This time he really looked at her. Sand dusted her bare feet and calves. Some of the red hair tucked behind her ears had slipped out and framed her ruddy cheeks.

He asked the obvious question anyway. "Where have you been for the last hour?"

"At the dentist. Where do you think?" She dropped the shoes to the floor and walked over until only the sectional sofa separated them.

"Someone out there killed Manning. You need to be more careful."

"Were you planning on sending a search party after me?"

"Do I need to?"

Since he knew exactly where she'd been and who she'd been with, the search party wasn't necessary. A leash might be more appropriate. Maybe a lecture. He wasn't ready to rule out using the handcuffs again.

Dietz. He'd stalked Annie on the beach, then made himself at home by her side. Sat there talking and sharing all of his theories with her. Kane couldn't hear the conversation, didn't really want to, but he knew Dietz well enough to know the subject.

Kane wondered who Dietz thought he killed today. Bastard.

None of that surprised or disappointed Kane. No, he didn't expect much from Dietz except anger and blame. But, he expected more from Annie.

That she hadn't gotten up right away and come back to the house made every muscle in his body clench in frustration. After she'd heard all Dietz had to say, she still sat there and listened some more. Conducted a conversation. Took in the view.

Her eyes narrowed. "You saw me. You were watching me on the beach."

"How is Dietz doing today?"

"You actually spied on me." There was no heat behind her statement. She said it more like a fact than an accusation.

"I haven't let you out of my sight since I found you. So, yeah, I watched. I also noticed you didn't push him away. Did you enjoy that back rub? Having his hands on you?"

She dropped onto the couch with a sigh. "It's not what you think."

"I think you found a new friend." With Kane's hands on either side of her head, he leaned over her from behind. "Maybe one who doesn't ask as many questions."

"Get a clue. He was just—"

The front door opened after one sharp knock. Kane jumped almost as high as Annie did. When he saw the visitors, he didn't feel any relief. Josh and Derek walked into the family room looking pissed and aiming their joint rage in Annie's direction.

Kane knew she noticed. She stood up and edged around the couch until she stood beside him. The closer Josh and Derek got to her, the closer she moved to Kane. One more step and she'd be inside him.

"I have to start locking that door," Kane said in an effort to ease the building tension.

"We both have keys." Josh didn't spare Kane a glance. No, his attention centered on Annie.

"What did I do?" she asked.

"What did you do?" Josh took one last step until he faced Annie across the couch. "You lied. Again."

"Josh, maybe there's an explanation." Derek put a restraining hand on Josh's forearm.

Annie shook her head. "I don't know what you're talking about."

The comment infuriated Josh even further. His face flushed with rage, and his hand moved to his gun.

Kane knew Josh would never hurt Annie. The gesture was unconscious, but it was too much. "Everyone cool down. Josh, back up."

Josh didn't move.

"Josh!"

Josh finally took the hint and moved. A firm tug on his arm from Derek helped.

"What the hell is going on?" Kane asked, but when Josh looked as if he was going to speak, Kane cut him off. "Not from you. Derek, you tell me. You seem more rational than Josh at the moment."

"We saw her." Derek's gaze flicked to Annie, then back to his uncle. "She was with Dietz. He wasn't forcing her, and she didn't try to leave."

"Do all the men on this island get off on spying on women?" Annie asked.

"Get off is too strong. Enjoy, maybe." Nobody laughed at Kane's joke.

"I wasn't spying." The frown on Josh's face showed

exactly how much he disliked that description. "We drove by and saw Dietz hanging all over you."

"Hanging on me?"

"I thought it looked 'cozy' but 'hanging' is probably fair," Kane said.

"You're both wrong. I was there first. Just sitting there on the beach watching the ocean. Dietz came up to me."

"Warrior Boy, do you see what I mean now? You can't trust her." Josh leaned in toward her again. "Dietz hates Kane."

Annie rolled her eyes. "Yeah, I got that part, Josh. I may not be from here, but I'm not an idiot."

"So, why were you talking to him?" Derek asked in a much calmer voice than the one Josh used.

"If everyone will settle down and listen, and stop jumping to conclusions"—she pinned Josh with a glare—"I'll tell you."

"Right. Can hardly wait to hear this story." Josh crossed his arms over his chest.

"I knew she was with Dietz." With that admission, Josh and Derek both stared at Kane as if he'd finally lost it. Maybe he had, but he believed the meeting between Dietz and Annie to be innocent. "Annie and I were just talking about what happened with Dietz."

"Are you kidding?" The shock on Josh's face matched the shock in his voice.

Kane gestured to Annie. "Go ahead."

"As I said, Dietz approached me. He told me about his sister and Kane's wife—"

"What did he say exactly?" This qualified as Kane's least favorite subject on the planet. But, now that the information was out there, he needed to make sure Dietz had at least attempted to be honest.

"That your wife was young and had a problem with alcohol."

"There's an understatement," Josh mumbled.

Annie's cheeks flushed, but she kept going. "You worked a lot and missed the signs. Dietz said you knew but didn't want to deal with it. He talked about the accident. Blamed you."

"Like Josh said, nothing new there." Derek sprawled out on the coffee table like only a young man comfortable with his surroundings could do.

"What did you say back to Dietz?" Josh asked.

Somehow Annie managed not to wither under Josh's harsh glare. "I said Kane wasn't to blame for his wife's drinking or the accident. The accident was just that, an accident."

Josh visibly relaxed. Some of the tension left his face. "Anything else?"

Kane wanted to ask the question, but Josh beat him to it. From what Kane saw, the conversation on the beach went on for a while. He knew there was more to it than the car accident.

She nodded. "He told me Kane pushed him out of the police job."

"And?" This time Kane asked the question.

She sat down on the armrest of the couch. "He asked me to provide him with information on Kane in exchange for whatever I wanted. A quid pro quo."

"Fuck! I knew it. Let me kill him." Josh fell back into the chair. "One bullet. Ten minutes."

Annie looked horrified, which made Derek's smile even bigger.

Kane couldn't help but smile, too. Josh's boast didn't have anything behind it but a guy's big talk. He'd never shoot anyone in cold blood. No matter how much he wanted to.

"He's kidding," Kane assured her.

"No, I'm not," Josh said.

"What type of information?" Kane asked.

"Where you go and with whom. He wanted to know if you talked about Watson and what you said. Typical Hawaii guy spy stuff as far as I could see."

"And you told him no." Kane felt that certainty down to his feet.

"No." She smiled as she said the word.

But the answer pulled Derek away from whatever buttons he was fiddling with on the MP3 player on his lap. "Did you just say no?"

Her grin gave Kane a silent warning not to panic. He didn't. He might not know much about Annie, but he knew he could count on her to be able to identify an enemy when one landed right in front of her. Unfortunately, she'd had a lot of practice. Too much.

"I told Dietz to kiss my ass." She looked toward the ceiling as if she were contemplating the most important question in the universe. "I may have told him to grow up and stop wallowing in the past. Probably something in there about hell and damn, too. I included most of the oldie-but-goodie swear words in my response."

The remaining tension in the room fizzled out as all three men laughed. With all that behind them, Kane was ready to move on. Dietz's position wasn't going to change. No use in wasting time trying.

"Look, we have something more important than Dietz to take care of at the moment."

"I can't imagine what that would be." Derek adjusted the headphones around his neck.

Kane came out with it. "Howard's resurfaced."

"What?" Josh jumped to his feet.

So did Annie. "You've been holding back that information. What exactly were you waiting for, an invitation?"

Josh nodded his head and grinned in what could only be described as admiration. Lucky for him Annie couldn't see it. She probably would have flattened him.

She could do it, too. Had the stiff stance and clenched fists for battle.

"Roy called a few minutes ago. I'm going to the station to pick him up and then—"

"Count me in." Josh's hand went back to his gun.

"Me, too." Annie walked over to her sneakers.

As if Kane would let her step into danger. Never going to happen. She stayed here, safe and locked in. Until he knew all of her plans for Howard, she'd be staying here. He didn't need a civilian and potential target in the way. Especially one with a secret agenda.

"Josh." Kane pointed to his friend and usual backup. "You're coming along. Annie, you're grounded."

Bent over with one shoe on and the other one off, she stopped. "Like hell."

"No arguments. This could be a trap or a dead end. Any number of things. You stay with Derek."

"What did I ever do to you?" Derek meant it as a joke.

Annie wasn't laughing. "I don't like it either. I should go along, Kane."

"No." Holding his ground was the only option. If she came along, he'd spend the entire time trying to protect her, and protecting women never worked for him. More importantly, it never worked for them.

She limped over to Kane on her one shoe and grabbed on to his shirt. "You know why I should be there."

"I don't. Tell me," Josh said.

Annie ignored Josh and Derek. "Please, Kane."

"Watch out, Kane. She's pulled out the big guns. Begging." Josh checked his phone, then shoved it back in his pocket. "Hate when women do that."

"We'll be back. I'll call you as soon as I know something." Kane tried to walk around her, but she didn't let go of his shirt. "Annie, stop. I need to get going."

"You need to take me with you."

"Can't. You stay with Derek." When he loosened her

hold on his shirt, he was surprised not to see two holes where she had held the cotton material in a death grip.

"Maybe I should give Derek a gun. You know, to protect himself from her." Josh rubbed his beard.

"She'd probably use it on me," Derek said.

"The sooner I go, the sooner you'll have whatever information I have." Leaning down, Kane whispered in her ear. "Don't make me use the handcuffs."

She pulled back, refusing to relax. "This isn't funny."

"No, I can see that it isn't." He kissed her then. Not long. Not hard. Just a quick peck on the lips. Enough to throw her off balance. Long enough for him to leave.

Kane slid into the passenger side of Josh's car and waited for the warnings. Annie stood on the porch arguing with Derek about something. Derek solved the problem by kicking back in a chair with his headphones on.

The car door opened. Josh slumped into his seat but didn't say anything. Just turned on the engine and started backing out of the driveway.

"Damn, just say it." Kane lowered the window. The rain had stopped, taking the humidity along with it.

Josh shot him a quick look, then concentrated on the curving road again. "What?"

"The I told you so."

"Ahhh." Josh smiled behind his sunglasses. "You mean Annie."

"Of course."

"The lady does have you chasing your tail."

"She'd kick your ass if she heard you say that."

"I'm not dumb enough to say it to her face."

"I believe her about Dietz." Kane reached into his back pocket and took out his cell phone. Roy was supposed to call if he found out any other information.

Josh's smile disappeared. "So do I."

Kane stopped dialing. "Thought you hated her."

"I want to."

"But?"

"Can't."

Kane sympathized. Blocking out Annie was an almost impossible task. "Any reason?"

"I figure she's going to be around for a while, so I should get used to her."

This time Kane was the one who lost his smile. "She's going home eventually."

"Come on, Kane. This is me. Josh. Annie means something to you. For the first time in a long time, you've let a woman stay at your house. Meet Derek. She isn't a fling."

Wrong road. Kane knew where Josh planned to take this conversation, and they were headed in the wrong direction.

Kane had tried that life once and it didn't work. "She's leaving. Her life is somewhere else, which is better for her. Kauai is a dead end for her."

"Not that I-kill-every-woman-I-know bullshit."

Josh didn't live it. Kane did.

"My life is fine the way it is," Kane insisted.

"You're hooked on her."

Kane tried again. "She's going back to Seattle."

"You keep telling yourself that buddy. Ten years from now when I'm going to your kid's baseball game, I'll remind you of this moment."

For some reason, the thought of a future didn't fill Kane with the dread it once had. Kids and Annie. Little smart-mouthed kids with deep red hair. He could almost picture them.

It had been years since he'd let his mind wander in that direction. Seeing more than a week ahead of him had been impossible. Since he'd buried a woman he cared about.

Yeah, no thanks. He'd hosted enough funeral lunches for a lifetime.

"Like hell," Kane muttered and turned to look out the window.

"Keep denying it, Warrior Boy. It will make your fall all the more fun when it happens."

"Just drive."

"You won't make me wear a tux to the wedding, will you?"

"You're not invited."

Chapter 25

"He cares, you know."

Derek's cryptic statement stopped Annie before she could walk back into the house. She assumed the "he" in the sentence was the same "he" who just drove off. Kane.

"About anything in particular?"

"Dietz and what he thinks." Derek slipped his headphones off. "Kane acts like the crap Dietz says doesn't matter. It does."

"No one likes to be blamed for other people's mistakes." She stepped back onto the porch and leaned against the railing by Derek's feet.

"Kane does that all on his own. It's Dietz's vendetta. He never lets Kane forget. You know what I mean?"

She thought she did. "About Leilani?"

"About everything bad that's happened to Kane. He broke up a drug ring, won all this praise and got his job. Dietz spun it to try to make it look as if Kane called in favors." Derek rocked on the back two legs of the chair. "Kane stopped kids from selling drugs to other kids. All Dietz does is preach about how Kane killed Sam Watson. I mean, hell, Kane knows the kid is dead. He also knows the kid was about to shoot Josh in the head."

All this time she'd been looking for the missing information on Kane. She should have pressed Derek. The kid was happy to talk about Kane. They clearly loved and admired each other. That Kane couldn't take that feeling and focus it on . . . Yeah, her. That was the thought that went through her mind. She wanted Kane to focus all the attention and love on her.

Love? Cripes, how the hell did that happen? Why now?

She stood on the edge of accomplishing everything she'd set out to do. To avenge her mother and put that life behind her. Then in walks Kane and ruins everything. And she was dumb enough to fall for him.

Looked like bad taste in men ran in the women in her family. Sure, Kane was solid and smart and handsome. All those things. He also lived in a different state from her, carried a badge and would likely arrest her as soon as she got rid of Howard.

"Kane did everything he could for Sam and Leilani. Both of them set their lives on these impossible paths," Derek explained.

"Leilani did drink, then?"

"More and more. She got married young and viewed Kane as her ticket out. He had been to college in Arizona. Left Kauai. Landed an impressive job. She hoped he'd take her away from here. From being poor. When he settled down, instead, and turned into a bit of a local hero, she lost what little composure she had left."

"I can't see Kane marrying that type."

Derek flashed her that soft smile Kane used on her all the time. On Derek, the look came off as sweet. On Kane, it was anything sexy and hot and everything she'd always wanted from a man.

"Can only see him with a feisty redhead from Washington state, huh?" Derek chuckled.

She had to stop that type of thinking right now. "No—"

"I'm kidding." He waved her off. "The real answer is that people tend to marry young here. I guess Kane thought it was time. Either that or . . ."

"Or?"

"He wanted to save her."

She didn't have an answer for that. She never thought of Kane as the savior type, but the role did fit. From his career choice to the way he handled her, he showed his tendency to protect.

"Dietz can't understand any of that. He's too busy nursing grudges. He wants someone to blame for his life. Kane fills the role."

"Competing for the same job probably didn't help."

"Honestly? Dietz was a terrible police chief. Totally unqualified. The newspaper ran editorials arguing that the Police Commission needed to clean house following the scandal of the previous guy. Dietz coming from Internal Affairs, and not having any recent street experience, didn't fit the bill."

To Annie, the most pathetic part was that Dietz fought the battle alone. Kane didn't participate. "I think your uncle is impervious to Dietz. Kane's not the most emotional guy in the world."

"That's where you're wrong. That's the part you're not getting. You didn't see Kane. You weren't there when my mom died and when Leilani died." Derek cut off and swallowed a few times before starting again. "He lost it."

Lost it, all right. Lost his ability to care and feel. Annie understood that part even if Derek did not see the connection. "He learned a hard lesson from those deaths."

"Being?"

"To shut himself off." She stared at the water, got lost in the sound of the waves. "Other than you, I can't imagine what or who could bring out his emotions."

Derek sighed from shoulder to stomach. "Maybe you're not as smart as I thought."

"Maybe not."

This one would turn into a heartbreaker one day. A tall, dark and handsome sweet-talker just like his uncle.

"You're ignoring reality."

"Are you trying to impress me with your college psych knowledge?" she asked.

"I'm getting a Master's in marine biology. Freshman psych was a long time ago."

"Whatever. I'm going to make something to eat. Want a sandwich?"

"You know, with that kind of talk I could get used to a woman in the house again."

She ruffled his hair. For some reason, the action felt right. "You only love me for my food."

"I'll let you know later." He put his headphones back on. "After I've tasted it."

Fifteen minutes later while mixing her tuna salad and staring at a spot in the middle of the kitchen table, she continued to analyze Derek's perception of Kane. She'd seen flashes of Kane's softer side. For the most part, he played the role of tough cop well. Other times, he joked and laughed.

She still couldn't help but think that he held a part of himself back. Maybe he only hid that part from her. Maybe other people, people he loved, got to see that private, vulnerable side. Not her. She ranked as a guest. A nuisance even.

"Annie."

She spun around at the sound of her whispered name and nearly dropped the bowl. She caught the lip in time, slamming it against the side of the chair before the bowl could crash to the floor.

"Careful." Dietz reached out his hand as if to perform a miracle catch, but she beat him to it.

A heartbeat lodged in her throat. "What are you doing here?"

Crouching down, Dietz hid next to the kitchen doorway, gun in his hand and a grim frown on his lips. He ducked down and peeked into the hallway outside of the kitchen.

With a finger pressed to his lips, he said, "Quiet."

She would not. "Have you lost your mind?"

He glanced into the family room one more time, then back at her again. "He'll hear you."

"Who?"

"I saw him come in here after he did something to Derek."

The surprise at seeing Dietz washed right out of her. "Derek?"

She glanced into the family room, trying to remember if she heard Derek come in the house or if he still sat out on the porch.

"No, not in there. Move over here with me." The nonthreatening guy from the beach had vanished. This Dietz was jittery and unsure, all cockiness gone.

"No way. I'm calling Kane right now." Unfortunately, the phone sat closer to Dietz than her. Reaching for it would put her in his direct firing line.

"Come. Here," he ordered.

Sit. Stay. Give me the journal. She'd had just about enough of being ordered around by men on this island. Yeah, she'd dealt with enough law enforcement bossiness for a lifetime.

"Kane will arrest you if he finds you in his house."

"You gotta stop talking." Dietz's voice never ventured above a whisper. Only the intensity grew.

This time, before she could back away, he reached out and snagged her. Grabbing her arm, he pulled her next to him.

"He's here." Dietz's hot whisper echoed in her ear.

What she noticed was the desperation behind the sound. Maybe he'd finally lost it. "Who?"

"In the other room."

"Yeah, but who?"

Phum.

Phum.

Plaster and wood exploded from the doorframe in front of her. Less than a second after she heard the strange, muffled noise, Dietz went facedown on her white sneakers. His gun clanked against the tile floor. One arm stretched out above his head, and he stopped moving.

Blood seeped out in circles, expanding on his back and the chunk of plaster missing from the wall. Beating down the panic, she fell to her knees and felt for Dietz's pulse.

"Dietz?"

"It's too late, my dear." Sterling Howard strolled into Kane's kitchen looking every bit the rich yachtsman in his navy pants and spotless deck shoes.

He even had a blazer with one of those stupid seals embroidered on it. Every hair in place. Nails buffed and fake tan distributed to perfection. At fifty-something, if that was how old he truly was, Howard was fit and in control.

The gun gave him away for the slime he was. A big gun with what she assumed was a silencer on the end.

"You killed him," she said as shock filled her veins.

Howard shrugged. "Collateral damage."

Her thoughts went to Derek on the front porch. She had to get to him. Jumping to her feet, she tried to run past her attacker.

"Ah, ah, ah. I don't think so, Ms. Parks."

She skidded to a stop when Howard aimed the gun right at her heart.

"Let me go," she pleaded. Derek needed her.

Howard grabbed her upper arm and dug those manicured nails deep into her soft skin. "We need to get acquainted, you and I."

Reality dawned on her. She saw the smug recognition on his face.

"You know who I am," she said.

"Of course. I know everything about a mark before I go after it."

That was what her mother was to him. A victim. "My mother."

"Yes. The perfect score. Rich, attractive and disconnected from her family or anyone who should really care about her. I hadn't counted on her mental instability. The woman was frighteningly crazy."

"Go to hell!" Annie made sure to spit in his face.

His composure slipped, and he snarled like the animal he was. As soon as it appeared, it left. Almost instantly a calm washed over him again. It was as if he trained his mind and body to act with complete control, and could switch his mood without thought.

Within seconds his rage turned into disdain. Howard wiped his face with his jacket lapel. "So vile and underclass, my dear. Your mother raised you better than that. The finest schools. The best activities."

"Shut up!"

Not from him. She wouldn't take this from him. He didn't have the right to talk about her or her upbringing. Every word he said cheapened her life. Every sentence made a bigger mockery out of what her mother's life had become.

"All those opportunities spread before you, open to you if you would only have taken advantage of them. And, what did you do instead? Waste them." He shook his head. "It's a crime, really."

"You're a condescending prick." She edged back toward the counter, trying to remember where Kane kept the knives.

Howard pursed his lips as if he tasted something rotten. "Language. All this time with these police officers has ruined you."

"Where's Derek?"

"We were discussing your mother and what a disappointment you were to her."

How could her mother ever be taken in by such a creep? How could any woman? "Don't talk about my mother. Don't talk about me. Don't talk about Kane. Do you hear me?"

"You're shouting. I have a gun, and you're shouting." Howard made a tsk-tsking sound. "That is not your smartest move, my dear."

"I'm not your dear."

"No, but you could have been my stepdaughter. Think about that. The family outings, afternoons listening to the orchestra together. Yachting. You could have benefited from some respectable fatherly attention."

"You killed my mother, you sick bastard."

He pressed the hand with the gun against his chest. "Such concern from the prodigal daughter."

"She's my mother."

"You never cared enough to actually call her or visit. Really, Ms. Parks, who is the bad guy here?"

"I didn't cheat her or steal from her. I never used her."

"Worse, you pretended she didn't exist. And, last I checked, your mother was very much alive."

Breathing, but not alive. Her mother existed, ate and stared. That was all she had left. "You ruined her."

The gun aimed right at Annie's heart again. "Interesting that you pretend to care. You who abandoned her and left her alone with her pills. See, Annie, I did her a favor. I showered her with attention and then removed the one thing that caused her pain. Do you know what that was?"

Annie refused to respond. Not when she needed all of her focus and wits to get out of this situation alive. Howard had likely killed everyone on his yacht excursion but her. He probably had something to do with Jed's disappearance, too.

The vile man needed to die.

Keeping her body as still as possible, she felt around the counter behind her. Her hands shook as they skimmed the cool surface.

"No guesses, Annie? It was the money. See, without the money, your mother had no resources to buy the drugs. The money ruined her, so I removed that temptation as a way of forcing her to become a productive member of society."

The rage exploded behind her eyes nearly blinding her. "She went insane."

"Your mother's insanity predated me. I couldn't have known how unstable she'd become or that she'd take that option." He shrugged. "Live and learn."

She tried to stall for more time. "Where's Derek?"

"In the trunk of my car."

She accused Kane of lacking emotion. Wrong. It flowed from him like a river compared to Howard.

"Is he alive?" Her hand brushed across the countertop.

"I hit him with a stun gun and threw him in the car. The headphones helped. He never heard me coming."

With unexpected speed, Howard reached out and pulled her away from the counter. She looked down and saw just how close she'd come to the can opener. One shot to the side of his head, and Howard would be on the floor next to Dietz.

Dietz, who wasn't moving.

Derek, who was in Howard's car.

The scenario played out like a nightmare.

"Why are you here?" Bile formed in her stomach. She tried not to dwell on the fear. To deal with Howard, she had to stay in control. She needed to know his plan to see if she could stop it.

"That's an interesting story." His smile was feral and contemplative at the same time. "See, according to my information, Kane isn't known for engaging in anything serious with the ladies. My plan was to pick up the boy, blackmail Kane into leaving me alone, and then move on."

"Kane wouldn't—"

"The moving-on part is your fault. You'll pay for that eventually. Until then, you will be my insurance."

"What are you talking about?"

"Maybe the good police chief used to shun women, but he's taken quite a liking to you. Which, of course, is unfortunate for you."

One more loss Kane would have to accept. "We don't even know each other."

"I hope that's not true since you're sleeping with the man. I'd hate to think you turned into a whore on top of everything else."

"How do you know that?"

"I make it my business to know everything. I'm in the business of information."

The truth dawned on her. Kane's missing link and

her target were the same person. "You were Sam Watson's dealer."

"Alas, no. If I were, the child would be alive and the business would be running." Howard glanced at his fingernails, as if to make sure the murder hadn't messed up his cuticles. "No, not me. I know who, but that's a story for another time. To the extent you have more time, that is."

"You'll never get away with this."

"That's where you're wrong." He grabbed a piece of plastic out of his jacket pocket. "Hands in front of you."

"Why?"

He didn't wait for her to comply. After grabbing her hands, he wrapped the tie around her wrists and yanked. "We're going to take a little trip."

"Why don't you just leave? Take the car and whatever money you haven't spent and go."

"I no longer leave loose ends." He touched the tip of his gun against her nose. "That's a lesson I learned from you, my dear. Now I can never assume the dysfunctional relatives won't show up because they always do."

Numbness settled in her hands. "You're going to get caught."

"I never have before."

"Kane will find me. He will kill you if you hurt Derek." She knew Kane would track her and do everything he could to hunt down Derek. It made her sick to think about Kane berating himself over the danger Derek was now in.

"That's the point, my dear." Howard grabbed her under the arm again. "Kane is the man I need."

"Why?"

He ignored her question. "It's a shame you no longer have your camera. Beautiful instrument. An unexpected and unfortunate victim of your charade. When you walked into that meeting room on my yacht and I realized who you were . . ." He shook his head. "Not very smart, Ms. Parks. You lost the element of surprise."

Things, she could replace. She couldn't remake Dietz or Derek. "You knew who I was from the beginning."

"As soon as I saw you."

"How?"

"Your mother had your photo next to her bed."

That information stunned Annie as much as everything else that had happened in the last few minutes. She never saw a photo. Never had any indication that her mother even cared enough to keep one.

"I figured you and Manning were working together. That you were working on the same exposé as he was. That meant you both needed to disappear. You were supposed to go first, but that didn't work out. Your mother failed to inform me about your swimming skills."

She'd caused Manning's death. She'd dragged him into this mess. Now he was dead. The guilt stacked up on her. "So you killed him."

"No."

"Why lie now?"

"Oh, I killed him. Just not for the reason you think." He guided her around Dietz. "That's right. Step over the dead officer."

"You're sick."

"Resourceful."

Sick. The word was *sick*. "Where are we going?"

"Have you ever been to Waimea Canyon? It's a lovely site. I hope you aren't afraid of heights."

Chapter 26

When his home answering machine rather than a human picked up at his house for the third time, Kane knew something had happened. Something bad and final.

He closed his cell phone with a snap. Tried to think over the pounding inside his skull. Less than ten minutes after they left the house, a sense of wrongness settled over him. He fought the feeling for a few miles, then gave in and called home. And called. And called.

The only voice he heard was his own on the machine. No one picked up. No one called back.

He tried again with the same results. The fourth time confirmed what he knew the first. Derek and Annie were in trouble.

"Still nothing?" Josh took his eyes off the road for a split second.

"No one is answering." So stupid. Kane had watched Annie every second. By stepping away he'd left her vulnerable.

Josh turned off the radio. "Maybe—"

"Turn around."

"What about the lead Roy called you about?"

Kane unloaded his rage. He whipped the cell phone in front of him. It hit the dashboard and split apart.

"Feel better?" Josh asked.

"Turn the damn car around and get back to my house."

"Right."

Kane wiped a hand over his face. "Sorry."

"It's okay."

"Something's wrong. I can feel it."

Josh tapped his fingers on the wheel. "There could be a reasonable explanation. They could be at the beach or—"

"They're not at the beach."

"How do you know?"

"I do." Kane knew because he always knew. Before the police called from the accident scene in Oahu, he knew. Leilani had kept pushing. Acting as if she could beat the odds and outlive everyone. He'd tried to get her into a program. Even scared the hell out of her by dragging her through the rehabilitation hospital and the morgue to show her what could happen.

And then it did. Leilani died before her twenty-sixth birthday. Married for two years. Widowed for almost five.

Josh grabbed his cell phone. "Here. Call the station. Ask for backup."

"You believe me now?"

"I believed you the first time. I just hoped you were wrong."

When the car roared into Kane's driveway ten minutes later, having broken every traffic law in the state, no one sat on the porch or beach. The front door, usually open to let in the ocean breeze, stood shut.

Kane's anxiety morphed into fear. Someone had taken them. He knew it down to his soul. He didn't let Josh stop the car before he jumped out the door.

"Damn it, Kane. Wait!"

Kane was already moving. He slammed the door and ran up to the porch.

Josh grabbed Kane's shirt from behind just as he reached the top step. "Stop it. You're acting like a madman."

Kane tried to shake Josh off. "We don't have time to waste."

"What if they're in there and fine?"

"They're not." A breath hissed out of Kane.

He couldn't regulate his lungs or his mind. Everything ran in circles in his head. His usual calm abandoned him. He didn't have any control and didn't care.

"Protocol." Josh slapped him on the back. "Get it together. For them."

The final phrase sank in. Embarrassed and shocked by his lack of restraint, Kane could only nod.

Josh took over, leading them up to the door and, after a quick check in the windows, inside. Crouching and covering, they moved through the family room, opening the closet door and checking for hiding places.

The crash of glass sounded in the kitchen. They both ran, weapons ready. When they hit the doorway, they saw Dietz. With blood running down his back, Dietz tried to drag his body up to the kitchen table. Shattered glass and something white and sticky covered the floor.

As they reached Dietz, the chair toppled over, throwing the man back to the tile. He yelled in pain as the chair fell against his head.

"What the hell happened?" Kane shoved the furniture out of the way.

"Damn it." Josh helped Dietz turn over on his side and propped up the older man to ease his choking coughing. "Take it easy."

Kane grabbed some clean towels and pressed them against the man's back. "Can you talk?"

"Annie . . ." Dietz choked out her name.

"Where is she? And Derek?"

"Took them . . ."

Josh balanced Dietz with one arm and grabbed for his cell phone with the other. Josh remained calm as he called for help. "Officer down. I repeat, officer down."

Kane worked to stop the bleeding. His stomach twisted and turned. Someone had Derek and Annie.

"Couldn't stop him . . ." Dietz's weak voice grew even weaker.

"Who? Bill, tell me who has them."

With a last burst of energy, Dietz grabbed the front of Kane's shirt in his fist and tried to sit up. "Have to—"

"Bill, no. Stay still." Kane's anxiety increased. Dietz wasn't going to make it if they didn't get him help. Soon. "Where the hell is the ambulance?"

"They're on the way." Josh helped to wrestle Dietz back down to the floor and stem the flow of blood.

The older man wouldn't be deterred. He kept trying to talk. To get their attention. With a pain-filled groan, he fought them until he drew Kane's face down. "Ho . . . Howard."

Something inside Kane crashed. A heavy darkness fell across him from the inside out. "Sterling Howard? He has them?"

"Yes."

"Are they okay?"

"For . . . now . . ." Dietz spit out the words, then slid to the floor.

Kane didn't bother to hide his terror when he faced Josh. "Where are they? Where could he have taken them?"

Sirens sounded in the distance. The whirring and bells swelled, getting closer and louder, until they screamed right outside the front door.

"I'll go," Josh said.

Kane could hear shouts and a murmur of voices. The front door banged, and something rolled across the floor. A few seconds later medics trampled through the house. Men he'd known for years flooded into his kitchen.

With a minimum of words, they loaded Dietz onto a stretcher. They ran around, pumping plasma, medicine and fluids into him. Everyone had a job to do but Kane. He wasn't sure where to start. Still unconscious, Dietz lay there unmoving. Kane couldn't help.

Too late. The two words spun around in his brain.

"Hey." Roy fought his way through the crowd to get to his chief. "What happened?"

"Didn't you get the bulletin?" Worry made Josh's voice more gruff than usual.

"I meant the details."

"Sterling Howard tried to kill Dietz. Took Derek and Annie." It physically hurt to say the words. Kane rubbed his chest to try to ease the pain.

"Why?"

"Revenge. He's a nut." Josh threw up his hands. "Who the hell cares, Wallace?"

"We don't know where he has them." Kane spoke the words that circled in his mind.

"What about the lead? The ranger cabin in Waimea Canyon?" Roy lifted a computer printout from his pocket. "This is what I called you about. Here."

Kane grabbed the paper out of the younger man's hand, and Josh read it over his shoulder. A map. They studied the directions and location.

"I know this place. I've hiked around there a million times." The memory of his conversation with Annie came back to Kane. They had talked about the area, its beauty, so recently.

"I can take Kane. Josh can—"

"No. Call Ted. Secure the scene until Ted can get

here and work out a strategy and backup. Josh will come with me." Kane was already moving for the door with Josh right behind him. "If there's any news, call Josh's cell."

Roy jogged after them and down the front porch steps. "What are you going to do if you find Howard?"

"When," Josh corrected.

Kane was two steps ahead and at the car door. "If we're lucky, kill him."

Roy stopped in the middle of the driveway. "If you're not lucky?"

"We just arrest him." But Kane hoped for luck this time.

Chapter 27

They drove for what felt like forever. Behind the dark windows of the large sedan, Annie watched miles of shrubs and rocks disappear as the car climbed the twisting road up to the canyon. For forty minutes they drove on, passing only a few cars and no houses or people.

She saw signs for pull-offs to scenic lookouts. She knew from her study of the area that the canyon stretched for miles and sat at the northern end of Kokee State Park. The deep cavern cut by water through volcanic rock spanned two miles across and dove thirty-five hundred feet down to the river below.

The canyon walls were not visible from the drive, but she knew the landscape. Few people other than hikers. Only a few cabins, and all of those occupied by park rangers. Miles and miles of sheer rock colored brown and red and green from the elements. Wind sheers that could topple the average man.

Howard skipped all that and kept his eyes on the road and his mouth shut, except for an occasional show tune hum.

With her hands and ankles tied, the doors locked from his side and nothing but air above her and a steep cliff below her, Annie didn't have anywhere to go. As uncomfortable as she was, her seat beat Derek's. He remained locked in the trunk.

They finally turned off the main road and followed a muddy and uneven lane back to a cabin. From the route, Annie guessed they had stopped on the northeastern rim of the canyon.

There was not a human in sight. She scanned the area, looking for a tourist, a hiker, even a lost dog. Every now and then she heard the buzz of a helicopter touring the canyon. The noise always retreated before reaching them.

Howard turned off the car. "We have arrived at our desination."

"Since you're going to kill me anyway, tell me why Chester Manning had to die. What was the exposé?"

"You're not in a position to issue orders." Howard pocketed his keys and tightened his grip on the gun. "Unless you don't care about poor Derek and his diminishing oxygen supply that is."

She'd thought of nothing but Derek. And Kane. His face refused to leave her mind. Anxiety ate away at her stomach as she sat there in the leather seat, knowing Derek could be dead just feet away. Knowing the anguish Kane would suffer if he lost Derek.

She wanted to believe Kane would mourn her. She knew for sure if Howard succeeded, Kane would add two more deaths to a conscience already overburdened with guilt. How much pain could a man take before more than his emotions shut down? Until everything inside him failed.

"Let Derek out. Please." Begging Howard for anything made her sick.

"I make the decisions."

Wind whipped up the canyon and rocked the car. She hated waiting with Howard, sitting there and having to refrain from scratching his face. Hated not knowing if Derek had enough air. But, being outside the car scared her even more. Between the cold air and the almost guaranteed trip Howard intended for her into the base of the canyon on her head, she felt safer in the car.

"I'm going to come around to your side and get you out. If you try to run or cause trouble, I will shoot a hole into the trunk and keep shooting until you behave. Do you understand me?"

She understood he was a damn madman. "Yes."

"I knew we'd get along together, Annie. We both saw your mother for who and what she was. We're a lot alike, we are."

She refused to believe that was true. "We're nothing alike. You're a disgusting user and liar—"

The slap came out of nowhere. One minute she sat there venting her rage, knowing Howard intended to kill her. The next her head flew to the side from the force of his palm against her cheek. She tried to rub the sting away, but her bound hands made that difficult.

"That was your only warning. Unlike your mother, I do not tolerate disobedience." Howard slammed the door and stalked around to her side of the car.

He yanked on the handle. Crouching down, he dragged her feet out onto the gravel. "I need you to walk, so I'm going to break the tie around your legs. If you do anything, and I do mean anything, to upset me, I will shoot you, then start shooting into the trunk. Do you understand that, Annie?"

When she didn't answer, he pressed the barrel of his gun into her stomach. "I asked you a question."

If it were just her, she'd knock the gun away and take the risk. But, it wasn't just her. "Yes . . . yes, I'll do whatever you say."

"Good girl." He snipped the band and then pulled her to her feet.

The jerking movement sent her ankle in one direction and her sore knee in the other. A flash of pain shot up her leg as her left leg buckled underneath her. She would have fallen on her face if Howard hadn't caught her at the last second.

Bent over, her knee throbbing and her arm on fire from the stranglehold he had on her skin, she let out a moan. The cry was real, but she drew it out in order to give herself time to look around the area for a weapon of some kind.

Grabbing her chin, Howard twisted her neck until she looked up at him. "I am running out of patience with you. We are going down this trail to a rock ledge about a hundred feet below. We can do it the nice way or the hard way."

She glanced down. If there was a ledge there, she couldn't see it. "The nice way."

With a tug, he brought her back to his side and started walking.

"Why not the house?" She kept looking back at the car, hoping Derek would pound and scream. Anything to signal he was alive. "And what about Derek?"

"I have a meeting. Then I'll take care of Derek."

"Here?" She slowed down, trying to see if anyone else might be hanging around the house.

Another helicopter made a run up the canyon. She heard the flap of the blades and could see the dark blob in the distance.

"It will turn around before reaching us," he said.

Of course. Howard would have checked on that. He was a planner by nature. He made very few mistakes.

"Come along, my dear. I meant to show you the canyon during our yacht excursion. Of course, I expected you to be a real photographer. When that turned out not to be the case, I canceled the side trips."

"Except for the one into the water."

"You forced my hand."

"And I am a photographer," she mumbled. For the first time in her life she stood on the precipice of stunning natural beauty and didn't worry about a shot. All she wanted was to race to that trunk, free Derek and figure out how to call Kane.

Kane. Not her camera. Not revenge. No, the only person or thing on her mind other than fear was Kane. She wanted him here to reassure her, joke with her. Love her.

Another first. She'd fallen deep and hard for a man. One who protected his heart by burying it and forgetting he carried it inside him. One who would have to deal with yet another death, probably more, before the day was over. A heartbreaking loss that would convince him to keep everything on an unemotional level.

She hated Howard for so many things. She hated him most for the little remaining piece of soul he was about to steal from Kane. Panic and fear, yeah, she had those for herself. But, the ripple from Howard's actions extended far beyond her.

"You are doing very well, my dear."

She limped beside him, grating her teeth together every time she had to put weight on her sore knee. "You should leave. Get out now."

"Loose ends. No loose ends this time."

"You mean me."

"Among others."

The soles of her cheap sneakers slipped on the pebbles and branches covering the already rough terrain. "How many people do you intend to kill? Your entire crew—"

"Is waiting for me on a new yacht off Port Allen. That kind of help doesn't come cheap, but can be bought."

The hundred feet he'd talked about dragged on for what felt like miles. Every step mounted was a lesson in agony. She struggled not to scream as she fought against the barreling wind. She didn't know if it was the altitude or something else, but the breeze felt like an Arctic gust in the middle of a storm.

She knew she was going to die. She understood that, but maybe she could save Derek. The question was whether or not she could figure out a way to take Howard with her.

They rounded the corner and stepped down onto a ledge that amounted to an outcropping of rock about twenty feet long and ten feet wide. The perfect place from which to throw a woman over the edge and into the deep valley below.

"There's no one here," she said.

"There will be." Howard sat her down on a boulder. "Be patient."

He flipped open his phone and pressed a button. "Bring him down here."

"Who was that?" she asked. There were too many men who could be the "him" in the sentence. Howard could be talking to and about anyone.

"Patience, my dear."

He dialed again. This time his message was much more brief. "Back up."

She snorted. "Can I call someone? You know, my last chat since I don't get a last meal."

"You can be happy I haven't killed you. Consider that my good deed for the day."

"Haven't killed me *yet*." She said the word since it hung in the air. There was no need to pretend.

He made that annoying tsk-tsking sound again. "It's very discouraging to see pessimism in someone so young."

She judged the distance from Howard to the edge of the rock wall. One good shove might do it. But, if she failed . . . She inhaled deeply, trying to calm her nerves. The situation called for one of her stronger traits. She needed to bide her time and wait for the right opportunity.

A huge grin split across Howard's face. The same smile he'd likely flashed at her mother to win her over. "Some of our company has arrived."

Howard aimed the gun at the far wall. A second later, Mike stepped onto the ledge, dragging Derek over his shoulders.

Please let him be alive. She tried to get up to help Derek, but Howard stopped her with a curt shake of his head. Pointing the gun at her forehead telegraphed his message as well. She guessed the intimidating move was to ensure he had her attention. He did.

Panting and shuffling his feet, Mike looked up and stilled. "What is she doing here?"

Mike's shirt had pulled out of his pants. Sweat stained the area under his arms. Streaks of dirt splashed across his ruddy cheeks. The supposedly stable businessman's gaze looked frantic, almost wild.

In some ways Mike's appearance here, with Howard, shocked her. In other ways it didn't. Something had happened to the man. Something that destroyed who he was and altered his relationship with Kane. When Josh took a shot at Mike, Kane had insisted Mike was one of the good guys at one time. It looked as if that time had passed.

"She can't be here!" Mike insisted in a harsh shout.

"Insurance. Drop the young man over by Annie."

Mike hesitated, then followed the order. He dropped to his knees and unloaded Derek by sliding him onto the ground.

"We need to get rid of her."

Howard cut him off. "Quiet."

"We had a deal." Desperation filled Mike's voice.

She heard it in the breathy tone, saw it in the way he rubbed his hands together and shifted his weight from side to side. No doubt about it, Mike's career in crime was new. Probably one he didn't enjoy all that much at the moment.

Yeah, well, she didn't feel too sorry for the guy. If this kind of stuff scared him, he should have stayed in legitimate business.

"The terms have changed." Howard motioned with his gun for Mike to take the position closest to the canyon. "Over there, and stay on your feet."

"You can't—"

"I hold the gun, so I assure you, I can."

She tapped Derek with her foot. When he didn't move, she slid down on the rock, desperate to feel Derek's pulse.

Howard forbade that as well. "Don't touch him."

"But he could be injured."

"Do you really think I care about that?"

Mike gestured wildly, pointing above them and to the side. "Are you crazy? We have to get out of here. Kane will kill us."

A wind gust raced up the canyon. Rocks and dirt kicked up in a swirling cloud. All three of them turned to the side to evade a full blast in the face.

Howard regained his composure almost immediately. His biggest concern seemed to be the dirt on his jacket lapels. Removing a handkerchief from his pocket, he snapped it in the air with a crack and started blotting off the stains.

"I'm a bit tired of hearing about Mr. Travers and what he'll do to me. Rest assured he will do as he's told."

"You don't know what the hell you're talking about." Her goal was to stall for time. To figure out how to keep Howard focused on Mike instead of her.

"My information is that he cares a great deal for his nephew. Isn't that correct, Mike?"

Just when she thought her anger had peeked, it rose again. She faced Mike and vented her rage. "You told him? You put Derek's life on the line? For what, money? I thought you were Kane's friend."

By the end, she practically screamed at him. The anger and disgust were real, but the increase in volume was meant to attract anyone who might wander by. She heard scuffling sounds above them. Probably the wind, but she hoped for a stray hiker or anyone smart enough to know how to call for help.

"Her indignation is cute, but I wouldn't be offended, Mike. She has a great deal of experience in abandoning loved ones. Those in glass houses, and all that." Howard tucked the cloth back in his pocket. "Now, I believe you have something for me."

Mike's gaze darted to her, then back to Howard. "Not with her here."

Howard exhaled with a great deal of drama. "You still don't understand. See, I will be leaving your lovely little island very soon. In order for me to stay quiet about what I know, I need something from you."

"I have the money."

"Yes, well, that is no longer sufficient."

Mike took a threatening step forward until his gaze fixed on Howard's gun. "You bastard! We agreed."

"Smart move, Mike. Trusting a con man," she said.

"The lady is correct, I'm afraid. See, the person with the gun sets the terms. My gun. My terms."

As hard as she tried, she couldn't figure out what was happening. Howard clearly had information on Mike. Information Mike wanted kept quiet. If she could get them arguing, get their attention on each other, maybe she could do something. What, she didn't know yet.

"You've moved into blackmail? I'd think that was a lower-class of crime." Her mocking tone got Howard's attention.

"You don't even know what you've stepped in, do you?" he asked.

"I know you're a fraud and a thief. Apparently you're a blackmailer and a murderer, too." Wind pushed up the Canyon again, forcing her to close her eyes and tip her head away from the gust.

When she straightened, Howard stood only a few feet away from her. The crowding made her insides tense. If he touched her, she'd make a move to send him over the edge. At this point, there was nothing left to lose.

"It's Mike's fault, and yours, Annie, that Chester had to die. What a waste. The man played a fantastic game of polo."

Everything kept coming back to her. "Me? What did I do?"

"You showed up with him. See, Chester came onto the yacht to tell me about an exclusive. A story he planned to use to build his reputation and have people see him as more than a millionaire playing at publishing."

If only Chester had gone to the police with his tip. The *if onlys* were so easy to see in hindsight. Like, if only she'd trusted Kane a little more. If she had worked with him, not through him.

"Seemed a prominent businessman had gotten himself all wrapped up in the local drug trade. Ice, I believe. Then one of his young dealers got shot."

"Sam?"

"I believe that's the name. Mike, can you help me on that?"

"Shut up!" Mike spat out.

Howard disgusted her, but, in some ways, Mike had him beat. Howard knew only one way to live. Not Mike. He seemingly had everything.

"You're the guy at the top of the drug sales?" she asked Mike.

"Well, he was. Then I was. Now, no one is, thanks to you," Howard explained.

Mike's shoulders dropped with every word Howard uttered. With his head bowed, he actually looked contrite. Annie didn't buy it for a second.

Her head started to spin. So many people. So many sins. "I don't understand. Why would you do it?"

"Tell her." From his wide grin, Howard was enjoying Mike's distress.

"That's enough," Mike said.

"I will decide what is enough. Tell her."

"Stop. Just take the money and go." Mike tried to be rational, but his agitation put him at a distinct disadvantage.

And for her it provided the perfect distraction. Without Mike and Howard going after each other, she might not have felt Derek's hand on her sneaker. Might not have seen pebbles and rocks rain down from above Howard's head.

Her turn to distract. "You may as well tell me. Howard plans to kill me."

"True." Howard nodded. "It's simple, really. Mike found a side business. He ran into some financial problems. Seems he got involved with a phony land deal."

"By you."

"Yes, that's true, too. Mike was an easy target. Rich and, well, easily conned. Once I had his money and his signature on the fraudulent papers, I had my scapegoat."

She listened, growing more disgusted by the minute. Such a waste. People dead because of greed. That was what this amounted to.

With Howard enthralled in his story and Mike growing increasingly irritated, she saw her opening. Whenever Howard tormented Mike by waving his gun or smiling in victory, she glanced around the ledge for a rock. She needed one small enough for her to pick up but hard enough to do some damage. Howard planned to kill three people.

Three *more* people. She knew it even if Mike hadn't figured it out yet.

"Chester told me he had a big story. I gave him more credit than he deserved and assumed I was the headline. When you came on the boat with him, I thought I had my confirmation. The original plan was to have Chester take the fall for your death. Unfortunately, you refused to die."

"I'm funny like that."

"Then I realized, a bit too late, Chester was there to talk about Mike. That changed things. Made me think more in terms of a new business venture myself."

"And Mike helped you by putting Dietz on Kane's investigation. With Kane discredited, you had an open shot."

"No!" Mike's head shot up. "I did it to keep Kane occupied."

"Then I guess I should thank you." Kane walked out of the same outcropping of rock where Mike had appeared.

Relief swept through her, turning tension into hope. Seeing him, being close to him again, helped her focus her thoughts. Tough and tall, Kane walked into the middle of the catastrophe.

She wanted to cry and throw her body in his arms. Do all those girlie things she never imagined would appeal to her.

Kane's gaze traveled over her face. He must have been satisfied with what he saw, because he nodded.

Then he looked down at Derek's body on the ground. If he felt anything, he hid it well. As usual. Other than the tightening of his fists, she didn't see any sign that the scene tested Kane's control.

"More company. Excellent." Howard motioned to Kane to step close to Mike.

Kane ignored him.

"Move!"

"No."

"Hands up and turn around." This time Howard's voice shook. Something about Kane threw Howard off balance.

She worried an out-of-control Howard would result in a bullet in the middle of Kane's chest. She could not tolerate that result. If she had to throw her body in front of his, she would.

"The game is over, Howard, or whatever you're calling yourself these days," Kane said in a deadly calm voice.

"I don't think so. See, my idea was to have Mike kill your girlfriend. You know, as a bit more insurance for his silence. Derek was coming with me to ensure your cooperation."

Kane actually looked bored. "And now?"

"You've made Mike irrelevant." Howard pulled the trigger.

The roar of the gun echoed in the small area and through the canyon. Kane used the chaos to lunge at Howard, but it was too late. A red splotch appeared on Mike's white shirt. His mouth dropped open as the stain increased in size. After a second or two, Mike dropped to his knees. Then fell facedown onto the hard rock floor.

"Bastard!" Kane slid to a stop.

Howard turned his weapon on Annie. "One more step and she dies."

"So much death and pain. Annie kept her fingers pressed to her mouth to keep from throwing up.

"You didn't have to kill him," Kane said through clenched teeth.

"I'm afraid I did. You should thank me. Mike was hardly a decent friend to you."

"I am going to kill you." Kane delivered his vow in a low and steady voice.

"Only if you want to watch your precious Annie die." Howard smiled when the color left Kane's face. "Now. You have a great deal to lose here. Mike told me Derek was your only concern, but I'm thinking you'd be upset if I dropped Ms. Parks into the canyon, correct?"

No. She would not be the reason Howard got away. Not this time. "Kane, kill him. Do whatever you have to do to kill him."

Howard frowned. "Really, my dear. You have better breeding than this."

"Go to hell."

"A policeman." Howard shook his head in disappointment. "You should have done so much better."

As far as she was concerned, no man ranked above Kane. If he would have her, she'd be blessed.

"There's nowhere for you to go, Howard." Kane balanced his hands on his hips. "You actually think you're going to kill the police commissioner, the police chief and a visitor without someone noticing?"

For the first time since Howard showed up in Kane's kitchen, Annie felt a surge of confidence. Kane wouldn't come alone. Josh roamed around these mountains somewhere. Maybe some of the other officers, too. Probably Ted.

And Kane had a gun behind his back. She'd bet everything she had, which wasn't much, but still. Howard was too busy killing and threatening to pat Kane down.

Kane sent Howard a look that should have scalded him. "You know the one thing you don't understand?"

"Enlighten me," Howard said in a voice dripping with sarcasm.

Kane gave a slight nod. "I'm not here alone."

With that, a rain of stones fell behind and around Howard. He jumped and yelped.

Annie didn't get to see anything else, because Kane leapt on her, covering her and Derek with his body. Her side hit the ground hard, but Kane protected her head with his hands. When she looked up again, Josh had Howard sitting on the ground with his hands folded behind his neck. Blood trickled out of the corner of his mouth. The pants, blazer and shirt now had dirt stains all over them. The sleeve of the blazer was ripped, exposing the shirt underneath.

Annie figured Josh had tackled Howard from above. Josh must have kicked Howard's gun, too, because the weapon lay just outside of her reach. No one scrambled to pick it up.

Kane checked Derek's pulse and leaned down to whisper something. Annie figured Kane wanted to reassure himself, and maybe Derek, that everything was going to be okay. When Kane jumped to his feet and headed for Howard, she wondered if that was true.

She could see the hate in Kane's eyes. In that moment, she wasn't the only one who wanted revenge.

Her eyes went back to the gun.

This was her fight. Her presence had led to Chester Manning's death. Everything could be traced back to Howard. The method and timing had changed, but the goal remained the same. Howard had to die.

She reached out and snagged the butt of the gun

with her fingertips. With as little motion and noise as possible, she slid the gun to her and hid it under her legs. If she stayed seated, no one would know.

Just as Kane moved in on Howard, the older man raised his head. "You forget one thing, Travers."

"What's that?"

"I'm not here alone either."

Chapter 28

*A*nnie. Kane whipped around ready to protect her. Too late.

Again.

Roy stood behind her with a gun pointed at her temple. Shocked and wide-eyed, she sat there with her hands folded on her lap.

Kane couldn't look at her. Not now. Seeing her fear would debilitate him. He had enough trouble taking in the scene. Everything jumbled together in his mind, facts and memories, until none of it made sense.

His sergeant. A policeman. An inside man. The kid who almost wet himself when Annie smiled at him.

Roy kept his gun on Annie.

Josh aimed at Howard.

"It would appear we have a standoff," Josh said. The pretense that he would sacrifice Annie was just that, a pretense.

She didn't know that. Her pale skin blanched, and her gaze darted around as if searching for an escape.

Kane wanted to reassure her, but now wasn't the time. Howard needed to think Josh was in complete control. That he didn't have a vested interest in Annie or in keeping her alive.

"Lower your gun, Josh." Roy called out the order in a sure voice.

"Fuck. You." The only sign of Josh's anger was the small tremor in his voice.

Kane suspected anyone who didn't know Josh would never even notice. But, that was part of the problem. Roy did know them. Kane had thought they knew Roy. Wrong.

"Are you working for Howard or were you working for Mike?" Kane asked his former sergeant.

Howard lowered his hands. "Roy is a young man who can be bought by the highest bidder. He started out with Mike, feeding him inside information so that Mike could evade your drug sweeps. When I saw how valuable Roy could be, I convinced him to throw in with me."

"Why, Roy? Why do this?" Annie's question came out as a plea.

"Ever try to make it here financially? It's impossible. I wasn't about to sit around and wait for some kernel to be thrown my way in the department. Not when I have a golden ticket straight to the top."

Roy's usual aw-shucks way of talking had disappeared. A new maturity and sense of purpose stood behind his words. The boy had become a man. A very evil man.

"Gentlemen, it looks as if we need to strike a deal of sorts," Howard said.

Kane had one more secret. Derek. Howard thought Derek lay there unconscious. Wrong. The kid was primed and ready to go. When he saw Derek's hand move, Kane realized Derek was waiting to be a hero. And he would be, but not in the way he thought.

"I suggest that the DEA agent retire his weapon. We wouldn't want Ms. Parks to be the victim of an accident." Howard's charming tone didn't cover the threat behind his words.

When Derek's fingers moved, so did Kane. He clapped

his hands together. At the sound Derek reached out and grabbed Roy's shoe and pulled until the younger man fell. Kane whipped out his weapon as Derek rolled to the side and pushed Annie behind him.

Josh made sure Howard never moved, but Roy didn't go down in silence. He came up off his stomach with his gun loaded and aimed. Kane dropped him with one bullet to the forehead.

"You killed him!" Howard shouted.

"Damn right." Kane waited for the guilt to hit him. This time it didn't come.

"Might want to keep that in mind." Josh shoved Howard.

As Kane lowered his gun, he saw Annie stumble to her feet with a gun in her hand. "Annie, no!" He shouted, but it was too late. She had already aimed the weapon at Howard and looked ready to fire. With her hands tied, her fingers barely reached the trigger.

"Yes." The barrel waved in the air as she closed in on Howard. "He's got to die."

"Don't do this, honey." Kane tried but his voice didn't break through whatever spell held Annie in its grip.

"Annie, please." Derek stood behind her with his hands out.

Kane knew Derek waited for a signal. If Kane gave a nod, Derek would grab her. This would end. But, this wasn't Derek's fight. Annie had to wrestle with her own demons and silence them once and for all.

Annie kept walking until Kane stepped in front of her. He stood two feet away, so that the gun pointed at his chest. "Don't do this."

Those beautiful green eyes clouded with hate. "I have to."

"No, you don't. You don't want this." The more she nodded, the more he shook his head in denial. "You don't want what this will do to you."

She finally looked straight at him. "You asked why I was here, and I gave you a bunch of reasons. They were all true, but there really was only one main reason I came here."

Kane knew why. He could see it in her eyes. Feel it pulsing off her body. He understood the vise grip of vengeance. It grabbed you and did not let go. He fought off that grip for years after his wife died. He'd wanted someone to pay. When he finally figured out that the one person who could have stopped the accident was already dead, he let some of that anger go.

"Tell me why you're in Kauai," he said in a soft voice.

Tears formed in her eyes. "To kill him. He deserves to die."

"Stop her for God's sake! She's mad!" Howard pleaded with Josh for assistance.

"Shut up or I'll give her my gun." Josh stepped behind Howard and stuck the barrel in the back of his head with enough force to push Howard's head forward.

Kane blocked them all out. Blocked out the wind and rustling trees. In that moment, only Annie existed. He was the only thing standing between her and the loss of her humanity. If she insisted that Howard die, then he would do it for her. He could handle murder and what it did to the shooter's mind and soul.

The guilt and remorse would kill her. He couldn't tolerate that. The idea of her bright light burning out over someone like Howard . . . No, it wasn't going to happen.

He couldn't save Leilani or Kaia. He could save Annie from herself.

"Give me the gun, Annie." He held out his hand. He could grab it from her at this distance, but she needed to be the one to make the decision.

"No, I have to do it."

"You're a cop. Stop her!" Howard kept up his demands and threats.

Kane focused only on her. "You can't get it back, honey. You think this will solve something, but it won't. Killing Howard won't make your mother well or give you back your childhood."

"Listen to him!" Howard shouted between whimpers.

Josh shoved Howard one more time. "I said to be quiet."

Kane kept talking, trying to soothe and comfort her as well as convince her, "This isn't who you are."

"I promised." Tears rolled down her cheeks now.

"Let the guilt go. You didn't make your mother sick. You didn't cause what happened to her. It's time to forgive yourself."

The gun shook, and her arms lowered a fraction. "She left me."

"I know, honey."

"I hated her and stayed away, and she found him." Annie leaned around Kane and pointed the gun at Howard.

Kane adjusted his stance and tapped on the end until she lowered the gun to a point at his waist. Progress. They were making progress.

"Let the police have him."

"He has to die." She repeated the phrase a few times as if lost in a past he couldn't enter.

His heart broke for her. This beautiful, smart, lovely woman. The woman who'd taught him to believe again. To feel again. If she did this, he'd lose her forever. She'd lose herself.

He held out his hand. "Then let me kill him for you."

"What? You're the damned chief. You can't kill me." Howard's composure broke.

"Kane, you can't." This time, Derek made the plea.

"Josh?" Kane didn't have to form the question. Josh would know what he was asking.

"I'll support you," Josh said.

In that moment, only Annie mattered. "If Howard has to die, then I'll do it. I've killed before."

She frowned. "You can't."

"If you need him to die, if that's the only way you can leave this canyon, then I'll do it for you."

"You'd do that?"

"I will do whatever I have to, and take however long I need to do it, to make sure you walk out of here the same person you are right now."

Her hands dropped in front of her until the gun pointed at the ground. "I'm so tired."

Kane watched the tension leave her body. He sighed in relief as his hand covered hers. "I know, baby."

When she fell into his arms, crying and rambling nonsense, an aching tenderness swept over him. This need to protect her, to love her, only grew stronger when she buried her fists in his shirt and cried.

"It's okay." He kissed her hair. "We'll work this out."

He said the words, wondering if they were true.

Chapter 29

The last twenty-four hours blurred into a haze of doctors, police, press and questions. Sitting on the hard hospital bench in the hallway outside of Dietz's room, Annie buried her head in her hands and tried to find her equilibrium.

Nurses ran around the hallways carrying trays and medicines and clipboards. Phones rang. The intercom buzzed with chatter. The smell of stale antiseptic filled the air.

She stared at the newspaper on the floor beneath her feet. The headline and front page stories talked about corruption and deceit in paradise. She had to smile because she knew Chester Manning would have loved this part. He'd thrived on the spotlight and bringing attention to Hawaii. In his death, he'd managed to excel at both.

Too many men had died for this cause. Jed could be dead. A man she'd brought into the fight simply by hiring him to run an investigation. Howard wasn't talking, so she didn't know.

Jed's wasn't the only death that weighed on her mind. Roy. Young, misguided and greedy. She couldn't help but wonder if he'd gotten messed up in the world that destroyed him because of all those reasons Kane had given her for the drug trade problem. Maybe Roy had felt lost and bored. Something had driven him to the wrong side of the law. No one would ever know what that something was now.

Everything else left her feeling blank. Sterling Howard, or whatever the hell his real name was, faced a life in jail. Only now the vastness of his financial and land scams were coming to light. He'd tried to pass off government land as his own and sell it off and brought Mike down with him.

Yeah, she wouldn't miss Howard, but having him caught left a hole. One she never expected. For almost a year, unmasking and killing Howard had ruled her life. With Howard behind bars and likely to stay there for a long time, nothing had changed for her. Her mother still stared into space. The sun still rose each day. Life on Kauai pressed on. Relief never came.

Kane got this part right. Her mother didn't miraculously get well when Howard admitted his con. Annie knew now that her guilt was her own. Being a grownup meant forgiving and moving on. She had to find a way to accept her mother for who she was. And what she'd become.

Wiping Howard off the planet had been the goal, but this ending worked better. Mission accomplished. Now she wanted a different mission. Really, she had since Kane took her in.

Somehow she'd managed to regain her dignity but lose her heart. Of all of life's unfairness, this seemed the harshest. To fall in love with a guy whose view of moving on and regrouping did not include a permanent place for her.

She looked up as Kane walked out of Dietz's room. Kane's usual jeans and T-shirt outfit had been replaced by a black suit with a bright green tie. A series of press conferences and interviews forced Kane to wear his big boy clothes.

The business attire highlighted his handsome face, but she preferred him in casual clothes. The more serious the clothing, the more serious Kane became. It was the laughing, joking and,ʼ yeah, annoying Kane who captured her heart.

He slumped down on the bench next to her and balanced his head against the lime green wall behind him. Exhaustion weighed down his limbs, making his shoulders slump. Stress showed on every inch of his face from the frown lines on his forehead to the flat line of his lips.

"How's Dietz?" she asked.

Kane kept his eyes closed but reached out for her hand. The warmth from his palm seeped into her skin. "Better. He's stabilized. The first shot collapsed his lung. The second didn't hit the chest cavity as feared. More like under his arm."

Touching Kane filled her with a desperate longing. She hadn't left him yet and already missed him. Every hour put her one step closer to losing him. The flight back to Seattle was going to kill her.

"Is he awake?" She could hear the tears in her voice. She almost didn't recognize the sound since before yesterday it had been years since she cried.

"Yeah. He's talking."

A typical cryptic Kane comment. "Anything interesting?"

Kane squeezed her hand as he opened his eyes. "That I should get back to work because the death toll on Kauai was on the rise."

That relief she yearned for finally hit home. Not because of Sterling Howard getting what he deserved. Because of Kane.

"Dietz cleared you?"

"Yeah."

"I'm so happy for you. You must be relieved." He needed a celebration. She just wished she could be part of it. Part of his life.

"It will be good to get back to work."

Disappointment rushed right in behind the relief. He still couldn't let go and enjoy. This news should have sent his world spinning upright again. But, after everything that had happened in the canyon, that rein he had held on his control had tightened, not loosened.

She had to leave. It was either that or blubber all over him, and that was just not going to happen. With one last touch of her palm against his cheek, she leaned over and kissed him. Soft and warm, unleashing her loss and need. When they broke apart, she rubbed her nose against his.

"I need to go," she said in a soft voice against his lips.

She lifted her head, expecting him to crack a joke and offer her a ride. He didn't do either. He sat there staring at her with an unreadable expression. He could be happy or sad; she'd never be able to tell.

That was the problem. His emotions stayed locked inside. She'd lived like that for years. She couldn't do it anymore. A few months ago, the physical part would have been enough. Not now. She'd lived half of a life for too long.

"Thank you for everything." When he didn't say anything in response, she stood up and started down the hallway.

She'd gone five or six steps, forcing her feet to lift and move, then repeat again, when the tears began pushing against the back of her eyes. The lesson of her life was that love hurt. Always.

"You're actually going to leave." His husky voice, so low and unemotional, hit her like a fist to the stomach.

She turned back around to face him. He should see what emotion looked like. "There's nothing else for me here."

Almost as if in slow motion, he stood. His face, tense before, drew tighter now. Something that looked like pain moved behind his eyes.

"Nothing?"

"My life is in Seattle."

Five feet of emptiness and baggage stood between them. People walked around them. The loudspeaker continued to squawk. They ignored it all, looking only at each other.

"What's there? Your business? You can take that anywhere. Your mother? Move her here." His arms hung loose by his sides.

Here? "Kane, we've been through so much in such a short time. It's not real. It's . . ." It was very real for her. That wasn't the issue.

"What?"

"Not going to work." She stared at the ceiling, trying to force the tears back down her throat long enough to talk. What she needed right now was some of that patented Annie attitude. Only, she couldn't conjure it up. "We're different. I need something else."

"What?"

"Emotion. Passion. Love."

"And I can't give you that."

His ready agreement touched off a new feeling inside her. Anger. "No, you can't. You don't feel anything. You don't allow yourself to care and get hurt, and all those other wonderful and horrible human things."

"Annie—"

"No," she held up a hand to keep him from moving

any closer. If he touched her, she'd lose her composure. Weakness could not be his last memory of her.

"Annie, please listen to me."

"Let me finish. See, I grew up with that hole. The one where my physical needs were met but nothing else. I can't do that again." When she said the words, she finally understood them to be true. "I deserve more, like a man who can tell me he loves me and accept that life includes pain without hiding from that."

"You don't think I can do all that?" He stood right in front of her now.

She worried her heart would stop. Right there. On the spot. On the side of the hospital hallway. "You lost your mother, sister and wife. Those deaths are a shield you use to keep everyone, except Derek, and maybe Josh, outside."

He stared at her with those intense dark eyes. The usual spark had burned out leaving only flatness.

She couldn't look anymore. With a nod, she turned away and tried to force her legs to move again.

"You're wrong," he whispered to her back.

She stopped.

"Do you know what happens on the first day after you bury the woman you love? You die. Shrivel and die. You wonder if anyone would notice if you crawled into that hole in the ground and joined her."

His tears fell now. When she turned around, she saw something else in those eyes. Desperation. Despair. Maybe a flicker of hope.

"Kane, you don't have to—"

"But you realize, even though most of you is dead, that you can't jump in that hole because it will upset other people. They're grieving over one loss and can't take another. So, you exist for them. Not for you. You aren't alive anymore, so for them."

He stopped and rubbed his forehead. She figured he

was done talking until the words started again, this time surer and louder. "You get up and breathe and eat because the other people you care about beg you. You do it even though you curse every sunrise. You wonder how kids can dare laugh in the park or anyone can go to the beach, how life can go on as normal, when all you feel is darkness. But you go through the motions for them."

Every word made her heart ache for him. Emotion moved through his voice and showed on his face. Kane felt it all. Lived through it all, and it stayed with him.

Closing the distance between them, he stepped forward and crowded her to the side of the hallway right against the wall. "Then one day you get up because there's nothing else to do. You realize you won't be lucky enough to die. You're stuck living. You start functioning on autopilot."

She reached out and ran her fingers down his arm. He didn't move to touch her. His body stayed stiff as his shoulders drooped.

"The people who care about you start to think you're coming around. Really, you're just learning how to exist without thinking. Without a heartbeat." When his voice cracked, Kane swallowed and started again. "Then the coldness settles in. With the color gone, everything looks and feels the same. Bland. Days pass, one into the other. Then it happens. You don't think of your wife every fucking minute of every fucking day. That should be a good thing, but it's not. You know why?"

Tears clogged Annie's throat. She could only shake her head.

"Because it means you're losing her. You've lost her body. Her touch. The pillow no longer carries her scent. The bathroom only smells like you. The memories fade. The sound of her voice no longer rings in your head.

You, the person who vowed to love her forever, forget parts of her and who she was."

Annie choked on a sob but didn't let go of Kane's hand.

"One day you realize all you have is photos. A few memories. The things you wished you'd done or said stay with you. Yeah, that stuff, the guilt, doesn't fade. You date because it's expected, but the part of you that died is still dead, and every new relationship is an opportunity to lose that last little piece of you that lives on."

She had been so wrong. He felt with an intensity that ran deep and consumed his life. The pain for him was permanent, crowding out room for anything or anyone else.

He continued. "And that's how you live—"

She brushed her hand over his lips, "Kane, please. Don't."

He kissed her palm. "Until one day a redhead from Seattle drops on your beach, all mouthy and tough, and those feelings come back. The ones you vowed never to have again. The ones you thought you never could feel again."

Hope. The emotion that radiated from him was hope. She wanted to believe something else lingered there in that beginning of his smile.

"Kane, what are you saying?"

The smile spread across his beautiful mouth. "That I love you. That I started feeling and living again when you washed up in front of my house."

"I can't—"

"You can't leave me," he pleaded as his grip tightened on her hand. "You don't need Seattle. You need me and Derek and Kauai, and heaven help him, Josh."

Love. The look on his face and in the glow on his cheeks. Love. He felt it, too.

Everything she wanted sat right there, at her fingertips. All she had to do was grab it. For her. Not for her
mother or for anyone else. For her.

"I need—"

"Me."

"Yeah, you. I love you." She said the words. She'd
never said them before. Never met anyone worthy of
them until now. "Forever, put-me-in-the-ground-with-
you type of love."

He grabbed her around the waist and lifted her high
in the air. Spinning her around in a circle and shouting
a cheer. She could hear the murmur of approval from
the nurses. Laughter mixed with tears as she wrapped
her arms around his neck and held on. She pledged her
love as she kissed his face and neck.

The twirl stopped, but her head kept spinning. When
she finally landed, her heart lodged in her throat at the
look of pure pleasure on Kane's face. Gone were the
lines and frowns.

"Well?" she asked. If he came this far, he could go
the final step.

"What?" He actually had the nerve to look serious
with that question.

"You have something to say to me."

"See, now, I'm thinking your bossiness is going to
be a problem."

"Kane." The man was two seconds away from a kick
to the shins.

"Really, I'm the police chief, and you're going to
have to show me a little respect."

"I'm going to show you my shoe in your butt if you
don't tell me what I want to hear."

"That I love you? Yeah, I do. I love you." That sexy
grin of his came back in full force. "I am a bit worried
that I'll strangle you before the wedding, but I'll work
on that."

"Wedding!" The idea stole her breath.

He was handing her everything. Love. Loyalty and a real home.

"This is a family-oriented island. The chief of police can't be living with some haole girl." He pulled her tight against him.

The love he felt was right there. Easy to see.

She tried to look stern. "I'm looking up that term soon to see what it really means, so don't get used to it."

"Have I explained that as the wife of a town official, you get a job?" He kissed her then with a love and longing that made her head spin.

"Did you propose?"

"Good point." He nodded with mock seriousness. "Better ask and get you to say yes before I describe the job duties."

Excitement and happiness screamed inside her, begging to get out. She'd say yes to anything he asked. "Tell me the duties first."

He leaned in as if he were telling her a secret. "The chickens."

"Chickens?"

"Your job is to round up the chickens."

She threw her head back and laughed. "For you, I'd even hunt down those stupid beasts."

His laughter joined hers. "Wow. You are in love."

She was. The forever kind.

Check out more of HelenKay Dimon's fabulous heroes!
This undercover agent's HOT AS HELL . . .

She's mad as hell.
He's the reason.
The desert may not be big enough for both of them . . .

Tell Me More . . .

Lexy Stuart is nobody's fool . . not since she wised up
to the fact that her fiancé, Noah Paxton, wasn't just sport-
ing the hardest bod this side of the Ironman competi-
tion. No, he was also harboring enough secrets to make
a CIA operative blush. Little things he never thought
worth mentioning like, oh, a previous marriage. So Lexy
gave back the ring—with extreme prejudice—and made
sandy tracks straight to a remote desert spa. Problem
is, with a man like Noah, a girl can run, but she can't
hide. Nor does she particularly want to . . .

Alexa Annabeth Stuart. The stuffy name couldn't be
less suitable for a woman as fiery and free as Noah's
Lexy. And Lexy is his—always will be—the tricky part
will be getting her to realize it. Of course, Noah's always up for a challenge. Which is a good thing, since
between the crazy heat at this God-forsaken "retreat"
and the looks Lexy's shooting him (not to mention the
shockwaves he's getting from her hot-pink bikini),
winning his ex back could be one dangerous mission.
But if Noah doesn't survive it, well, he intends to die a
very satisfied man . . .

There's triple the pleasure in
HARD AS NAILS . . .

**What's better than a man who's good with his hands?
Try a trio of hard-bodied hunks
who'll be happy to flip
your house, your heart . . .
and anything else you have in mind . . .**

This Old House

Architect Cole Carruthers's mission is simple—visit his company's latest rehab project and cajole the sweet old lady who once owned it into vacating the premises. But the sultry, sledge-hammer-wielding woman he finds is far from old, nor particularly sweet. For reasons she won't reveal, Aubrey Matheson refuses to leave the house she claims is her birthright. As far as Cole's concerned, there's only one thing to do with this squatter: hunker down with her and discover every single one of her sexy secrets . . .

All About Adam

The last meeting tough-as-nails Becky Carter took with sharp-witted, wicked sexy lawyer and real estate rehabber Adam Thomas culminated in a scorching-hot game of kiss-and-run. Becky was the one running, and she's regretted it ever since. Now Adam's back to do some actual business . . . or so he says. If Becky has her way, this weekend of negotiation will speed from boardroom to bedroom—and stay there . . .

Man at the Door

After finding herself famous for all the wrong reasons, artist Erin McHugh just wants to fix up her house, open her art studio, and settle down out of the spotlight. Then job foreman Ray Hammond walks through her door and Erin recognizes broad-shouldered trouble. Hot, young, and always in the news, Ray is everything Erin wanted to avoid. The challenge is how to resist a guy who can build anything, fix anything—and make Erin feel everything . . .

Keep an eye out for HelenKay's new book,
IT'S HOTTER IN HAWAII,
coming in April 2009 . . .

"Does watching the rain help?" she asked.

Help what, was the question. "It looks like we're stuck for awhile."

"At least we're not outside."

Yeah, because being alone in a cave with her was a better solution.

Cal glanced over his shoulder. Cassie sat hunched in the far corner, her upper body curled over her bent knees. In the fading light, he could see she was trembling. The sexy shorts and thin T-shirt that distracted him during their hike and kept her cool despite the sun's heat proved even less practical now.

He beat back the images floating through his mind. Mental photographs of skimpy wet clothing clinging to her trim frame, followed by visions of the same clothing strewn all over the cave floor. Cassie naked and backlit by the fierce storm.

Jesus, he was in trouble.

"Do you think—"

"You need to get out of those clothes." He had no idea when the words formed in his head or how they escaped his mouth.

They must have surprised her too since her head

shot up and a sharp gaze pinned him where he stood. "I'm fine."

That made one of them. "This is serious, Cassie."

"No, it's not."

"We could be here for a long time."

"So?"

He knew many ways to talk a woman out of her clothes to get her into bed. Doing so for practical reasons clearly was not his strength. "You'll get sick."

"Figures you'd think about that now. After I'm drenched."

He tried the less controlling route. "How about you slip out of those before you get cold?"

A seductive smile crept across her lips. "Are you trying to sweet talk me out of my clothes, flyboy?"

He had no idea what he was trying to do, except engage in a bit of self-torture. "I'm only trying to help."

"How?"

How? "Huh?"

She leaned back, opening up her body to his view and balancing her upper body on her hands. "How would you help?"

What the hell was happening? "You need to get dry and warm."

"You have any suggestions how I do that?"

Lots of them. They all involved her being naked and strapped to him. He could see the entire scene unfold in his head. Their positions changed, but the results stayed the same. He was making love to her, slipping deep inside her, as the storm raged around them outside.

Cal closed his eyes, trying to block out the sexual fantasy spinning through his mind. Instead, the mental pictures seared right onto his brain, gnawing at him to abandon his control and take her.

Imagining her sexy body, all pink and ready, made him groan. To keep Cassie from seeing his growing erection, he turned back to the opening. With his arms stretched above his head and his fingers digging into the cold rock, he watched the driving rain wash away layers of dirt around the canyon.

The evidence of how much he wanted her pressed against his zipper. His skin itched as if begging to get his clothes off.

He was in hell.

He tried to think of something witty to say but his tongue jammed his throat closed. When words failed, he tried reciting the alphabet to gain his composure. He never got past the second letter, whatever the hell it was. He couldn't remember.

More by Bestselling Author

Lori Foster

More by Bestselling Author
Hannah Howell

__Highland Sinner	978-0-8217-8001-5	$6.99US/$8.49CAN
__Highland Captive	978-0-8217-8003-9	$6.99US/$8.49CAN
__Wild Roses	978-0-8217-7976-7	$6.99US/$8.49CAN
__Highland Fire	978-0-8217-7429-8	$6.99US/$8.49CAN
__Silver Flame	978-1-4201-0107-2	$6.99US/$8.49CAN
__Highland Wolf	978-0-8217-8000-8	$6.99US/$9.99CAN
__Highland Wedding	978-0-8217-8002-2	$4.99US/$6.99CAN
__Highland Destiny	978-1-4201-0259-8	$4.99US/$6.99CAN
__Only for You	978-0-8217-8151-7	$6.99US/$9.99CAN
__Highland Promise	978-1-4201-0261-1	$4.99US/$6.99CAN
__Highland Vow	978-1-4201-0260-4	$4.99US/$6.99CAN
__Highland Savage	978-0-8217-7999-6	$6.99US/$9.99CAN
__Beauty and the Beast	978-0-8217-8004-6	$4.99US/$6.99CAN
__Unconquered	978-0-8217-8088-6	$4.99US/$6.99CAN
__Highland Barbarian	978-0-8217-7998-9	$6.99US/$9.99CAN
__Highland Conqueror	978-0-8217-8148-7	$6.99US/$9.99CAN
__Conqueror's Kiss	978-0-8217-8005-3	$4.99US/$6.99CAN
__A Stockingful of Joy	978-1-4201-0018-1	$4.99US/$6.99CAN
__Highland Bride	978-0-8217-7995-8	$4.99US/$6.99CAN
__Highland Lover	978-0-8217-7759-6	$6.99US/$9.99CAN
__Highland Warrior	978-0-8217-7985-9	$4.99US/$6.99CAN

Available Wherever Books Are Sold!

Check out our website at
http://www.kensingtonbooks.com